# Dane's Mark

## *Berkley Titles by Lora Leigh*

### *The Breeds*

DANE'S MARK
CROSS BREED
ELIZABETH'S WOLF
WAKE A SLEEPING TIGER
BENGAL'S QUEST
RULE BREAKER
STYGIAN'S HONOR
LAWE'S JUSTICE
NAVARRO'S PROMISE
STYX'S STORM
LION'S HEAT
BENGAL'S HEART
COYOTE'S MATE
MERCURY'S WAR
DAWN'S AWAKENING
TANNER'S SCHEME
HARMONY'S WAY
MEGAN'S MARK

### *The Nauti Series*

NAUTI SEDUCTRESS
NAUTI ENCHANTRESS
NAUTI TEMPTRESS
NAUTI DECEPTIONS
NAUTI INTENTIONS
NAUTI DREAMS
NAUTI NIGHTS
NAUTI BOY

### *Anthologies*

TOO HOT TO TOUCH

OVERCOME
(includes novellas "The Breed Next Door," "In a Wolf's Embrace," and "A Jaguar's Kiss")

ENTHRALLED
(with Alyssa Day, Meljean Brook, and Lucy Monroe)

NAUTIER AND WILDER
(with Jaci Burton)

TIED WITH A BOW
(with Virginia Kantra, Eileen Wilks, and Kimberly Frost)

PRIMAL
(with Michelle Rowen, Jory Strong, and Ava Gray)

NAUTI AND WILD
(with Jaci Burton)

HOT FOR THE HOLIDAYS
(with Angela Knight, Anya Bast, and Allyson James)

THE MAGICAL CHRISTMAS CAT
(with Erin McCarthy, Nalini Singh, and Linda Winstead Jones)

SHIFTER
(with Angela Knight, Alyssa Day, and Virginia Kantra)

BEYOND THE DARK
(with Angela Knight, Emma Holly, and Diane Whiteside)

HOT SPELL
(with Emma Holly, Shiloh Walker, and Meljean Brook)

IN ISABEAU'S EYES

# Dane's Mark

LORA LEIGH

BERKLEY
New York

BERKLEY
An imprint of Penguin Random House LLC
penguinrandomhouse.com

Library of Congress Cataloging-in-Publication Data

Names: Leigh, Lora, author.
Title: Dane's mark / Lora Leigh.
Description: New York: Berkley, 2024. | Series: A novel of the Breeds
Identifiers: LCCN 2023025790 (print) | LCCN 2023025791 (ebook) |
ISBN 9780593098776 (hardcover) | ISBN 9780593098790 (ebook)
Subjects: LCGFT: Novels.
Classification: LCC PS3612.E357 D35 2024 (print) |
LCC PS3612.E357 (ebook) | DDC 813/.6—dc23/eng/20230616
LC record available at https://lccn.loc.gov/2023025790
LC ebook record available at https://lccn.loc.gov/2023025791

Printed in the United States of America
1st Printing

*This one is for you, Katie.*

*Always remember . . .*

*Stay strong and live your dreams.*

*Find your path and keep your step steady.*

*Life isn't easy. Adulting sucks.*

*And always remember, being happy starts with you . . .*

# THE WORLD OF THE BREEDS

If you're new to the Breed world, you don't have to begin at the beginning, starting here is fine. You just need to know a few things, then you're good to go.

The first, Breeds Were Not Born. Breeds Were Created. Those were the first words they learned to say in the labs where scientists performed their Frankensteinian experiments to give Breeds life. They mutated genes, spliced and diced them, gave them this and that, until they thought they'd created the perfect killers. Man and beast combined.

Breeds.

They were stronger, faster, far more intelligent than the scientists ever knew. Their flesh was tougher, their hearts were stronger and their healing capabilities exceeded anything they envisioned.

Physically, Breeds were everything and more that the scientists and military leaders overseeing the projects hoped for.

What they didn't understand was that by combining the best possible genetic makeup from the animals they used, and the human males who provided the sperm, the females who sacrificed their eggs, they weren't creating soulless beings. They were creating everything they were not.

The Lion, the Tiger, the Wolf, and Coyote. Jaguar, Jackal and Cougar.

The list is long, and in many cases the results were horrific. And through all of them, one thing remained true. Those given the best of the animal genetics, those whose beasts were strong and fiercer inside them, knew a degree of honor most humans could never imagine. Add that to the humanity they were given, and the genetics of some of the greatest warriors, kings, and statesmen, spies and assassins, and the creatures that rose to challenge them became invincible.

Breeds are savage in battle—which they wanted.

Breeds are merciless in battle—and this they strove for.

Breeds are cunning, deceptive, intuitive and calculating—and this they thought they could control.

No man controls a wild beast. For a moment, it may do as trained to survive, but the call of the wild can't be denied.

The beast will turn.

And when they turned on their creators, stood before the world and proclaimed themselves worthy of freedom, life, liberty and the pursuit of happiness, Breeds also held in their hands proof of atrocities that shocked the world.

Over one hundred and fifty years of experiments, torture, heinous acts committed against women; against strong, capable men; and against babes who died screaming in horror, could not be refuted.

The people rose against the nations whose militaries were involved, whose demented, psychotic scientists performed such evil against helpless beings. Proof of those creations and their battle to survive, to escape, to hide and to live, for more than a century, caused the masses to rise up in horror.

Countries were nearly toppled.

Individuals whose vast wealth spanned generations found themselves to be paupers when the dust cleared. That or hanging on to their fortunes by their fingernails and Breed mercy.

The world had no choice but to acknowledge them, and to sign the tenets of Breed Law that ensured their freedom and the financial ability to make certain they could protect themselves as well.

But Breed secrets could threaten that freedom, just as proof of injustice threatened and destroyed those who once funded the experiments creating them.

Breeds are nineteen years into fighting to survive against not just those who work in the shadows to destroy them now, but against the unknown long-term results of what they are.

Human or animal, or be they monsters?

And the most dangerous secret of all could turn those same masses against them.

Remember, Breeds are deceptive, calculating, spies and assassins and some are even great orators with just the right range, pitch and tones to their voices to ensure the world listens. Breeds can instantly seize opportunity to advance their cause, or bury the proof of what could hurt them most. They show the public that side of them that's protective, honorable. That hurts as they hurt, and dreams as they dream. And in secret they fight to hide newly discovered strengths, and nature's determination to see that they survive.

And that greatest secret is about to explode into the world.

They've used propaganda, gossip rags and social media to lay in the foundation, to aid in their battle when it's revealed. But can anything ever prepare the world for Mating Heat?

The reaction of combined genetics working to ensure that Breeds understand that they may have been created, but those who come after them will be born. Born to hide if they so choose, born to survive and to become the best of both worlds. Man and beast.

And if their greatest threat is the Mating Heat, then the proof of it could save them or destroy them.

Mating Heat delays aging, one year to every ten after a created finds his mate. A hybrid Breed ages normally, until he reaches his prime, and at that time, age delay kicks in with or without a mating.

Because conception is rarely easy, and sometimes takes years, or decades for the mating hormone to advance in the human mate's body and ensure conception can be possible.

Because they weren't created to mate. They were created to be sterile.

The mating hormone creates a physical bonding, two mates whose driving need to be a part of each other can't be denied. That hormone is then given to the mate the animal has chosen in a kiss, and from there, anything can happen. Anything but divorce, separation, or turning away from that one person nature has given to the Breed, that is solely theirs.

Their mate.

And now, the world is about to learn this secret.

This could be their final footnote in history. They may be gone when the dust clears, wiped away in the fear and fury that could grip humanity.

But to kill those known to exist will do no good.

Breeds will still remain.

But that is for another story, another battle, another Breed to tell.

This is my story.

The first-born hybrid Breed. Son of the one they call the first Leo and his human mate. This is the end of my denial that I can refuse the woman everything inside me reaches out for. Has reached out for years to possess. Nature couldn't make me reveal myself to her, so Fate's stepped in.

God help us all!

# • PROLOGUE •

Katy Chavos refilled coffee cups and made her way around the small diner in Broken Butte, New Mexico, heading for that last table at the far corner, placed before two plate glass windows that looked out on the lower end of the main street and the sheriff's office.

There were rumors that one of the occupants took that table for the sole purpose of catching sight of the sheriff's wife. But what man would do that while flirting with only her and no one else consistently for three years?

Over the years, he'd nearly kissed her several times and she'd known that had been his intention before he'd pulled back from her. He usually came in during the late shifts she worked and spent several hours talking to her. His gaze always seemed to caress her, and he'd touch her hand, her arm. But he always ended up pulling back then as well.

Dane Vanderale sat facing the window and his bodyguard, Ryan

Desalvo, or Rhys, as Dane often called him, sat with his back to it, and the sheriff's office. Which could be one of the reasons the gossip was so nasty about why he always took the same booth: so he could watch the sheriff's office and hopefully glimpse the woman it was said he was really interested in.

That day, despite the busyness of the diner, the chatter wasn't as excessive as normal, allowing Katy to enjoy the dark rasp of Dane's voice as he spoke. That voice haunted her dreams. As did the rest of him.

Over six feet tall and broad-shouldered. His skin was a golden bronze from the sun that contrasted with the thick, overly long length of his dark blond hair as it lay along his neck.

He sat with his powerful forearms on the table, the fingers of one hand holding his coffee cup, the sleeves of the desert tan shirt he wore folded to just below his elbows.

He didn't look like the heir to multinational business Vanderale Industries, which owned either controlling interest in, or near controlling interest in, weapons manufacturing, military machines and vehicles built for rough terrain for law enforcement as well as the military.

But it was the Breeds they were most known for providing advanced vehicles and weapons to. The head of the company, Leo Vanderale, Dane's father, was said to take almost a paternal interest in the success of the Feline Breed community, Sanctuary, and the Lion Breed leader Callan Lyons and his family. Callan and his wife, Merinus, had been the first to tell the world of the Breeds nearly twenty years before. Callan was still a driving force in Breed rights and their fight for survival.

More than once it had been mentioned that Leo Vanderale's and Callan Lyons's physical looks were similar enough that they could be related, but that was said about several other powerful figures as well. The Vanderales weren't Breeds, but like those other powerful families, they backed the Breeds fully.

She'd met Dane and Ryan just after turning eighteen. She remembered the first evening he came into the diner, his gaze meeting hers and sending her senses flooding with excitement and sensations she didn't understand. Then he'd asked her how old she was.

How many times had she wished she'd lied to him?

She was twenty-one now; surely whatever male sense of decorum had stayed his intent to touch her then wouldn't apply now.

"We need to be heading out soon," Rhys mentioned, the words barely reaching Katy as she refilled coffee cups several tables away.

"In a moment," Dane answered, his voice sounding a bit distracted.

"Come on, Dane. Katy's just going to invite you to dinner at her place again, you're going to refuse and then you'll get pissed because it hurts her. I don't want to deal with it today," Ryan growled back at him, and though his voice was low, Katy heard him.

She paused, keeping her head down as Mrs. Clyde, an elderly retired teacher, muttered something about dessert.

"She'll stop soon." Dane didn't sound concerned.

"She's certain she's in love with you," he seemed to point out.

"She's a child," Dane scoffed, his tone touched with disgust. "She has no hope of fitting into my world . . ."

Her head came up quickly, her gaze turning to the corner and meeting Ryan's as he lifted his head as though sensing her regard.

Pride and anger filled her, her heart shattering in her chest. Katy knew she'd faced condemnation in the past, but nothing had ever hurt like this.

She had no hope of fitting into his world? God help her, she'd never thought that far. She'd only dreamed of feeling the warmth of him against her, his kiss, his touch. She hadn't given a damn about his world or knowing anything about it.

Evidently, she wasn't worthy to even share that much with him, though. What had ever made her believe he was different from everyone else in her life?

She bypassed the next table and stepped to Dane's as his head turned to her almost warily. Those green eyes, bisected with just a hint of amber, held regret as he stared up at her. As though he sensed the fact that she'd heard the cruel words.

*Oh yes, I heard you*, she wanted to assure him. *Every. Single. Word.*

Dry-eyed, fighting just to breathe, to hold in the pieces of her heart trying to dig their way out of her chest, she filled their cups. Her hand was shaking, so a bit spilled here and there, and she couldn't bring herself to care. A cry lay trapped in her throat, fighting to escape. And she couldn't allow that.

"May I get you something else?" she asked with almost formal politeness.

"Katy . . . dammit." There was a growl in his voice that had the potential to do the Breeds proud as he wiped his hand over his face and looked at Rhys as though demanding he fix it.

"Mr. Desalvo?" It was almost impossible to meet the compassion in his blue eyes.

"No, thank you, Katy," he said gently before looking at his cup and shaking his head.

"Very well." She pulled their bill from the gaily printed apron she wore and placed it on the table, light as air. "We hope you return soon."

Turning on her heel, Katy walked away, her head held high, shoulders straight.

She was breaking apart inside and didn't know how to stop it, how to hold on to her sense of decorum and pride long enough to get out of there.

Placing the coffeepot on the burner behind the diner's front counter, she stepped through the EMPLOYEES ONLY entrance and moved to the kitchen, where the owner, Costas Santiago, and his wife, Sylvia, worked to get the orders together.

"Katy?" Sylvia looked up from a salad she was preparing, her gaze instantly concerned.

"I'm not feeling well," Katy whispered, pressing her hand to her stomach as she felt it pitching with the effect of the pain roiling through her. "Can I just hang back here for a minute?"

"Of course, dear." Sylvia placed the finished salad in the opening between the kitchen and waitresses station. "Go lie down in the office."

She shook her head. "I'll be okay in a minute," she said faintly.

From the mirror at the side of the kitchen service opening she could see the dining area and checkout. She watched, miserably aware that she was hiding like a coward as Rhys checked out and glanced through the window in concern, as though he knew she was watching.

He paid for their meal, then moved behind Dane to the exit.

Lowering her head, she gave them time to reach their vehicle and drive away before returning to the dining area and once again feeling the terrible weight of aloneness she'd felt for the past few years threatening to engulf her.

Tracking the car Dane and Rhys were in, she watched as they pulled into the parking lot of the sheriff's department and entered the building. Sheriff Jacobs and his wife, Harmony, had arrived as well. Their cars sat in their designated area.

She still couldn't imagine Dane pining after a married woman from the diner window, but evidently, neither did he come to the diner for the twenty-one-year-old misfit who had loved him since she was eighteen.

As she cleared the table and lifted Rhys's cup and saucer, four folded hundred-dollar bills stared back at her. Their normal tip was usually half that, and most often left by Rhys rather than Dane.

She'd kept the other tips because each time she returned them, Dane would seem almost hurt by it. He'd urge her to put it toward the college classes she was taking, or to buy a pretty dress So she'd kept them, thinking he left them because he cared.

She was such a fool.

Picking up the bills, she strode to the checkout, found an envelope and hurriedly scribbled a note before shoving it and the bills inside and sealing it. Promising the other waitresses she'd quickly return, she left the diner and all but ran the short distance to the sheriff's office.

Making certain Dane and Rhys weren't in the reception area, she entered, left the envelope with Dane's name on it with Lennie at the front desk and turned and left. She didn't want the obvious charity. Pity money, she thought. She'd been so pathetic, unable to hide how she felt for him and so obviously a complete failure where he was concerned.

And why shouldn't he believe she could never fit in his world? She didn't know how to wear makeup. She didn't fix her long, heavy fall of hair or dress in anything but her waitress uniform.

She didn't do anything but work.

For what?

For the house she rented on the edge of town? The yard was mostly dirt and desert sand, the wood aged and paint peeling. It was drafty, too cold at night sometimes and too warm through the day. It was just a shack and little more. A place to sleep, to escape to, where she didn't feel judged. She just felt an aloneness that weighed at her soul instead. Not loneliness. Loneliness was curable. But aloneness, that sense of having no one. That was far different, and she'd found no way to cure that.

◆ ◆ ◆

The girl didn't return.

A loner sat by himself, head lowered over his coffee, and drew in the scents of the diner, identifying each person there, and he knew she hadn't returned.

He'd caught the sound of a pickup, decades old, pulling out behind the building earlier and had known it was her.

The pain had been too much to bear facing others with, he thought. Such pride she had that the thought of anyone else seeing or knowing her pain was unthinkable.

Digging into his pocket he pulled free some ragged bills, placed them on the table after ensuring there was enough for a tip, rose to his feet and left.

He stopped in the diner just because of the girl. He liked her quiet. She didn't flirt or talk too loud. She refilled his coffee, asked if he wanted anything further, then moved on when he shook his head.

There was something about her that was almost regal, a personal pride that refused to allow her to give in to what he sensed was a less than happy, fulfilled life.

She never felt sorry for herself, never mentioned whatever her circumstances were, despite the other waitresses' constant harping over their lack of funds or lovers who were inexperienced in love or just too uncaring.

And unlike the others, she was innocent. It was there in her eyes, in the subtle grace of her body. She wasn't yet a woman who had known a lover's hand. Probably because she was unwilling to settle for less than that which her heart ached for.

He'd felt her pain this time, and it offended him. Even he could tell when her face lit at the other man's arrival, pure joy sparkling in her gaze, and whether he deserved it or not, it was this man her heart sought.

And with a single uncaring sentence, he had shattered girlish dreams and a confidence far more fragile than it appeared. The man responsible for it surprised him as well. Because Vanderale should have known better. He should have been more protective . . .

He breathed in heavily, turned in the direction her truck had gone and began walking, wondering where she went, where she found solace.

If there was any solace to be found . . .

Wondering if perhaps it would be better to still her pain in that worn little shed she lived in rather than the restaurant. No, that wouldn't do, he thought firmly. At least, at her place of work she'd be found, taken care of properly perhaps. In that horrid little shack she might never be found. And that just wouldn't do. It wouldn't do at all.

✦ ✦ ✦

The rattling of her windows and the sound of the porch swing hitting the side of the house on her front porch drew Katy from the bed she'd been tossing and turning in and onto the rickety front porch of the house she rented.

The large craft settling in her front yard barely made a sound. A heli-jet, the stealth kind that the Breeds used. This one was being piloted by none other than Dane Vanderale himself.

He stepped from the pilot's seat with no Rhys in tow, and holding her gaze he crossed the expanse of barren yard until he stood at the bottom of the steps. Still, silent, his expression somber as his green eyes almost seemed to glow in the dark, they were so intent.

Katy crossed her arms over her breasts and just watched him. She knew the braid she'd woven into her hair for bed wasn't the neatest. The overlarge T-shirt and loose gray pants weren't sexy sleep lingerie, but she didn't exactly have need for such items, did she?

"Will you invite me in?" he finally asked, his voice a dark male rasp that still had the power to affect her.

"Sure. Won't you come in, Mr. Vanderale?" She stepped back, pushing back pride and embarrassment, realizing now how harshly he'd judge the little house, which was no more than a shack.

She pulled the door open and entered ahead of him, knowing what he'd see when he came in.

A small television hung across from the threadbare couch and matching chair. A table for two, scarred but polished, not far from the sitting area. A narrow kitchen and a few thin rugs.

Her bedroom wasn't much better. But it was clean. She kept the small house as spotless as possible. She taped or stuffed any cracks she found that allowed the fine dust to flow in with the drafts. She swept the wood floors, mopped and waxed them to a dull shine. But it was still what it was: an old shack with running water and a bathroom.

"How can I help you?" She watched as his gaze went over the kitchen and living room, his expression never changing, but she could feel his sense of distaste at where she lived.

He pulled the white opened envelope from his pocket and placed it on the table, revealing where his name had been scrawled in a hasty hand.

"This was left for you to keep. Rhys leaves the tips, but have no doubt exactly from where they come," he told her with an edge of displeasure in his voice.

"Your pity?" she suggested, barely holding back the anger ripping her apart as energy seemed to surge inside her, threatening to obliterate her control. "I don't need your pity. Take it and your outrageous tips and give them to someone else."

He looked around again and she knew he was seeing all the things she did without.

"I pay my own bills," she told him fiercely, challenging the disapproval she felt coming from him, drawing his gaze back to her. She pointed her finger in his direction, feeling as though she were being torn apart. "No one has to pity me any longer and give me a place to sleep. I pay my own rent and I bought my own furniture, and you can take your judgmental attitude and hop right back in that pretty little heli-jet and fly right on back out of here."

He didn't show surprise or anger, just that solemn knowledge that she couldn't decipher.

"I'm well aware of the fact that you take care of yourself," he told her before sighing heavily with a slow shake of his head. "Come on, Katy, let's not be angry with each other."

Angry with each other?

He thought she was angry?

She wasn't angry. She was broken.

Not heartbroken, but broken in a way she had no idea how to navigate. The one person, the one person in her life who she'd been certain hadn't pitied her . . .

She'd been such a fool. The large tips should have been an instant clue.

"You think I'm angry?" Her fists clenched as she fought the hot, scalding pain that seemed to explode inside her. "I'm not angry with you, Dane. 'Anger' is just a mild, weak word for what I feel right now."

He shook his head, dragged his fingers through his hair, then stared down at her again. What filled his expression she wasn't certain, but the sight of it only made the pain worse.

"No, Katy . . ." He shook his head again.

"If you come back to the diner, someone else will wait on you," she whispered, fighting her tears now. "If you leave another of those stupid tips, the other girls can share them."

Anger flashed across his face, in his gaze then.

"They were left for you," he snapped, disdain filling his tone as his accent thickened. "To buy shoes, clothes, whatever pretty girls need. I didn't feel sorry for you, Katy. I'm your friend . . ."

She shook her head desperately, fighting the tears and the wound she could feel ripping through her soul. "No."

"Yes, Katy," he retorted firmly, as though believing it could ever make it true. "I know you think you feel more. You're young, you don't know . . ."

"I don't know how unsuited I am to your perfect life?" she cried out, throwing a hand to her side in an encompassing motion as the tears threatened to fill her eyes then.

"You're right, Dane, I'm not suited to it," she agreed, fighting not to cry. "And you're not suited to mine, so why don't you stay the hell out of it."

The pain surging through her very veins heated, making her feel flushed, making the night feel hotter than it actually was, as though she were on the edge of being ill. Yet an icy chill surrounded her as well, and she felt as though she were dying. Being ripped apart from the inside out.

She was going to break apart, splinter into a million tiny pieces and fill the oceans with her tears, if he didn't leave. She needed to press her hand to her chest to ease the stabbing pain there, but she'd be damned if she'd give him the satisfaction.

"Katy, come on, girl," he chided her then, as though she were a child, a stupid little kid who had no idea what she was doing. "We don't throw away three years of friendship—"

"You knew what you were doing," she rasped, nearly sobbing with the unfairness of it. "Flirting when I worked the late shifts, reaching out to tuck my hair in place, urging me to sit and talk with you when no customers were there, watching me as though I were a treat you wanted . . ."

He stepped back, a frown working over his brow as confusion creased his face.

As though he hadn't known . . .

"That's not what it was." His voice hardened.

Katy stilled. She knew she hadn't been wrong. He had done all those things for years.

"Ask Rhys," she suggested, her voice sounding as brittle as she felt. "Go ahead, Dane, when you return to wherever you came from, ask him if you didn't." Her fingers formed fists at her side. "I was an amusement for you, nothing more," she accused him furiously, her stomach tightening with the pain. "You didn't want me; you couldn't have cared less. You just wanted a ready excuse for being at that diner where you could watch the sheriff's office and moon over the woman you do love."

Oh God.

Katy stared at his face, stared at the truth that revealed itself when he took that hasty step back, his face clearing of all expression.

It was true.

She had been no more than a handy female to distract others.

The laugh that escaped her throat was ragged, coarse.

"It didn't work." She fought the scream that wanted to escape. "No one believed you were there for me. Except me." She gave an ironic little laugh. "Poor, stupid, desperate Katy, believing the big bad Vanderale heir wanted her in any way."

It was laughable. She bet he and his Breed friends laughed at her often.

"I wouldn't use you like that, Katy." And he even sounded as though he believed it.

◆ ◆ ◆

Dane stared at Katy, uncertain what to do, what to say. He hadn't done what she accused him of. He'd held back his lust, the heated arousal he felt around her. She was a child. A baby, compared to him. If he dared to take her to his bed, to take the innocence that was so much a part of her, he'd never forgive himself.

Would he?

He could feel her pain, though, ripping at his chest, tearing at his guts with unforgiving claws. And he knew, never in his long life had he ever hurt another woman as he had this one. And to do it to her . . .

He stared around the house once again. He had no idea she lived like this.

He kept a safe house in town, a little unassuming two-bedroom. It wasn't drafty. And he'd always know she was safe. Or he'd have Rhys get her an apartment, or perhaps a small house less plain than the safe house. Something pretty, with a yard. Something secure, so no one could invade her home.

*Protect her.*

The need to protect her was like a hunger inside him since the day he'd met her.

*Mating hunger?* he wondered, not for the first time, checking the glands beneath his tongue for itching, swelling, any change that would indicate she was his mate, and there was none there. She wasn't his mate. To take her, to allow her to care more for him, would be unconscionable.

But he could provide the house. Rhys could buy it under an assumed name, make it available to her. That he could do.

He watched as she moved to the table, stared at the envelope, then picked it up and turned back to him, extending it with a hand that trembled from the emotions he could sense pouring from her.

Dane stared at it, shaking his head.

She needed that money. He knew she did. She had books to buy for her classes. She needed food.

"Please don't come back while I'm there," she all but pleaded with him, her voice quiet, hoarse. But determined. She meant every word of it. "Don't do that to me, Dane. Give me a chance to forget . . ." She swallowed tightly. "To forget you."

Stepping forward, she reached up and gingerly tucked the envelope in the pocket of his shirt. As she did, he saw the tear that fell from her eye and felt it splatter against his left hand, between his thumb and finger, like a spark of fire.

Tears. What in the hell had he done to his proud little Katy, because he knew she hated to cry.

His hand moved until it tucked beneath her chin and lifted her head. And another tear fell.

Before it could run down her cheek, his head lowered, his tongue touching it, the subtle taste of chilis and honey, and pure innocence.

As Dane's lips lingered, Katy's parted, the sudden need for his kiss like a hunger raging out of control. She saw his breathing grow quicker, felt her own grow shallow as she fought to draw in needed oxygen.

She wanted to beg, to cry, to do whatever it took for one kiss. Just one kiss . . .

He jerked back with a grimace.

"I'm sorry . . ."

Of course he was sorry. He could use her to cover his attempts to lust for another woman, but he couldn't ever allow her a single shred of what she needed in exchange. Even if he did want it himself.

"Get out!" Anger surged inside her, a tidal wave of it mixed with the pain, loss and humiliation of needing something, someone so bad it was eating away at her heart. And she knew she would be as much an embarrassment to him as her shack was to her. "Just go. You were so right. I can't understand your life. I'm not good enough for it and I'm not sophisticated enough for you. Go find someone who understands your brand of cowardice, Dane. Because I don't want to be a part of it."

He shook his head as though shaking away some thought.

"Katy, listen to me. Please . . ." He pushed his fingers through his hair, stared around and once again she saw the distaste in his expression for the only place in the world where no pity for her had existed.

"Go." She stomped to the door, emotions shredding her chest as she fought not to cry. "Please don't make me humiliate myself further. Please, Dane . . . Please . . ."

As though all she had to do was beg him.

He gave a sharp nod of his head and moved past her, onto the loose boards of the porch and then straight to the heli-jet awaiting him. Seconds later, the craft threatened to shake her little shack apart as it lifted soundlessly, banked and flew away.

She fought to breathe, to keep from sinking to the porch and wailing like the five-year-old she had once been, realizing no one really loved her.

She breathed in ragged gasps, reentered the shack and closed the door, which she had to lock with a padlock. Not that it would deter anyone that wanted to come in. A good hard jerk of the door would tear it from its rusted hinges.

It was all she could afford. The pretty, carpeted apartments cost more in rent than she made in a month, and she had to ensure enough was left to pay for the books she needed for classes at the community college, for electric, water.

She needed that business degree she was working so hard for. It was her only ticket away from there, away from everyone who saw her as the whore's daughter. The infant even social services hadn't wanted. The child her foster parents had felt sorry for. And her foster mother told everyone in the small town exactly that.

Her foster father, John Moran, had never said much, either way. He'd just watched Katy with heavy, saddened eyes. He'd never known what to do with the little girl who had too much energy and too many questions.

They had to take her in, she'd overheard her foster mother, Marie, say piously. It was her Christian duty after Katy's mother had died, not even knowing which of the men she'd bedded was the girl's father.

Everyone the Morans had known in the church had heard that story. Other children weren't allowed to play with her, because only God knew how Katy would turn out. But those that tried were often turned away at the Morans' door anyway. And Katy had learned to keep to herself.

She was different, one little girl had told her, and she hadn't been the first. Not bad different, but too different. Though she could never explain how Katy was different from other kids.

Once she'd developed breasts, suddenly men leered at her, and women glared at her. Katy had chosen clothes too baggy and concealing when her adopted mother took her to the local Goodwill after that. She didn't like how dirty the men's looks made her feel, and how ashamed the women's looks could make her of the body she had no control over.

She was just different . . .

The words filled her mind, her soul, as she stared up at the ceiling that night, unable to sleep. Too cold outside as well as inside.

She was just different.

She wished she could fix it. Wished whatever made her different would just go away and leave her alone.

The only friends she had were the Santiagos, and that was a friendship born of their compassion, not love.

And now, the only person she'd believed had understood that difference had only been using her as a smoke screen to hide his need to watch the sheriff's wife.

She was just different . . .

And it was killing her.

"I love you . . . ," she cried out into the night. "I just love you . . ."

But only the beast waiting in the darkness beyond heard her.

And he shed his tears with her.

◆ ◆ ◆

He returned to the diner the next night after the young woman hadn't shown up for the day shift. She worked every damned day. It was just finding the shift she had taken. He'd learned she chose her time before the other girls and often took the shifts they didn't want.

Rain or shine, holidays, weekends and every day in between, he'd heard, she worked. And though she'd never make enough to afford more than a shack and the ragged clothes she owned outside her uniform, she still tried.

The night shifts paid less in tips, he thought, which would make it harder for her to meet the demanding cost of the schoolbooks that her small grant for business school didn't cover. He'd slipped into that shack she called a home after she left earlier that day and had to control his rage at the primitive conditions of it. The cabinets and refrigerator were nearly bare of food. And though it was spotlessly clean, he could feel the fine grit and sand invading it. Even worse, he could sense the hopes and dreams, the valiant battle she was waging to be more than others believed her to be. And in the scents he found there, he'd found the subtle presence of one that had torn at the heart he didn't believe still existed within him.

He'd learned quite a lot about her over the months he'd been in the area as well. Not that it had been hard. Whenever some of the townspeople saw her, if they weren't alone, then they'd gossip. And he was good at listening.

Her mother, Amora Chavos, Marie Moran's distant cousin, had been a whore, they said, and didn't know who Katy's father was before she was killed. Stabbed to death, probably by some john. They said the girl tried to tempt good men to lust after her, just as she had the cousin who took her in after the Morans had died.

From what he'd learned, Katy had been underage, barely sixteen, when her foster parents died and another cousin, Charles Moran, and his wife, Lisa, had assumed responsibility for her. They sold the store and the home Katy had grown up in and swore taxes and debts took all the money. Truth was, it had gone in Charles's pocket. But nothing had been left to the girl anyway. Legally, it had been his right.

Morally was another story.

The diner owners had tried to help with school, a better apartment, whatever she needed, but he'd heard she politely declined each offer. The only thing they'd been able to force her to take was the minimum wage for the hours she worked on the midnight shift.

When he stepped in that night, he immediately knew the young man working the kitchen was actually sleeping. Katy sat at the corner table where Vanderale always sat when he came in, a book opened and a notepad beside it.

As he entered, she smiled in welcome. A warm little curve of her lips that didn't make it past the haunted depths of her brown eyes.

So much sadness.

It filled her to her very soul, and yet she still smiled, still hoped, still fought.

"You're out late tonight," she said quietly, moving for the coffee and cups stacked behind the counter as her concern and subtle warmth wrapped around him. Odd, that, he thought, the way he could sense the gentleness of her soul as though such a thing were a strength rather than a weakness to her.

"Just coffee or anything else?" She kept her voice quiet, unintrusive.

He'd never answered that question before—just sat down, took the coffee, paid for it, then left.

"Pie." He cleared his throat when she turned back to him in surprise. "Apple. Warm, please."

He'd been tempted by the apple pie many times.

"Of course." She gave a little nod, placed his coffee on the counter as he slid onto the barstool, then moved to the cooler for the pie.

Cutting a slice much larger than he knew was normal, she placed it on a saucer, then slid it into the microwave. When it was finished, she collected it and placed it in front of him with a fork and spoon.

"Just let me know if you need anything else . . ." She turned to move away.

"Who are you?" he asked her.

What was it about her that confused him? What puzzle piece did she hold in the overall scheme of his life? And why did he find it so hard to do what he knew must be done?

Wariness crept into her eyes. "I'm your waitress, remember?"

"Did I know you," he demanded curiously, rubbing at the scar that still marred his temple, "at any time?"

Few people made him curious, especially humans. But there was just something so damned different about her. Something that went beyond what he already knew.

"No. My name's Katy, though." She pointed to the small name tag near the collar of her uniform. "Were you hurt?"

Compassion swept over him like a gentle wave. He wondered if she knew she did that.

Her name was actually Katelyn. A very pretty name.

He took another bite of pie, enjoying the taste of it as he considered how to respond. Never give anyone enough information to betray freedom.

Finally, he gave a little nod. "I'm okay now." At least he thought he was at the moment. There were good days and bad days. The last couple of days he'd seemed saner than normal.

She was obviously waiting for his name. She'd have to wait until he remembered it, he guessed.

"You study." He turned his head and nodded to her books before looking back at her.

She just watched him, her pretty brown eyes filled with concern and compassion.

"Business school." Another of those sad little smiles. "Office managerial courses."

He nodded. That seemed to suit her.

He ate his pie, glancing back at her a few times, and tried to figure out the puzzle of her.

As he did, he saw the slight blemish on her cheek that hadn't been there before and frowned, wondering what it was.

"Did you hurt your cheek?" he asked in unfamiliar concern.

Goddammit, what was it about her that bothered the beast stalking inside him, that had it pacing, uncertain about what he'd come there that night to do?

He could feel the claws pushing beneath his fingertips, feel the "other" demanding he free it. He had to leave soon; he may not be able to get to her when her time arrived. Killing her now, taking her sweet life, was the greatest mercy he could show her. And mercy was something he doubted she'd known often.

Or he could fight for her. The sudden thought had him as well as the "other" pausing.

No one else in her young life had fought for her, he thought. He could give her a chance to know, if not true happiness, then at least a life she had no idea could exist for her. She had time, he thought.

To take the life of one so precious without fighting to save it was surely a mortal sin.

If he fought, perhaps he could save her.

She reached up and touched the mark with a shrug. "I'm not sure . . ."

She wasn't exactly telling the truth, but he could tell she was confused by the mark.

He inhaled slowly, carefully. It was a risk, taking her scent in this way, all the way to the depths of his being where all secrets were laid bare to him.

Then again, taking her scent deeper inside him where he allowed few scents to actually reach was the only way to be certain of his suspicions. There, in the deepest part of his brain, where he broke it down, and began analyzing it.

A gift he'd acquired. Not one he liked, but he knew how to use it.

Then he stilled.

She was busy making fresh coffee, taking care of small chores as he sat there.

He tipped his head to the side, drew in her scent again and the pieces of the puzzle slowly settled into place. And the sorrow he felt wasn't just his, but the beast's that raged inside him as well.

She was an unmated mate. Lost. Alone. And not even knowing who and what she was. There was more to her, though. So much more than anyone could possibly guess. A pretty little angel drifting through life with no one to sense, or to understand that such creatures paid a horrible price for the beauty within them and the incredible gift they had been cursed with.

This little angel was unique among all others, though. So unique, so very special that at first, he had trouble believing she existed there, in such a bare little place, devoid of support or the care she should be given.

"It's hard to be here, yes?" he said softly when she turned to him. "This small town. It's hard being more than they are and being made to feel as though you are less."

There was no fear in her, only acceptance, but the bitter irony in the curve of her lips oddly touched him.

"More?" she questioned him as she poured him a cup of the fresh coffee, the sadness that filled her threatening to rip through her soul. "It's much harder being less than everyone else and being constantly reminded of it."

And she believed that. She believed she was less, but still she fought, hanging on by her fingernails and fighting to rise above whatever the petty minds of those around her believed of her.

"You should leave here." It was no fit place for one such as her.

She wasn't just Vanderale's mate; she was more. She was so much more, and that little bastard had just walked away from her. Left her to her fate and to an agony the beast had seen only once and sworn he'd never allow another to suffer.

"One day," she stated. "I have to finish classes first and begin sending out applications."

She didn't sound as though it would help much, and likely it wouldn't.

He remembered the errand he'd run earlier, the phone call he'd made, despite his "other" raging at the hopelessness and the added grief they would feel. If Vanderale wasn't going to mate her, then he was going to kill her long before her time if he continued to come around her. What awaited her, both he and the beast would grieve over, but she had time to find some measure of happiness, of satisfaction. To know she had succeeded at attaining at least one dream.

"Tell me, have you heard of Tech-Corp?" he asked her.

"Who hasn't?" She worked as she spoke, wrapping silverware. "Based in San Francisco and holding multinational contracts despite its being a relatively new start-up. They work in AI and hardware components for military and law enforcement organizations all over the globe."

"Even the Breeds." He watched her carefully.

"They need them more than most," she said, compassion coloring her voice. "It's terrible how hard they have to fight to survive."

Even the Breeds who came into the diner often shied away from her, he'd seen. And still, she spoke of them with compassion. They were friendlier than many of the citizens, though, he gave them that.

Silence filled the diner then. He drank his coffee; she refilled the cup. He weighed his options, weighed her options and the demands of the beast snarling inside him, ripping at his mind.

"You've been coming in for months and only now spoken," she commented as she placed the pot back on its burner. "Everything okay?"

He looked at his coffee, frowning.

Concern. She was concerned for him, even though she couldn't possibly guess who and what he was. He was no benefit to her, she would believe. Yet her compassion and concern were like a gentle wave of warmth passing over him.

"Sometimes," he answered as honestly as possible before lifting his head again. "Do you know who I am?"

She shook her head, once again putting distance between them.

Of course she didn't, he thought. He hadn't told her.

He pulled the items he'd gotten earlier from his jacket, looked at them for a second, then extended them to her.

The plane tickets he'd gotten that morning, the letter he'd written to Tech-Corp's HR, and a small envelope of traveling money.

She looked at the items, then lifted her gaze to him questioningly. He could see the hunger and the fear, the doubt and the suspicion in her gaze, and he could scent the hope she immediately squashed.

"Three first-class tickets to San Francisco. One for you, and two for the Santiagos, because your safety will be a concern for them. A suite at Tech-Corp's new employee training center, for a three-day stay, and traveling money. A car will be waiting for you, or if you prefer, you can get your own ride at the airport. Should you decide to accept a position in their training program, then you'll begin immediately."

The scent of hope, of fear and a desperate need suddenly whipped from her like a whirlwind of pain-filled emotion. He could see the small tremors that shook her body, feel how she fought a hope that she was terrified would be destroyed.

"Who are you?" She shook her head in disbelief.

"One of Tech-Corp's founders and owners." And some days, he actually remembered that. "You're far too intelligent, too intuitive to smother in this little town, Katelyn Chavos. Tech-Corp has begun a program that trains managers as well as their own PR staff. They're growing rapidly and have the ability to meet several different needs within the business community. I believe you'll fit there. It's an opportunity to succeed beyond the boundaries of this little place." He pushed the papers forward. "Take it. I'm heading back tonight, and I'll meet you there when you arrive."

She took the papers and the envelope almost fearfully.

"Who are you?" she repeated more firmly, and he could hear the unconscious resonance of the demand in her voice.

"I'll tell you when you arrive," he promised, standing and tossing just enough money for the coffee and pie to the counter. "I'll see you in three days, hopefully." He paused, meeting her gaze. "This is your future, Katelyn. Grab it with both hands or simply give up now. You have a choice: Choose for you, no one else."

# ✦ CHAPTER 1 ✦

BROKEN BUTTE, NEW MEXICO
EIGHT YEARS LATER

Broken Butte had changed, Katelyn Chavos thought as the black Tech-Corp SUV she rode in entered the city limits. There was now a large, chic hotel with attached shopping and a conference center as well as several other popular tourist stays on the outskirts, between Broken Butte, New Mexico, and Window Rock, Arizona. A mall outside of town, updated sheriff's department, as well as a sleek new city police department and courthouse.

The dusty town she remembered had all but been transformed and appeared to be thriving. Even the diner the Santiagos had once owned was gone, and in its place a chain restaurant known for its American-Italian food.

From the file she'd gone over on the flight there from San Francisco she knew that the Breed groups settling in the area, the new Western Division of the Bureau of Breed Affairs in Window Rock, Arizona, along with the accompanying businesses to support the

Breed influx and their needs, had transformed many of the poor counties along the Navajo Nation reservation land and nearby towns.

Prosperity was beginning to show itself not just in the communities surrounding Window Rock, but all through Arizona, New Mexico and Utah, where Wolf, Coyote and Lion Breed communities had begun to spring up.

The majority of many of the Breed bloodlines were found to have contained a high concentration of genetics from the area. The young women kidnapped from the tribal communities in the decades of Breed research and development had come from this area. Their connection to the land and what were considered psychic talents were prized by the Genetics Council scientists who had been given free rein to choose the young women used to carry the fetuses created from the genetic modifications.

The horrors and atrocities committed on the women taken from the area were often reviewed in the press as well as by governments around the world. Lest anyone ever forget the monstrous acts of the scientists who created the Breeds.

They were nearing the twenty-year mark of Breed knowledge and awareness. The day Callan Lyons stood before the world with his small pack of Feline Breeds and proclaimed their demand for freedom wouldn't be forgotten for decades, if ever.

And the closer that twenty-year mark had come, the more Katelyn had seen interconnected events and possibilities and knew that soon, possibly too soon, change would be coming. She wasn't certain which side the scales would tip in that, but she knew neither Breeds nor non-Breeds would be unaffected.

"Mr. Parker asked me to remind you that he and Mrs. Parker will join you at the hotel restaurant for dinner this evening," the Bengal

Breed driving the SUV reminded her as he glanced in the rearview mirror.

This Bengal still retained a shadow of striping along his rough-hewn, handsome features, an indicator that he had been one of the last to be freed from the labs some ten years before.

Bengals were most often testy, hard to get along with and exceptionally brutal in battle. Thankfully, this one was rather polite and strikingly handsome to boot.

Breed males weren't classically handsome. They were rugged, the strong bones and angles in their faces giving them the ultimate bad-boy look. Their gazes were penetrating, often with hair that sometimes resembled the animal their genetics came from, and they normally wore it a bit overly long. Their voices could often hold a latent growl or become low and resonate with sex and sin.

The Breed females, few though there were, were absolutely beautiful.

Katelyn had yet to meet one over five feet six inches. They were delicate and appeared vulnerable and in need of protection. They were anything but. They'd been honed in the fires of cruelty and sexual abuse, considered no more than playthings for the upper echelon Council ranks or the soldiers that ran the labs where they were created.

"Thank you, Drew. I'll contact Mr. Parker myself and let him know when I'll be available this evening," she told the Bengal as she glanced up from the electronic pad and the files she was going over. "Would you slow down as we drive by the office site? We won't be stopping; I'd just like to see how it's progressing."

"Of course, Ms. Chavos," he murmured, slowing the SUV to a crawl as he turned up the side street the Tech-Corp offices sat on.

The three-story white stucco-and-redbrick building sat amid several office buildings, rising a story higher than the others and appearing stately, waiting to be finished and filled with activity. Sun-dimming windows gleamed beneath the harsh sunlight drawing her gaze and her need to investigate the interior.

"Looks quite nice," she said in satisfaction as she sat back in her seat and closed out the files on the electronic pad.

She would get out by herself and walk along the streets to absorb the changes in the town one day soon. She doubted there were many people she'd recognize, or who would recognize her. She'd changed, Katelyn reflected; she was still different as she'd once been accused, but that difference was now buried and the world only saw a woman confident and certain of her place in the world.

"Should we go to the hotel now?" her driver asked politely.

Katelyn gave him a small smile. "Of course. Thank you for taking the time for me."

He shot her a look of surprise through the rearview mirror but said nothing else. Within minutes they were pulling beneath the hotel entrance, the shaded awning relieving the bright sunlight that would have spilled onto the dark gray and cream tiles that lined the entrance floors.

"Ms. Chavos." A hotel steward opened her door and lifted the leather briefcase from the seat next to her, then handed it off to her driver, extending his hand to help her out.

Katelyn stepped from the vehicle, the four-inch heels she wore with the cherry red snug business skirt that ended just above her knees and white chiffon sleeveless blouse giving her the added height she always felt she needed. Not that the four inches helped around Breeds. They were tall enough, broad enough, to remind any woman exactly how feminine they were, she thought with an edge of amusement.

"Your suite's ready, ma'am," the steward, Bert, the name tag proclaimed, assured her as he led the way through the entrance and motioned to a porter to collect her bags. "Should you need anything, please let us know, and we'll make sure it's delivered immediately."

They moved to the bank of elevators where he pushed the button inset between two cubicles, the doors opening immediately.

The ride to the top floor was made quickly and soon the elevator doors were sliding open, the cool, pristine hallway opening before them.

Katelyn could feel the exhaustion she'd been putting off for the past week catching up with her. She wanted in her room, in one of the comfortable silk pajama sets she'd packed, and stretched out on a bed for a nap.

She'd been going full tilt for the past two years as she prepared for the move to Broken Butte, coordinating and overseeing the completion of both the Tech-Corp production facility as well as the offices. Vetting construction companies and future employees for the new Tech-Corp location and making certain everything went smoothly was a time-consuming job. The agreement between Tech-Corp, Breeds and the Navajo Nation made things doubly difficult at times. And if she thought Tech-Corp was tough when it came to security, well, they had nothing on the Breeds.

Tech-Corp itself had a strict vetting process, but only Breeds required the many DNA samples she'd been advised she'd need from not just those employees, but herself as well.

Blood, urine and saliva swabs as well as a vaginal swab that would be taken in the Bureau of Breed Affairs medical facility rather than by a private doctor.

The background checks were completed, thankfully, and she had only to go over a few of them with the man who had taken her under his wing eight years ago, Graeme Parker, before submitting them to the Bureau when she arrived for her appointment at the medical facility. Everything was running smoothly, without a wrinkle in sight.

And that alone was worrying.

Within minutes a porter arrived with her luggage and placed it on the luggage racks awaiting them in the bedroom. Tipped, smiling in pleasure and assuring her all she had to do was call for him, he left the suite, and Katelyn slid the secure lock on the doors in place before sighing in relief.

God, she needed to sleep.

She felt that she could sleep a week and it still wouldn't be enough to renew the energy she needed some days.

"Hello, love."

Katelyn froze.

She knew that voice, smoother than sex and sin and flavored with a dark, heady rasp.

Please, God, what had Graeme done?

Releasing the doorknobs to the double doors, Katelyn turned slowly and stared at the man standing in the middle of the living area, close to the bar and balcony doors.

Six-four, dressed in a white dress shirt, sleeves rolled back on his forearms and tan khakis with his ever-present scuffed brown boots. His green gaze was somber, the color almost emerald though shot with warm amber tones in his sun-bronzed face, his thick dark blond hair falling over his brow and growing nearly to his shirt collar.

The ultimate bad boy, she'd always thought.

He should have been born a Breed.

"Did they put me in the wrong room?" She fought to ignore how her heart raced, how memories tried to push to the surface from that deep, dark place she'd confined them to.

"And here not even a *hello*, or *How have you been, Dane?*" he asked, his voice somber. "It's been a long time, love. Far too long."

It hadn't been long enough.

"Hello, Dane. How are you? Why are you in my suite?" She rattled off the questions, torn between throwing her arms around him and raging in fury that he was there.

"It seems we've a shared suite." His lips quirked with a bit of mockery.

Katelyn could only shake her head. "I'll call the desk . . ."

"Sorry, love, already tried that," he assured her. "There's not a spare room to be found."

Great.

Katelyn gazed around the room. The long conference/dining table and seating area with a bar and electric fireplace. The kitchenette was tucked in the far corner and divided from the room by a short counter.

It was to be her home until the house she'd leased in town was ready. A few weeks, she'd been assured, no more than a month.

"So stay at the Bureau. I thought you had a suite there." Graeme had told her several times the Vanderales had their own personal suite at the Western Bureau.

"The parents are currently in residence, and the twins are, quite frankly, little terrors at present," he said, the hint of his South African accent washing over her senses even as she noticed that despite his grimace, she could detect a smirk at the edge of his lips.

He was lying to her.

For whatever reason, he was determined to share her suite with her.

"For how long?" She forced herself to have patience.

She'd been certain there wouldn't be a chance of running into him. There were no Vanderale projects in the area, no news reports of their arrival. Yet here he was, right where she didn't need him to be.

She didn't want him there, didn't need him there, but beyond that, this was going to be more inconvenient to her than simply risking running into him on a regular basis.

He shrugged, his wide shoulders lifting as though it didn't matter. "Well, the parents haven't given me their itinerary yet. I'll let you know when they do."

This was going to cause problems. Her assistant, Portia, was due to arrive in a few days and was supposed to stay in the other room. Once the business for the day was over, she'd need Portia there so they could keep up with problems arising or last-minute concerns.

"Dane, I realize you must have your own reasons for deciding to steal the connecting room"—she stated, fighting to keep her tone icy, refusing to play along with whatever game he was playing—"but in two days' time, my assistant will be arriving, and she'll need it. I need her here."

He pursed his lips regretfully. "Sorry, love, but I can't exactly camp out in the hallway. I'm certain there are still rooms in one of the nearby hotels that Tech-Corp can get for her."

She wasn't in the mood for this. Wasn't in the mood for his outlandish humor or his perverse amusement at her expense. She had two days to fix this, but if she didn't shower and sleep soon, then she would miss her chance until well after midnight.

Graeme had a shopping list of details he wanted to go over for the production facility and new offices. This was her baby, and she would be in charge of the majority of decisions made. She couldn't afford to allow this problem to interfere.

But it was Dane, a part of her whispered. She hadn't seen him in eight years, other than online or in news programs. She hadn't spoken to him, hadn't felt that curious warmth that always seemed to reach out to her.

He was her weakness, even now, all these years later. But she'd never expected anything less.

"This isn't going to work," she informed him, fighting to remain calm. "Find yourself another hotel, camp in the desert, I don't really care. But vacate this suite."

"Come on, Katy . . ."

"My name is Katelyn," she snapped before he could go further, causing him to look at her sharply, his gaze narrowing. "I'm sorry, but Katy simply doesn't exist anymore, and I'd appreciate it if you'd remember that while addressing me."

She hadn't used "Katy" since she'd left Broken Butte. Graeme called her Katelyn from the beginning and had addressed her as such when introducing her to Tech-Corp's leadership team. She'd been Katelyn ever since, and she'd found she liked it.

"Katy." His voice lowered while he stepped across the room, his gaze holding hers as his expression turned somber. "You'll always be my Katy . . ."

She laughed at that. She couldn't help it.

"I'll always be that stupid little girl that believed you could do no wrong and had no hope of fitting into your life?" She rolled her eyes at the idea of it even though a part of her knew that twenty-one-year-old still lurked inside her, still doubted her value despite her changes. "No, thank you, Dane. I believe I much prefer Katelyn."

She stared up at him as he stopped in front of her.

"I never meant to hurt you," he stated, reaching up to brush her hair back from her cheek. "You don't know what my life was like then, baby. It wasn't safe for you."

For a moment, she was that young woman again, staring up at the man she was certain was coming to care for her, watching his eyes darken, the oddest golden striations gleaming in the green, mesmerizing her.

When his thumb brushed against the odd reddened mark on her cheek, a sizzling burst of subtle sensation shot through her body, causing her to jerk back and stare up at him in surprise.

"Don't . . ." She shook her head and stared around the room now in desperation. "On second thought, just take the fucking suite . . ."

She'd taken one step to escape him, to escape the remembered hunger for every touch from him that she could experience and fantasies of so much more.

Before she could get farther, he caught her elbow, turning her back to him, his lips lowering until they brushed against hers. That light caress held her immobile, her eyes wide and locked with his as she watched the amber lights gleam in the emerald color.

"Katy." His lips brushed hers, holding her still more effectively than chains. "I missed you."

His thumb brushed over the mark on her cheek again and she caught her breath at the pleasure.

"How?" She forced herself to break contact, to ease her head back as she fought to breathe, to calm her racing heart. "You can't miss someone you never knew, Dane. And we're both aware of the fact that neither of us knew the other."

"That isn't true." He frowned down at her. "Come on, Katy, it's been too long. Let's not be at odds . . ."

"At odds?" She nearly laughed at the words. "We are not at odds, Dane. One can't be at odds with a stranger. And that's what we were, what we are. Strangers. Now leave me in peace. I'm tired and simply don't have the energy to deal with you. Find another room while you're at it. Quickly."

This time, he allowed her to go, releasing his hold on her as she walked to the bedroom the porter had placed her bags in, entered and locked the double doors behind her.

Leaning back, eyes closed, she forced herself to breathe. Just breathe. No memories, no wishes, desires or remembered fantasies.

Because in them lay the road to madness, she admitted.

She'd been here before, fighting that need to just see him, hear his voice, know just the brush of his fingers against her cheek again and the hope that soon, she'd know his caresses, his kisses.

Pushing away from the door, she moved to her luggage and opened the leather case that contained the silk pajamas she normally slept in. She kicked off her shoes and headed to the shower even as she wiped a single tear from her cheek.

◆ ◆ ◆

"You've upset Katelyn." Graeme's voice came over the call, the faint rumble in it a sign of his displeasure.

Dane grunted at the accusation. "Trust me, it was a two-way street."

Seeing her again, seeing the changes in her, the sadness in her whisky brown eyes, the lack of a smile . . . She'd always smiled when she'd seen him, until the night that he'd arrived in the heli-jet at the poor excuse for a house she'd been renting.

He remembered seeing that damned shack where she lived and having to fight the impulse to force her into the jet and take her immediately to the safe house he kept in Broken Butte in case of emergency. As far as he was concerned, she needed to be safe from her living conditions.

But he'd known if he'd done so, he'd have only ended up hurting her worse. She'd be filled with hope, believing it meant far more than he was certain at the time that it had meant.

"I don't care in the least if you were upset." The growl deepened in

Graeme's voice now. "You've upset her, and it won't happen again. I didn't bring her back to you to allow you to hurt her."

That damned Bengal's inflated opinion of his actions and the reasons behind them amazed him sometimes.

"Stay out of this, Graeme," he warned the Breed as he stepped back into the spacious bedroom next to Katy's. "I won't tolerate your interference."

Silence came across the line before the Bengal chuckled.

It wasn't a pleasant sound.

"Tell me, has your animal begun shredding your guts again, demanding you fix what you hurt inside her?"

He froze at the question as well as the knowing tone.

"What the fuck are you talking about?" Dane growled, but he knew very well what the other Breed meant. He just didn't know how Graeme could have been aware of it.

"That mark on your hand," the other Breed drawled. "Do you even remember the night you acquired it?"

Dane glanced at his left hand before he could stop himself, at the red mark, in the form of a small starburst, between his thumb and forefinger. He frowned. He remembered the morning he'd seen it, but not how it had come to be there.

"Did your mother ever swab it, or did you just not tell her how you acquired it?" The silky edge in Graeme's voice warned him that the Bengal at least thought he knew where it had come from.

"Stop playing games with me, asshole." Dealing with Graeme was never easy, even at the best of times.

"The mark on her face," Graeme continued. "Is that not where you kissed a tear from her cheek just after that teardrop hit your hand, the warmth of it nearly stinging? Your tongue touched her cheek that night. I was there. I saw the exchange from the front porch as the monster I carry fought to escape and rip you limb from limb for the sheer agony that had torn through her. The next morning the mark was on your hand when you met with a Wolf Breed, Lobo Reever, and the mark was on her cheek that evening when I arrived at the restaurant and offered her a job at Tech-Corp."

He was the reason Katy had disappeared from Broken Butte? Dane had never known why she'd left, and the Santiagos had played dumb as hell, even though the Breeds who asked them about it said they'd lied.

They'd left town with Katy and then returned alone. They'd flown to San Francisco, then just disappeared, and Dane had been unable to track their movements.

He'd been enraged when she'd disappeared and the Santiagos refused to reveal where she had gone. She didn't want anyone to know, especially him, Costas Santiago had told him angrily when Dane had made a trip to his house. Dane had broken her, he'd claimed. For years the people in Broken Butte had tried and hadn't even dented her will and her spark. But he had done more than dent it. He'd nearly destroyed it.

The man had been determined to tell Dane nothing, and short of torture, he would never have revealed Katy's whereabouts.

And now that he'd found her again, there was a part of him determined to keep her from ever running away from him. A very matelike response from a Breed that wasn't her mate.

And that fucking crazy-as-a-hatter Graeme refused to tell him anything now. Smug, smirking ass of a Bengal. Dane swore he hated Bengals—not one of them that he knew was sane—but Graeme was the king of Bengal insanity, it seemed.

The fucker.

It had been years before he'd learned, entirely by accident, that she was working with Tech-Corp.

When Dane had called the CEO and asked about the senior managerial analyst, a man by the name of Ross Monahan had asked him to allow his partner to discuss her. As the partner was in Window Rock, where Dane was reported to be through several news reports, he'd likely just meet up with him.

It had been Graeme who met him, and he'd made a deal with Dane. Give Katelyn two years and she'd begin arriving in Broken Butte to start putting their offices and production facility together there, then he'd not interfere while Dane attempted to fix whatever he'd broken in Katelyn. And he knew Dane had done it, because Katelyn refused to consider any work with Vanderale Industries the few times the companies had consulted.

Dane had agreed.

He didn't know if he would have done so if he'd been aware Graeme was the reason and means behind her disappearance from Broken Butte.

"I'll make certain not to forget that it was you who hid her all those years," Dane promised him.

The odd, knowing chuckle had the hairs at the back of Dane's neck lifting in primal warning.

"You weren't the only reason," Graeme assured him. "But hurt her again, and I'll make certain to see if I can't rearrange that pretty face of yours. What did you do anyway?"

If the question hadn't been merely concerned rather than threatening, Dane wouldn't have answered him. And though the remark that Dane wasn't the only reason had his instincts flaring, he assured himself the Bengal meant the treatment she received as a young woman. He couldn't mean anything else.

"I called her Katy." He frowned at that.

Graeme was silent, and Dane had the sense of sadness or regret in his sigh moments later.

"Her name is Katelyn," Graeme said quietly. "Katy was a child, lacking confidence or choices, fighting just to survive in a world that often made no sense to her. She's the girl who loved a man who believed her to be without worth and having no hope of it. You should remember that."

The line disconnected, leaving Dane standing in the middle of the bedroom, his Breed senses rioting.

As a hybrid, his Breed senses were recessed unless he let them free himself. His ability to do that always confused his mother. Those senses were strong even when hidden. Those senses of smell, sight, hearing and awareness. Even his sense of taste was more sensitive. But after he'd arrived in Broken Butte when Katy had been a tender eighteen, it had become stronger, especially when he was in her presence, though he hadn't connected it at the time. Once she'd left, it had eased away about the time he'd realized what he felt for the Breed he'd protected for so long, Harmony Lancaster, hadn't been the love he'd thought it was.

His mother, once a leading Genetics Council researcher, had always feared hybrid Breeds wouldn't mate. That idea had been tossed out the window years ago with the mating of Kiowa Bear and the then US president's daughter, Amanda Marion.

In the years since, they'd learned hybrids experienced mating differently, in varying depths and strengths, until that final bonding occurred. Not that there were many hybrid Breeds in existence who had yet to reach their adult age, but there were a few, such as Kiowa, Dog Latrans and Cassie Sinclair.

He hadn't thought of Katy as his mate, though. And he still didn't. But what he'd done to her all those years ago haunted him. It wasn't that he hadn't wanted her. He had. Very much so. But she'd been far too young for the man he was.

As with Harmony, he was quite fond of her. He'd desired her when she was far too young for him to touch, worried him, often fascinated him, but to suspect Mating Heat was ludicrous, even now. Wasn't it?

Mates couldn't stay away from each other. The Breeds' animal instincts wouldn't allow it. And there were definite signs to mating. The glands beneath the tongue swelled with the mating hormone. Even hybrids experienced this. The male's inability to keep from touching his mate, marking her with that hormone, was a certain fact of mating. A mating scent that other Breeds easily detected.

Dane didn't carry that scent, or his father, Leo, would have informed him of it in no uncertain terms. The Breeds who had been around Katy the last day she'd been in Broken Butte hadn't detected a mating scent. And the glands beneath Dane's tongue had never been swollen.

She wasn't his mate. But still, his animal raged at Dane's actions, and his heart ached for the pain he caused her. He'd never forgotten her, or the lust he'd felt for her.

Shaking away the thought, he rubbed at the sensitive mark on his hand. It was no mating mark, and he'd be damned if he'd allow that crazy Bengal to convince him it was. And it couldn't have come from something as simple as a teardrop. No matter that mad Breed's claim.

Dane learned years ago to never attempt to probe too deeply in the minds of madmen; the complicated pitfalls could make a sane man suicidal.

But this was Katy, he thought, and he knew Graeme had a soft spot for her for some reason. He'd have to figure out why before he'd ever figure out what the Bengal was up to now.

The mind of a mad Bengal . . . fuck.

# CHAPTER 2

She'd grown up in the past eight years, Dane admitted as they sat through dinner and drinks with Graeme, the Western Bureau of Breed Affairs director, Rule Breaker, and the assistant director, Lawe Justice, and their wives the next evening. She wasn't the twenty-one-year-old who so obviously had to fight back her feelings around him as well as her discomfort in front of others any longer.

She was poised, confident and certain of herself in a way she had never been as a girl.

She'd always had a rather regal way of carrying herself, though, and that hadn't changed. A surfeit of pride had always refused to allow others to see her pain, or her discomfort, but it had always been there, all those years ago. At some point, she had discarded the discomfort and fear. She knew exactly who she was now, and how to navigate the world around her.

If she hurt, if she felt in the least uncomfortable, she didn't show it now.

She remained focused on the conversation, answering Rule's and Lawe's questions and socializing with their wives. She looked like a fucking princess the way she sat, straight in her chair, shoulders perfectly aligned, her head tilted just the slightest as she listened to Rule and his wife, Gypsy, discuss the new home they were having built not far from the Western Bureau of Breed Affairs.

He didn't notice her showing much of a reaction to anything else in the room, though he sensed she was aware of it, until the first strains of the band that had set up on the far side of the room filtered through the dining area.

Lights lowered until only those over the tables were lit to a soft dim glow. Turning her head, she watched as the lead singer, a young man that appeared to be in his late twenties, began crooning a soft country tune.

He saw her face soften for a second before her expression cleared again and she turned back to the table. But in that second, he saw something hungry, a longing he might have missed if he hadn't paid attention.

Katy wanted to dance.

Katy. Katelyn. God, it was hard to remember to call her Katelyn when he sensed so much of his Katy lying just beneath the surface.

He doubted she'd ever gone to a dance when she was younger; he knew she hadn't gone to her senior prom, or the graduation party the students held outside of town that year.

Sliding his chair back, he caught the quiet, somber look Graeme cast her before his gaze flicked to Dane. Standing, Dane stepped around to Katy's chair.

"Dance with me, Katelyn." He didn't give her a chance to refuse him.

Gripping the back of her chair, he slid her slowly from the table and caught one of her hands in his.

"Excuse me," she said softly as Graeme rose just slightly from his chair in an almost courtly manner.

"Enjoy, my dear," the Bengal murmured.

Placing his hand at the small of her back, Dane led her to the dance floor, aware of the uncertain look she gave him as she first stood to accept the invitation. And though she didn't appear or seem uncertain in any way now, he could still feel it, just beneath the surface.

It was the scent of her that held him captivated, though. A whisper of spice and sweetness, feminine longing and arousal, and barely there, almost unnoticeable, there was fear. Not a fear of physical pain or violence, but a fear of something entirely different.

Pulling her into his arms, Dane tucked her against his chest, inhaled her scent where it was more prevalent, at the bend of her neck, just above the hard beat of blood in her delicate veins.

"This game is going to get old quickly," she told him as he moved her around the dance floor, just enjoying the feel of her in his arms, the warmth of her body.

She felt warmer than he'd expected, but she always had. She'd been eighteen when he'd first met her, and he'd noticed it instantly, wondering silently if perhaps she was ill. But as he spent more time around her, he'd realized it was just part of her. Sometimes there, sometimes not, but prone to make an appearance at any time.

It was unusual, and when he'd questioned her, she'd brushed it off. She was just weird, she'd told him.

She was anything but weird.

"Unique" came to mind.

"I'm not a playing a game with you, Katelyn," he promised, nearly calling her "Katy" once again. "I had a need to hold you, to feel you moving against me. As you didn't seem inclined to share your room with me, I thought perhaps you'd share a dance."

Her pulse rate kicked up as he nipped her ear in admonishment, then licked over it gently.

God, the taste of her. Soft and feminine, spicy heat and rich, lush sweetness. Would she taste that good when he got her clothes off? he wondered. He knew she would. Sweet and hot, and damned if she wouldn't be addictive. He could sense it, feel it all the way to his soul.

"Do you want to hurt me, Dane?" she asked him softly, moving against him with a natural sensuality and grace that had his cock so damned hard, it was almost painful. "That's what you're going to end up doing if you keep this up. Wasn't it enough when I was younger?"

"Can you walk away from this now, Katelyn?" he asked, brushing his lips against her ear. "I watched for you, searched for you for years. Because I couldn't forget you. It wasn't finished, and we both knew it."

Her forehead pressed against his chest, and he felt her breathing, sharp, uneven, and scented the conflict building in her: to walk away, or to remain there, swaying against him. And she liked being against him. The warmth of him against her flesh, the feel of his heartbeat against her.

Katelyn fisted her fingers as they lay against Dane's chest, trying to tell herself she could walk away. She was strong enough. Yet she stayed there, the music, the man and his warmth wrapping around her.

"It was finished, Dane," she reminded him, but her heart was assuring her otherwise.

Dammit, she was supposed to be over him, finished with that silly little phase of her life. That phase where this man was the center of her universe and she spent her life waiting, watching for him so she could feel warm again.

"Enough." She gave a sharp shake of her head. "This evening is over."

The song slid into silence and she felt Dane give a little sigh.

"Very well, love." He sighed. "If you insist."

"I insist." Didn't she?

She turned away as he released her, aware that the music had begun again, another slow, sensual tune drawing yet more couples to the dance floor as they made their way back to the table.

She'd made a mistake in dancing with him, Katelyn admitted. Because she knew she'd ache for him well into the night now.

"It's time I call it a night," she announced as she reached the table, and her bodyguard rose from the table positioned behind her chair and Graeme and his wife, Cat.

Dane watched as Graeme came to his feet and wrapped his arms around her as though he experienced no discomfort in pulling her against him. Males and females knew strong levels of discomfort whenever they touched anyone else. For the females, it could be quite painful.

Yet Graeme's mate, Cat, gave Katy a quick hug as well.

"I'll be going up as well," Dane told them with a nod at the table. "Lawe, Rule, I'll see you in the morning."

He had an appointment with the two men to discuss several missions that were set to begin the next morning.

Handshakes were accepted, and before Katy made it to the restaurant exit with her bodyguard following closely behind, Dane and Rhys were just behind them.

"Miss Portia called earlier," the bodyguard was saying as they stepped into the lobby. "She sent the files you asked for to your personal inbox and said morning was fine to go over them."

"Excellent." Katy sighed, and Dane could hear the weariness in her voice.

"And Misters Vanderale and Desalvo are just behind us," the bastard reported.

"I'm aware." There was an edge of amusement but also uncertainty in her voice.

As they headed for the elevators, Dane noticed the older woman that stepped from the reception desk and began walking toward them. Harmless-looking, her head down, her salt-and-pepper hair short but bushy as it framed her angular face.

She walked with purpose toward the hotel exit, which put her walking past Katy, if she'd continued on her way. At the last second her head lifted and she moved to the side, directly into Katy's path.

Drew had less than a second to step in front of her, putting himself between Katy and the other woman.

"This is a fine way to treat family," the woman's coarse voice announced as Dane stepped beside Katy and felt her tense. "Really, Katy?"

Hotel security stepped from behind the registration desk, materializing instantly at the suggested confrontation.

"Step aside, Drew," Katelyn ordered the Bengal, forcing back the hard surge of excess energy she could feel building in her stomach and threatening to invade her system.

Adrenaline. For as long as she could remember, she'd had a problem with that hard, hot surge of panic-causing force that could erupt inside her.

She didn't panic anymore, she told herself. There was no reason to. And there was no reason to force it to her brain, where it would keep her awake for hours with all the various possibilities in every phase of work that she currently had in progress.

She was aware of Dane next to her, Rhys behind her, and wondered if his timing was a blessing or a curse.

"Drew, take Ms. Chavos up," Dane told the Breed.

Katelyn shot him a look of amusement, aware of Drew glancing at her for confirmation.

"I just wanted a minute, Katy. Please . . ." The woman tried to look around Drew as he did as Katy ordered and stepped aside.

Lisa Moran.

This woman and her husband hadn't wanted her in their home, Katelyn remembered. They didn't like kids. Kids were messy, Lisa would snap. The foster program didn't pay enough to keep her, but Charles had promised John for some ungodly reason, she'd claimed.

"What do you want?" Katelyn didn't bother with preliminaries as she faced the diminutive Lisa Moran.

Pleasantries were wasted on Lisa anyway. She wasn't a pleasant individual unless it suited whatever scheme she had formed.

The fact that the other woman had more or less ambushed her in the hotel lobby, where Katelyn was forced to be polite, all too aware of the journalists and sensationalists, not to mention bloggers and amateur smartphone video enthusiasts who could recognize Dane at any moment, wasn't lost on her.

"We're family, Katy." She smiled almost hesitantly, an odd look for her, Katelyn thought. "Surely you remember what family is?"

It was enough to make her stomach pitch.

"I have no family," Katelyn reminded her, satisfaction filling her at the discomfort she saw flash in Lisa's gaze.

"Charles was your family," Lisa tried again. "That made me family."

"Charles wasn't family," Katelyn denied. "Marie Moran, my foster mother, was my mother's distant cousin, and she married Charles's cousin, John. That does not make us family of any sort."

Lisa's lips thinned, and her eyes narrowed.

"Lisa, take my advice and walk away," Katelyn told her coolly. "You're wasting your time here. Whatever you think you want, it's not happening, and you should be aware of that."

"You don't mean that, Katy." Lisa tried to smile, but it just wasn't happening in any convincing form. "Trust me, you don't want to walk away from me right now . . ."

"Rhys, take care of this," Dane ordered his friend, and before Katelyn knew his intention, he gripped her arm and with Drew on the other side all but dragged her to the elevator.

Turning after he pushed her into the elevator, she could see Rhys and several security personnel escorting Lisa toward the entrance.

"You do not entertain that kind of poison, especially in public," he stated irritably as the doors closed. "I would have thought Graeme had already chewed your ass over that one."

Katelyn felt that gut punch of energy escape her control then. She had to clench her teeth, her stomach tightening as she literally pushed it up, past her heart, where it could rush to her brain instead.

She felt the sizzle behind her ears, the way her brain seemed to kick-start and begin pulling in information. And the dominant force she felt Dane attempting to exert over her pissed her off.

"Perhaps had you kept your nose off my ass, then it wouldn't have been an issue." She jerked her arm from his hold and slashed a furious look up at him. "You don't get to make these decisions for me. Walk the fuck away if I'm doing something you don't like." Then she turned to Drew, lips tightening at the wary look he directed at her. "Let someone manhandle me like that again and I will personally serve you to

Graeme with an apple in your goddamned mouth." She watched him swallow. Slowly. "Are we clear?"

"Crystal, ma'am." He cleared his throat and stared straight ahead.

She couldn't believe Dane dared to interfere the way he had. She knew what Lisa wanted, what she always wanted—money—and this was better dealt with sooner rather than later.

"Have you forgotten the hell that woman tried to make of your life?" he snapped.

The elevator stopped, door opening a second before she exploded. Compressing her lips, she followed Drew from the cubicle, then strode quickly up the hall as he quickened his steps to stay in front of her.

Once they were in the suite, she didn't have to restrain a damned thing.

"Let me tell you what I remember," she snapped, turning on him as Drew made his normal surveil of the suite. "I remember you, Dane, playing with a twenty-one-year-old virgin's emotions like they were your personal harp. Just as I remember you walking away when being called on it." She shot him a look of disgust as he frowned down at her and crossed his arms over his chest as though dealing with a child. "Now you don't get to tell me how to handle a damned thing. Are we perfectly clear?"

She swore she felt his denial, his confusion. She definitely saw it in his expression, in his eyes.

"Not how I remember it," he stated, his jaw tightening until the muscles bunched beneath his jaw.

"Of course it isn't," she retorted mockingly as Drew stepped back into the sitting area and walked to the bar across the room. "Tell me. How many times did Rhys have to warn you to walk away during those three years? How many times did he happen to arrive just before you kissed me, before you could touch me? How many times did he warn you to leave before the stupid little waitress could invite you to dinner in her pitiful shack again?"

Shame coursed through her now as she remembered. Half a dozen times she'd invited him, certain he was going to accept, that he only held back because of her age. But she was an adult, she'd told herself at the time. He'd realize she was an adult.

"Dammit, Katy, I couldn't stay away from you," he growled, his green-and-gold gaze slashing to Drew as he neared them.

Katelyn accepted the drink Drew handed her, giving Dane a tight smile before taking a sip of it, then lowering the glass.

She lifted the drink again, finished the shot in a single drink, then stalked to the bar, where she slapped the glass to the counter.

"You can leave, Drew," she told the bodyguard, unable to hide her anger. "I rather doubt you want to be here right now."

Drew grunted at that. "I love watching you tear ass, Ms. Chavos. Long as it isn't mine."

She almost laughed at that, which was surprising, as pissed as she was. He'd been her bodyguard for less than six months, and he seemed to be working out really well after all.

"How 'bout I kick your ass?" Dane suggested, his lips peeling back from his teeth in an almost Breed move that didn't surprise her in the least.

"Just go, Drew." She shook her head as she watched his shoulders tighten. "I'd hate to have to get upset because Graeme tried to fire you for damaging his little human self."

Drew shot her a vaguely surprised look.

What, he didn't think she knew Graeme frowned upon his men hurting humans he had need of? And for whatever reason, Graeme seemed partial to Dane right now.

"Yeah, Drew. Let's not hurt my human self," Dane drawled. "Just walk away like a good little Breed. I'm sure we can talk later and get all this squared away."

The bodyguard grunted again, the mockery in the sound a bit uncalled-for but not worth firing him over. He'd learned how to make her favorite chill-out drink. Only Portia knew that one besides him. She wouldn't fire him just because he was a smart-ass to someone else.

"I'll be right outside in the security lounge," he told her, referring to the wide lounging area across the hall on the right, just past the suite in front of hers.

Dane watched him leave, his expression tinged with challenge as the bodyguard gave him a warning glance as he passed him.

*Men!* she thought in irritation. There were times they still managed to amaze her.

"I'm not in the mood to deal with you tonight," she told Dane, reaching up to rub at the small red mark on her face, where it tingled as though the heat beneath her skin somehow irritated it.

"Your perception of the past is wrong." He caught her arm as she moved to pass him, his fingers warm against her skin, the touch more pleasant than she liked to admit.

"Is it?" she asked him. "I guess I also somehow misheard you when you said I couldn't possibly fit into your world. Right?"

He held her gaze, and she wasn't certain what she saw shadow it for a brief second, but it was something hungry, forbidden.

"You didn't understand," he told her, his gaze moving to her lips as they parted.

There was something she was going to say to that, because she knew she had understood perfectly. She'd known exactly what he meant. But the heavy sensuality that suddenly filled his face and darkened his eyes held her spellbound.

"I couldn't have you then," he told her, his voice somber, regretful. "You were so fucking sweet, so innocent, Katy. Destroying that and hurting your sweet heart further was more than I could consider."

His hand cupped her cheek, the rasp of his thumb over her lips causing her to part them farther in an attempt to draw in more oxygen. Hopefully, it would clear her head long enough to tell him to go to hell.

Or beg him to kiss her . . .

"I don't have to hold back now," he told her, his voice low, echoing with lust.

# ✦ CHAPTER 3 ✦

Dane tried to tell himself to pull back, to wait. To give her a chance to decide if this was still what she wanted. Then her lips parted, and that little pink tongue flicked out against her lips.

And he just gave it up.

Hell, this was his kiss.

He'd made the ultimate sacrifice eight years before. He was decades older than she was, more than twice her age. And at the time, his fear of a mating had ensured he kept his distance from her.

He couldn't have a mate. He'd known that for as long as he'd known what he was and what a mate meant in his life. Mating Heat was a scent that couldn't be hidden. A Breed couldn't recess his genetics far enough to hide that. And accepting his mate would be the possible death of his parents, those two precious little sisters of his and the Breeds in general.

Vanderale secrets were dangerous ones. Leo was nearing one

hundred and fifty years old, as was Dane's mother. Dane himself was seventy.

Mating heat delayed aging in Breeds and their mates. Hybrids were born with the aging delay, which kicked in around age thirty. Dane hadn't aged physically in forty years. And once he mated, and the aging hormones returned, aging would equal one physical year every ten.

Those secrets would destroy not just the Breeds but also the one known as the first Leo. The first Breed ever created.

Dane had lived in fear of Mating Heat, knowing if he found his mate, he'd have no choice but to take her to the Vanderales' African compound and go into hiding. The world would have to believe they had died.

Because of that, he'd been unusually diligent when his response to Katy had been so strong. She had been too young, too innocent, to force such changes on her.

Now, just as then, he couldn't detect the mating hormone in his system, nothing but the hot, lust-filled dreams he'd had over the years where she was concerned.

There was nothing to even hint that she was his mate.

He may well fall in love with her this time, he thought. Fighting that would be hell. He'd have to ensure she didn't fall in love with him, but he'd been told often he was too much an ass to actually love. And Katy hated him now, so he was certain he could keep her from loving him again.

She'd stopped waiting on him. She'd taken two lovers, he'd learned after finding her two years ago. A mate didn't do that, especially female mates. Another male's touch was so painful they didn't dare.

A woman in love didn't do it either, he thought. They waited. And Katy hadn't. She'd left Broken Butte, trained for who she was now and she'd had lovers. And now she could have him as her lover too. He could make up for hurting her. He could pleasure her, give her all of himself now, and know that Katy, as well as the Breeds, would be safe.

Before she could move away from him, before the hypnotic sensuality could ease, he lowered his head and covered her lips. His tongue pressed past the responsive curves, slid inside and nudged at hers.

And he was lost.

It wasn't Mating Heat. It wasn't anything mating- or Breed-related. But it was like nothing he'd ever known in his sexual lifetime either. And that was almost as terrifying as Mating Heat.

His arms went around her, and as fragile as she was, perched on those damned heels, she fit perfectly into them. Soft, heated, pillowy lips, already parted, were pierced by his eager, hungry tongue. And the taste of her was exquisite.

A hint of the peppers that had been in her meal at dinner, because she did like the spicy things, a taste of honey. And she had him aching for more. For a deeper, hungrier kiss. And he knew just how to take it, how to stroke her lips and tease her tongue, and tempt her to tease in turn.

And she excelled at it.

After a moment she melted against him, her arms going around his neck as she lifted closer to him, her tongue twisting against his, licking at it, drawing his taste back to her.

She was midnight and magic in his arms, he thought. And that was something he'd never known in his life.

◆ ◆ ◆

Katelyn was lost. The minute his lips touched hers, slanted over them and licked at her tongue with his, nothing mattered but that kiss. Then he pulled her to him, his arms wrapping around her, lifting her to him. One hand went to the back of her head, palmed it, then cupped her neck as though to ensure she stayed with his kiss.

The touch broke something in her. A hunger, once hidden, for touch. Not just any touch, but Dane's touch. And it was different.

She was no virgin; she didn't live on promises and dreams and hadn't since long before Dane entered her life. But what he did to her, she knew she'd want more. Crave it. Grieve every second she didn't have it once he was out of her life.

He was here now. And his lips and tongue met hers in such pleasure that she didn't know how to describe it, even to herself. He tasted like a dream, spice and honey and the tastes she loved the most, and she could become addicted to him.

The faint itch she'd felt under her tongue for most of the day eased, but a sucker punch of arousal-based sensation struck at her womb and released a wave of heat through her body that was impossible to control.

She heard her own moan whisper from her throat, as she became lost in the kiss and he dragged her closer, lifting her against him with a ragged groan as she felt her back against the wall.

His fingers smoothed beneath the chiffon skirt she wore, brushing it out of the way as his fingers curled around her thigh.

"Around my hips," he snarled, then nipped at her lips.

Katelyn moaned at the heat, the pleasure, as his hands cupped her rear, wrapped her legs around his hips.

"Oh, hell yes," he muttered against her lips, his hips bunching, flexing as he drove the hard ridge of his cock against the sensitive folds beneath her panties.

Her clit was swollen, throbbing with the need for orgasm. She couldn't remember a time when she had needed to be touched, taken, more than she did at that moment.

"Dane," she whispered his name as his lips moved to her neck, his roughened kisses and the rasp of his teeth and tongue sending shudders raking through her body as she felt the heat building against her skin.

Gripping his hips between her thighs, she moved with him, pressing to him, rubbing against the hard stalk of the erection his pants covered and fighting to breathe through an arousal so deep, so stark, she didn't know how much longer she could bear it.

"That's it," he groaned. "Ride my cock, sweet." The hint of South African accent slipped past his lips and stroked over her senses.

The soft cream chiffon of her blouse parted, surprising her. She hadn't felt him unbuttoning the fabric, but she had to admit, she'd been a little distracted by the excitement he was stroking between her thighs.

"Damn, Katy," he whispered, leaning back to stare down at her breasts as he kept her pinned to the wall with his hips. "Look at those pretty, hard nipples."

He released the front clasp of her bra, then pushed aside the lace covering her breasts. His gaze moved back to hers, the gold more apparent in the green of his eyes than before.

"Will you watch while I lick those pretty nipples?"

Her eyes widened, and she felt moisture spill from her vagina, dampening her panties further.

"Watch," he whispered. "Watch while I lick them. Then I'm going to suck them until you come. Right here. Just rubbing that sweet little pussy up and down my cock while I suck these pretty nipples . . ."

He was mesmerizing. The sound of his voice, rasping, a little graveled.

She watched. She couldn't help it. Fighting to breathe, drunk on the extreme sensuality wrapping around her, she watched as his tongue licked, prodded, lashed against one tight, hard point. He made it moist, made the ache go deeper, burn hotter inside her.

Once he treated the other to the same tortured pleasure, he moved back to the first one and sucked it into his mouth.

Katelyn's back bowed, her head thrashed against the wall, and her hands tightened in his hair, needing him, desperate for more. To be touched all over, to touch.

How many times had she lain in her lonely bed and dreamed of this? Needing him until the ache was like a firestorm inside her, torturing her, leaving her alone and staring into the darkness.

For so long . . .

She shook her head when he pulled back again, staring down at her breasts as she tipped her head back and closed her eyes.

She couldn't let him do this to her again.

She needed to think.

She needed to make sense of it without this heat burning inside her, without all the aching need and fantasies that filled her head, interfering.

He'd already broken her heart once. Could she risk allowing him to break it again? To break her?

"Stop," she whispered, nearly crying, feeling as though forcing the words past her lips would kill her. "Please, Dane . . . Please stop . . ."

His stared down at her, his expression savage and so hungry. As hungry as she felt but without the past haunting him as it haunted her.

"Katy . . . ," he whispered, touching his forehead to hers. "Baby . . ."

She could feel him fighting for control, fighting to do as she asked, to step back and release her from the pleasure both of them were feeling.

She could only shake her head and fight the tears she wanted to shed. Because she'd waited so long, so very long, for this, just to realize she was more vulnerable now than she'd ever imagined she would be.

He stepped back slowly, holding her as her feet touched the floor and she fumbled at her bra until the lace cups were secure once again.

She couldn't stop the first few tears that fell, but she made certain no others did. She'd cried for him once until her face was splotched, swollen, and her voice was hoarse. She would not allow herself to ever need anyone that much again.

"Why?" he asked, still watching her, the heavy proof of his erection still straining his slacks.

She shook her head.

"Tell me why, Katy," he growled.

Katy.

She lifted her head, staring back at him as she remembered how she'd ached for him, but she hadn't been good enough for him. The nights she'd lain alone, so certain he'd come to her. She'd known. All the way to her soul she'd known he'd be there, just to realize he wasn't coming.

"What makes you think I'm good enough for you now?" she whispered. "I didn't fit in your life eight years ago, and I'm certain I couldn't understand it now. How is sleeping with me excusable tonight but it wasn't then?"

When she'd needed him to hold her, to still the cold she always felt, to give her something more than his pity.

"My life was different then," he told her solemnly. "It was dangerous. And you were different, baby. A sweet little innocent." His lips kicked up in a mirthless smile.

"A dumb little girl who loved you," she amended for him.

He didn't say anything, just shook his head. Whether in denial or uncertainty, she didn't know.

"You're right. I told you, Katy doesn't exist anymore." She stared him in the eye, tears filming her vision at the haunted look on his face. "She doesn't exist because of you, Dane. And I don't know if I'm willing to risk who I've become to a man I know will have no problems walking away from me when the time comes. Just one of many," she whispered. "I'm surprised you even remember who I am. Maybe one of us should figure out why you do."

She forced herself to walk away from him, enter her bedroom and lock the door behind her.

She was too exhausted for this and too weak where Dane was concerned.

The heir to a multinational fortune. She wasn't marriage material where he was concerned, and she knew it. She had no illusions there. When Dane Vanderale married, it would be to someone as visible in the public eye as he was, someone who came from his world and knew how to fit into it.

It wouldn't be a former waitress, an orphan everyone watched to see if she'd become the whore they said her mother was. A woman who someone of influence had finally taken pity on and given her a job where she could excel.

And she did excel. She was almost unmatched in her field of expertise, and she knew it. No one could put together a team the way she did and, with just a little tweak here and there, make it a winning match.

She knew what she was doing. The tricks Graeme had taught her, four years of on-the-job training, professional psych courses and countless test phases before she ever took her first assignment under Graeme's eagle eye.

She could talk a prospective employee into moving halfway across the world and taking on a project that at first seemed daunting as hell, and make it look like a challenge or a premiere star in a résumé, whichever was needed.

She was good at it.

And she made a hell of a lot of money doing it.

But she would always be that poor little orphan when it came to qualifying as more than one of his flash-in-the-pan affairs.

That was the part she wasn't certain she could handle: when it was over, and she realized, in the heat of loving him, that she'd never been invited to a party, a social event, or dinner with the parents. And she was terrified it just may end up breaking her.

Pushing her fingers through her hair, she grimaced at the perspiration she encountered and the awareness that she was still too hot, her blood thundering through her veins with a speed that should have slowed down.

Walking to the mirrored dresser, she stared at the gold in her whisky-colored eyes, little pinpricks of color that Graeme told her only came out when she didn't direct the adrenaline rushing into her system properly.

At first, she'd been frankly disbelieving, but as he taught her, in small stages, how to direct the energy, she'd found that the panic attacks stopped, the stomach cramps eased, and the fevers that could leave her struggling to do anything but make sense of orders went away.

She closed her eyes, concentrated on the racing of her heart, her breathing, then she fought to allow her mind to open where all that energy raced and snapped inside her brain like a drug once again.

She was suddenly awake, energetic, her mind flooding with possibilities that existed in so many different areas that she had to force herself to direct the energy to the Broken Butte project.

Several different companies were already vying to get in on what they were doing there: building a small, eco-friendly economy that the Breeds demanded while providing jobs that in turn made those living around the Breed communities more prosperous as well.

Businesses and communities had a symbiotic relationship. And with Breeds, even more so. To be fully accepted, Breeds needed to be fully beneficial to the communities they were a part of—something they had known, but not to the extent she'd explained to them when she first proposed the venture.

They were all committed to Broken Butte now. And that had been Graeme's choice, not hers. Window Rock hadn't been an acceptable location because of the other support-based businesses springing up. This one was far enough away from Window Rock, and the economy was struggling against a lack of jobs and resources for both the people as well as businesses. It wasn't on the reservation itself because first, the idea had to be proven before it could be implemented there. It was connected to the reservation, though, in other, less legal or complicated ways.

Before she knew it she was sitting on the bed in a tank top and sleep shorts, going over the potential business files as well as the project spreadsheets her two assistant managers, Sabra and Catherine, had put together for her. Once they arrived, she'd have her full team there, and then things would get moving.

As she sat there, she heard the door to the suite close, indicating Dane had left.

Yeah, sleep was a little difficult, she admitted, turning back to the files and ignoring the dampness in yet another pair of panties. She was not changing again, she told herself.

At least, not yet.

# • CHAPTER 4 •

Nearly a week later, Katelyn stood in what would be one of the secured upper offices of Tech-Corp's Broken Butte location, frowning at the blueprints and comparing them to what she'd seen as the construction contractor and supervisor had walked her through along with the foremen in charge of energy installation, water and security wiring.

She was low on sleep, in a hurry and decidedly cranky from a lack of coffee, but so far, she'd held her temper in. It was being tested, in ways they didn't want to continue testing her. But she was in control.

Dane had thankfully been more absent than present in the suite he insisted on sharing with her, but the knowledge that he was there was making it nearly impossible to sleep. A lack of sleep and dealing with the problems she was facing now did not go hand in hand. Especially with a lack of caffeine as well.

She knew the men, had gone to school with them, and she knew the battle coming the minute she opened her lips and began speaking.

The contractor, Kevin Mosely, had taken every chance he could get to talk over her and make her look as stupid as possible in front of the others for the past week. He didn't care for the fact that she pointed out shoddy work and demanded it be fixed.

Frank Weldon, a beefy man and naturally gruff, was in charge of energy installation, while his brother, Mark, nicknamed Tank, was just big, with the largest hands of any man she knew.

Tank's once-thick blond hair was thinning now, and his gray eyes were bloodshot. He oversaw security wiring, while Chet Jones, a wiry man in his late twenties, with thick dark brown curly hair and a nervous habit of bouncing his leg if sitting or shifting constantly while standing, owned the plumbing and waterworks company Kevin Mosely had brought in.

The construction supervisor had surprised her, though. Joel Santiago was Costas and Marie's youngest son. She hadn't heard he'd moved back to Broken Butte. He hadn't been there before, so he was just getting a glimpse into the difficulties the men presented daily.

Joel was about six-one, trim, dressed as the others in jeans and a T-shirt beneath a long-sleeved shirt and heavy work boots. His black hair was cut short and neat, no doubt a habit from his recent discharge from the army.

He'd be about thirty-one or -two now, she thought. He'd watched her quietly each time Mosely had spoken over her, and once or twice had actually attempted to distract the other man.

Mosely wasn't a man to be distracted, though.

"We need to be getting back to work, girlie," Mosely informed her, in the insulting tone of voice someone would use for a nuisance. And not a particularly bright one at that.

"I decide when you go back to work," she stated firmly, her tone benign as she straightened from her perusal of the blueprints and checking her notes.

The silence that filled the bare-bones office was heavy, a bit oppressive. Evidently, she wasn't supposed to talk back to someone so much more intelligent than she.

"Now, look here, little girl," Mosely tried again with a bit more aggression. "We were hired to oversee this; let us do our jobs."

"If I remember correctly, Frank, I signed that contract and I sign the payments that go out on this project." Katelyn hadn't known Frank Weldon well when she was younger, but she knew she was beginning to not like him now. His crew had a good reputation, though, and Joel had been the deciding factor in her agreement when Graeme had argued for them. "You can return to the job when you tell me how you intend to fix the mess these men"—she looked at the others, with the exception of Joel—"made of the wiring and plumbing. They're within neither code nor the blueprints. You've promised me every day this week the problem was being dealt with." She stared him directly in the eye. "It's worse."

They were hastily installed with little care.

The broad face creased into a sneer as he let his gray eyes darken in anger and a mocking laugh left his throat.

He met her gaze. "Run back to your office, Katy. Let the men handle this and it will pass inspection just fine."

Anger and frustration edged Frank's expression as his brother muttered his agreement under his breath and the two foremen glared back at her.

"Frank, show some damned respect," Joel demanded, his expression angry as he put his hands on his hips and glared at the other man.

"Best remember who signs your checks, Santiago," Frank suggested with a frown. "You just got here. Remember that."

"Seems to me like Katy should just step aside and let us get back to work instead of flauntin' herself like she knows what she's doin,'" Tank muttered to his brother, voice low as the other men, all but Joel, smirked as though in agreement.

Katelyn wasn't in the least amused.

"What did you say?" Disbelief was impossible to keep out of her voice.

She had to have heard him wrong.

"You heard him," Chet snapped impatiently. "I don't have time to waste with you questionin' everything we do every damned morning and demanding we make changes when they're perfectly fine."

"Yeah, keep to what you know best. A little dress-up Barbie has no business stickin' her nose into our business," Frank growled as her head snapped up.

She watched Joel's body tighten as he took a single step forward toward the big man.

"You're fired," she informed them firmly as she stared back at the men before glancing at Joel. "All but Santiago. You're the new contractor if you want the job. You'll have a new crew here before the beginning of the week. My assistant will contact you with a time to meet with myself and Mr. Parker."

She was aware of her assistant hastily making notes on her electronic pad. Or perhaps calling for the bodyguard. Her Bengal shadow chose that moment to step inside the door behind her. The four men made the mistake of sneering at him too.

"Fuckin' Breeds," one of them muttered.

Joel remained silent, but she could see him tensing, preparing himself.

Oh yes, one of the four was going to make sure to attempt to retaliate before she left.

"The rest of you, check your contracts if you decide to fight my decision. You have thirty minutes to get off the property or Breed Enforcers will escort you off," she warned them.

"They'll be here in ten," Drew assured her, the latent growl in his voice concerning.

She almost sighed. No doubt his stripes were showing if the looks on the men's faces were any indication.

"You're not firing any of us, and we'll continue our job as normal once you get your twitchy little ass out of here," Frank snapped. "And you, you little fuck." He pointed his finger at Joel. "You *are* fired."

"Don't think so." Joel moved to come in closer to Katelyn and her assistant.

"Good day, gentlemen." She nodded to the furious faces of the men and gathered the blueprints and papers on the rough table together. "I expect this is the last time we'll see each other."

She hated this. Hated it.

Why in the hell had Frank had to open his big mouth and get the others started? Once they were barred from the site, they'd of course blame her for all of it. She'd warned Graeme that hiring local in this instance wasn't a good idea. She'd wanted teams from Window Rock or Flagstaff, or their own people brought in, but Graeme wanted to at least give them a chance.

Personally, she thought he'd been getting bored and wanted a reason to let the monster free. He was going to get his excuse if she didn't hurry and get out of there.

"I'm ready, Drew," she stated, turning to the Breed. "Portia." She handed the blueprints in her hands to her assistant, making the fatal mistake of turning partially away from the men.

She knew they'd try to retaliate, but she didn't expect what happened.

"Now just hold on . . ."

Before she could counter Tank, he gripped her arm, fingers digging into her flesh and turning her so fast, so hard, she lost her balance, her foot bending, the muscle straining as it felt as though her arm were breaking.

Heat shot from his hold, feeling as though flames were shooting up her arm, singeing it in the process. Adrenaline forced itself free, pushing to her muscles, her blood, before she could push it back, sending pain radiating through her system.

Her cry was joined with the savage snarl that left Drew's throat. He caught her as Tank literally threw her away from him, he and the others moving back quickly as Joel rushed between her and the group of still-furious men.

"Take her." Drew pushed her toward Joel.

"No!" Katelyn snapped, holding on to Drew's arm. "Joel, get Portia out of here. You'll ride with us back to the hotel to meet with Graeme." She glared up at the striped Bengal, watching the gold in his eyes snap like flames. "Get me to the car now."

Drew lifted her from her feet, his arms going beneath her legs and behind her shoulders. He turned so fast her head almost swam and stomped through the doors before moving quickly to the stairs.

She had to restrain her reaction at the touch. It was painful, and she didn't like it. Probably one of the new side effects of all the adrenaline she'd been dealing with lately.

"Third floor," he snapped into his earpiece. "Four men. The biggest just attacked Ms. Chavos. I want him detained and brought in."

And that was one thing she hadn't wanted. Unfortunately, she didn't have the power to rescind that particular order. She'd just hoped it wouldn't come to this.

As Drew rushed from the building, Katelyn realized her shoe was missing. It was one of her favorites too. And her ankle felt sensitive, though it wasn't swelling yet. It wasn't broken, thankfully. Four-inch heels were a bitch to fall in.

Joel held open her door and Drew slid her inside the passenger seat, then rushed to the driver's door.

"Ms. Connor, contact the hotel and have a doctor waiting in her suite," Joel snapped to Portia. "I'll be there later."

"Dammit, Joel . . . ," Katelyn said.

He'd turned and was striding back to the building as Drew pulled away from it.

"Don't even suggest I go back," Drew growled. "Unless you'll let me kill them."

This wasn't supposed to happen. Not to that degree. The four men had been angry before Katelyn had even arrived that morning. Joel had already been inspecting the work he knew she would have issue with. It had been a problem for the past week, the shoddy work not at all up to that crew's standards. It was the first morning Joel had been there, though. Perhaps if he had been there at the beginning this could have been avoided.

As they pulled away from the site, three SUVs sped past them, the Bureau of Breed Affairs emblem stamped on the doors. Hopefully, they were there in time to keep Joel from getting hurt. Four against one wasn't really a fair fight. Twelve Breeds against four men wasn't really a fair fight either.

# ✦ CHAPTER 5 ✦

Dr. Yollen and his nurse were waiting when Drew pushed Katelyn into the suite, the wheelchair he'd forced her into not really necessary, she'd told him. By the time they arrived at the hotel the sprain was slight, nothing serious.

He hadn't listened.

The mobile scanner the nurse used on her ankle and foot showed no broken or even cracked bones. A little inflammation in the muscles, but nothing that would be more than a twinge here and there.

Once he left, she watched Drew leave the suite to take his position in the wide, open lounge for security personnel. Coffee and chocolate were in plentiful supply for the Breed bodyguards that often gathered there.

"I'm going to shower and get ready for Graeme to show up," she told Portia, meeting her friend's concerned green eyes.

"What's going on here, Katelyn?" she asked quietly. "Those men acted like they hated you."

Portia was one of her best friends. They'd met, along with Catherine Terrione, and Sabra Moritz, their first year in the Tech-Corp training program. They'd roomed together during the first four years with Tech-Corp in the company housing provided on Tech-Corp grounds while they went through the intense business, managerial and business politics courses geared to prepare them for the positions they'd tested for.

She shook her head at the question, wishing there was an easy way to answer it. "They don't hate me personally." She sighed. "I left here the day before I arrived at Tech-Corp and never returned. The quiet, unassuming waitress who didn't create problems or talk back is suddenly being driven around by Breed bodyguards and dressing in ways they consider above her station." She shrugged at that. "A lot of them were waiting for the day that I became the whore it was reported my mother was."

She swallowed tightly at that thought. Portia knew the story of the years Katelyn had spent in Broken Butte, but until she'd seen it, Katelyn could understand why it wasn't so easy to believe.

Her friend watched her quietly for long moments, her green eyes still glittering angrily on Katelyn's behalf.

"That's no excuse for grown men to act like teenagers," Portia scoffed, pushing back the red-gold hair that had fallen over her shoulder. "What a parent does or doesn't do isn't the fault of the child. I remember when you arrived at Tech-Corp, too quiet and so filled with hurt. Sabra, Catherine and I despaired of ever getting you to smile, let alone laugh."

But they had, she remembered, a little smile tugging at her lips.

When she'd realized the lengths they were willing to go to in achieving that aim, she'd let some of the hurt go. Only someone who wanted to be friends would do such things. Pity wouldn't have gone to the lengths the three women had gone to in their attempts to ease the sadness.

"I'd never had friends," she reminded the other woman. "Joel's brother—Bennet—Joel, Costas and Sylvia were the closest I'd ever come to that. It seemed that every time I was close to making friends around here, someone would bring up my mother's past and insinuate that I would take the route she did. Or already had."

That she would sell her body to eat, to be warm. Perhaps if her mother's family had given a damn when her mother needed them, she wouldn't have resorted to such a thing.

A part of her hated Broken Butte for that. She'd lost her mother, any knowledge of who her father could be and anyone who may have loved her, because for whatever reason, her mother had left her home. Alone. Without friends, without someone like Graeme to help her.

"It sounds more to me like someone was too jealous, or just too damn mean to want you to be happy. You were a child. That's no way to treat a child."

It didn't matter; that was her childhood, Katelyn thought.

"Small towns," she muttered, making her way toward her room. "They can be a blessing or a curse. Now we need get that report ready. When Graeme gets here it will be rush, rush, rush. You know how he is."

Graeme had to be powered by a nuclear core or something, she often reflected. She'd known him to stay awake for days in the R&D department of Tech-Corp, working on some design or another. The other designers and engineers would be slumped across their desks, snoring. Graeme would be muttering amid what looked like chaos of some electrical or computerized component. She'd heard the same when he was buried in his lab, testing blood samples or DNA strands.

That Breed just didn't seem to have limits of any kind.

Entering her room, she closed the double doors and headed to the shower as she stripped. She had enough time to shower and get ready for Graeme's arrival; it wouldn't take him long. Once he was finished raging over the dumbasses in town, maybe he'd be nice and not argue when she insisted on getting dinner in her room rather than joining him and Cat in the dining room.

She should have refused this assignment, she thought as she stepped into the stinging warmth of the water. There were so many memories here, too many. And too many who still lived and worked here who had been present eight years ago.

The couple who had adopted her, John and Marie Moran, had owned a small grocery store and were well-liked. When the authorities had shown up with the eight-week-old infant, they had taken her in only because there was no other family.

They hadn't wanted children, were older and Marie often claimed Katy wore them out. She'd overheard her adoptive mother telling a friend what a chore and trial it was trying to raise a child destined to be no more than her mother was. A little whore.

It was in that moment Katelyn had realized she wasn't loved. She was tolerated.

*You're just different, Katy,* another child had once told her in school, almost confused by why she didn't like Katy. *It's like my skin has bugs on it when you're around.*

The other girl had walked away, rubbing at her arm and looking back at Katy, where she sat alone on the playground, the other children playing as though she didn't exist.

Katelyn didn't make anyone else's skin crawl after she left Broken

Butte, thankfully. She made friends easily; she'd even had a lover or two. Which had often made *her* uncomfortable, she thought in amusement.

Stepping from the shower and wrapping a towel around her, she took care of blow-drying and styling her hair, rubbing a rich moisturizer into her skin, then applying a light touch of makeup. Pulling on a pair of panties, she moved to the closet in the bedroom, knowing she may as well dress for dinner. There wasn't a chance in hell Graeme would allow her to hide in her room, no matter how much she insisted.

As she stood in front of the closet debating on the bronze shorter dress with the four-inch matching heels, or the cool tea-length gray chiffon, the double doors leading to her room burst open.

Dane stood just inside the room, green eyes blazing with anger, his body tight with it as his gaze went over her, then suddenly burning hot as he froze at the sight of her bare breasts.

She pulled the first thing she could reach from the closet. The long, loose gray shirt was quickly pulled on over her arms, and she began buttoning it.

"Don't believe in knocking, do you?" she snapped out. "You didn't see the doors were closed? Do you need classes or something?"

Or maybe she needed her head checked for even remaining in the same state she knew he was in. The man was going to make her insane.

# ✦ CHAPTER 6 ✦

Before Dane could properly examine her body for bruises, he became distracted by her breasts. A definite handful, they fit perfectly into his hands, he remembered, leaving her hard little nipples plumped above his grip for him to suck and lick, to sate his hunger for them.

He hadn't sated it yet, though.

The soft gray material of the shirt she pulled on hid those sweet curves from him far too quickly. She buttoned it with jerky motions, glaring at him. The bottom of the shirt fell to her thighs, the long sleeves covered her arms, and just that quickly, all that sweet flesh was hidden from view.

"Do you need classes in how to turn rabid bastards over to your bodyguard to properly dispose of?" His voice was louder than he intended.

Her eyes didn't widen; there wasn't a hint of fear. Just as her bodyguard had reported, she had known no fear at that farce of a meeting she'd had with four men intent on causing damage to her.

"They didn't deserve to die." She had the temerity to roll her eyes and allow a small laugh of pure amusement to leave her lips. "I heard far worse than that before I was fifteen. It just pissed me off that they refused to acknowledge their shoddy work. I've found I rather like honesty and respond to it much better than I do excuses."

The shoddy work had been a surprise at first, but over the course of the week it had just plain pissed her off, Portia had told him. As though she didn't know her job well enough to know what was going on.

Dane watched as she pulled a short bronze dress from the closet, then bent her knees to stoop down and retrieve the strappy, sexy-as-hell heels that matched it.

"Your bodyguard is there for a reason, dammit," he growled, giving his head a hard shake as the dress and shoes almost distracted him. "Let him do his job."

A short burst of air left her lips in a disgusted sigh as she straightened again. "Really, Dane?" she questioned him, her whisky brown eyes giving him a hard, quick look before she turned to the bed and laid the dress across the bottom of the mattress. "We'd be explaining it to the authorities and the town would have scheduled protests. The news services would be slobbering, reporters' eyes glazing in ecstasy. I really didn't think they deserved that particular pleasure this week."

The flippant unconcern in her tone had fury threatening to explode through his senses. He couldn't remember a single time when he'd been so damned mad at anyone. Especially a woman. Or so fucking worried.

"The first of the week, a Vanderale crew will be in place to complete that project. You will not enter that town again or deal with another of those deranged citizens." That was the perfect answer, he told himself. If a Vanderale company handled that job, then her safety was assured . . .

"The hell you say," she suddenly snarled, turning to him, her face flushing as her hands went to her hips and she stared back at him with an astonishing amount of anger. "Vanderale doesn't have a damned thing to do with my project." She lifted one hand and flipped it back toward herself in a decisive gesture. "And you damned sure won't be sticking your perfect, arrogant nose into it."

He stepped closer to her, his jaw clenching as his entire body felt strung tight. He stared into the challenge sparking in those pretty dark eyes and felt his cock throbbing in demand. In some distant part of his brain he realized that challenge was making his dick pound with lust.

"Vanderale is a silent partner in this little venture, sweetheart. And I will not have you going to that damned site and risking yourself again." His arms went over his chest to keep from jerking her over his lap and paddling her tight little ass. "You can oversee it from here. I'll make sure you get daily reports . . ."

"Hey, hard head, did you hear me?" she questioned him with furious disgust. "'Silent partner' means you keep silent. Tech-Corp is none of your concern, Dane. Zero. My job, my responsibility. Period. Now get the hell out of my room so I can get dressed. I have a meeting to make, and I simply don't have time to deal with you or your male histrionics right now."

She was dismissing him? As though he were a recalcitrant child stepping out of line? Like hell. Accusing him of male histrionics like some kind of diva with no knowledge or experience in what the hell had happened?

For some fucking reason that town had turned against her before she had ever left it. When she had been no more than a child. People watched her in suspicion, questioned everything she did, spoke to her as though they had the right to verbally abuse her.

She had no idea how many times he'd sent Breeds to knock heads together while still others went in and out of the diner almost on scheduled times to make certain she was protected.

He'd butted heads with Jonas, his brother, and the director of Breed Affairs more than once over the fact that Breeds he needed were being used by Dane instead.

Katy—Katelyn, he reminded himself furiously—acted as though she had no recall of the years she'd spent at the whims of the uncaring, judgmental pricks who had made her so miserable.

"Go away, Dane," she demanded as though speaking to a troublesome employee. "I don't obey your orders and I damned sure don't live for your approval, so you're wasting your time."

Wasting his time in his attempt to protect her? To ensure she wasn't hurt again? Did she have any idea what could have happened to her?

He'd heard about the big bastard who had grabbed her. If he'd attempted to strike her, he would have damaged her delicate body.

It was his job to protect her. He was the reason she was here. Him and that damned deal he'd made with Graeme because he was so desperate to fix what he'd done to her eight years ago.

Dammit, he'd missed her. She was one of the few women he'd known some fondness for, and he'd missed her warmth in his life. And now she was standing there, deliberately intent on being obstinate over this?

This stubborn streak she'd acquired was going to have to go. When had she acquired it? No doubt it was Graeme's fault somehow. That no-good Bengal Breed had somehow changed the sweet, caring girl she had once been into a woman who stood her ground and dared grown men to attack her.

"What the fuck happened to you?" he demanded. "You used to be sweet, baby. You used to . . ."

"Hang on your every word as though it were some unwritten law? Have no friends, no family? With no possible ability to fit into your perfect life?" Katelyn asked him, feeling the adrenaline racing through her brain now as every word out of his mouth hit the flames of her anger like gasoline to a fire. "Sorry, Dane, but I'm grown now, and I've learned how to make my own choices and fight my own battles."

That was never what she needed from him.

She had needed him, though. There were nights, especially before she'd left Broken Butte, that she'd lain and stared into the dark, crying silent tears and aching to be held, to hear his voice whispering in comfort.

She hadn't wanted his money, she wouldn't have argued if he ignored her in the cold light of day, if he'd just held her, let her feel his kiss, his touch. She'd been pathetic, and that was what he wanted to return her to?

She wasn't that girl any longer. She wasn't broken, desperate for just one person to care for her rather than feel sorry for her.

Worthless.

She knew her own worth now and didn't give a damn if he acknowledged it or not.

"You misunderstood what you overheard," he told her again, raking his fingers through his hair and staring at her, glaring at her actually. "You didn't understand . . . And I can't explain it to you. There was just too much danger then . . . and too much you don't know about me."

"It doesn't even matter now," she assured him, furious, even as she had to acknowledge to herself that it did matter. He'd said his life had been dangerous then but not how. And she found she didn't want to hear the excuses or the reasons. "Stay the hell out of my business. I don't need your permission to attend to my job or your approval. I sure as hell don't need you stomping in here swinging your big, bad dick around like I belong to you."

His control snapped. The second the word "dick" slipped past her lips.

"This big bad dick will do a hell of a lot more than that." Guttural, dark with the lust that exploded in his system, he rasped the words as he took that last step that allowed him to pull her into his arms.

He didn't wait, didn't pause for permission. He pulled her into his arms, one hand buried in the long, thick fall of hair, and pulled her head back to allow him to steal the kiss he swore he could taste.

No swollen glands beneath his tongue pumped the mating hormone into his system, but still, he swore he could taste a hint of chili peppers, honey and saffron. So subtle a taste that he swore if he could just kiss her deep enough, he'd figure it out.

His tongue pushed between her lips as they parted for him, thrusting against hers, tangling with it as she arched to him, her hands gripping his shoulders, holding him, kissing him back and fueling that hunger further.

He lifted her, so desperate to get closer to the heated warmth of her body that he stumbled the few feet to where he could push her against the wall and lift her until he could push the engorged length of his cock against her silk-covered pussy.

Her legs rose and gripped his hips, and he heard the hungry little moans leaving her throat as he pressed between her thighs, rubbed against the sensitive little pad of her pussy with the hard-on raging beneath his pants.

He cursed the clothing separating them. He wanted it gone, wanted to rip it from their bodies and bury himself as deep as possible inside the heated core of her body.

Kissing her was making him crazy. If there had been any control left before he'd pulled her to him, then it was gone the second he had her against the wall, desperate to fuck her.

His tongue pumped between her lips, a rumbled groan leaving his throat as she rubbed hers against it, suckled at it, and followed as he pulled back.

"Witch," he groaned, taking the few steps to the easy chair that sat just to their side.

He all but fell into the chair, holding on to her and forcing her thighs to stay in place around his hips as he arched against her and dragged her head down to meet his kiss again.

They didn't just kiss each other, they ate each caress, desperate, hungry and fighting for satiation.

Katelyn knew she was going to regret this. In the back of her mind the warning was pushing at her mind even as the pleasure washing through her ensured she ignored that last measure of common sense.

She broke the kiss to breathe, only to moan in rising pleasure as his lips found her neck, his teeth rasping over her sensitive flesh as his hands gripped her hips, rocking her against the steel-hard flesh, rubbing against the swollen bud of her clit as she cursed the clothes separating them.

"Get this off . . . ," he snarled, tugging at the shirt she'd hastily buttoned earlier.

He didn't bother unbuttoning it but pushed at her arms until she lifted them and he could drag the loose material over her head.

There was no time to be embarrassed or mesmerized. Not even a second to think before he was cupping one swollen mound, bending his head, his lips parting.

"Oh God, Dane." She arched as the heat of his mouth surrounded a hard, too-sensitive nipple and sucked it into his mouth as his tongue licked it.

He drew on her with hungry demand, each tug of his suckling mouth sending raging flash points of sensations to strike at the desperate flesh of her clit, making the need for release overwhelming.

Oh God, she was so close to climax. Her hips rolled against his, grinding against his cock, needing to be closer, to feel him so deep inside her that she'd never forget the sensation.

"Fuck, baby," he muttered against her breast, his hands gripping her hips, forcing her to ride him harder, faster as his lips moved to her other nipple. "That's it, darlin', ride me just like that . . ."

His hand slipped lower, pressed beneath the band of her panties, dragging the material over the curves of her rear, clenching in the flesh there before his lips and tongue possessed her nipple again, sucking at it with a firm, hot pressure that had her hands sinking in his hair, gripping the strands and holding him to her desperately.

Her gasping cries, his deep, rough moans, filled her head, and she was certain if she just had another minute, just that last final bit of pressure, she could come as sensation surrounded her clit with whipping talons of pure, exquisite pleasure.

Her head was pounding . . .

Not, not her head. She moaned in a desperate rejection of the sound making its way past the pleasure clouding her mind and her senses. Something, someone was banging against the door in imperious summons.

"No. Damn him," Dane cursed, his head lifting, his green eyes jade bright, staring into hers as she fought to understand exactly why they were stopping.

"Dane, dammit, let Katelyn go," Graeme's irritated voice snarled through the closed door. "We have meetings and no time for your interference."

She shook her head, desperate to deny the voice, the implications of the demand.

Then it hit her. She stared down at Dane, knowledge of exactly what she was doing throwing aside the mesmerizing pleasure.

She jumped from his lap, struggling with legs that felt weak, unwilling to obey her as she stumbled against the bed before righting herself. She looked around desperately for her shirt, only to have Dane hand it to her silently as he rose from the chair.

Graeme's fist pounded against the door again, and she knew he had no compunction against forcing it open if he felt the need.

Katelyn dragged the shirt over her head and had just forced the material over her breasts to her hips when Graeme's fist met the door again.

"Now, Vanderale," he snarled. "My mate requires food, and Katelyn has a report to give . . ."

Dane jerked the doors open and stalked past Graeme. Seconds later the doors to the hall slammed closed as well, assuring her that he had left the suite entirely.

She glared at Graeme where he stood with his wife, Cat. Cat's expression was resigned, if amused, as she gave Katelyn a helpless little shrug.

"There you are, dear," Graeme drawled, amusement flickering in his gaze. "Do get dressed and join us. I thought we'd have dinner outside tonight. The weather's lovely this evening . . ."

She closed the doors in his face as Cat laughed at whatever his reaction was.

No one, but no one, closed a door in Graeme's face as far as she knew. She wouldn't have dared if she weren't so frustrated, furious and thankful that he'd interrupted, certain she was going to die if she didn't manage to relieve the hot throb of hunger pounding at her clit, in her vagina.

The desperate need for his touch was like a craving now, one that felt as though it had a life of its own.

"Do hurry, dear," Graeme reminded her through the door. "You know how testy Cat gets when she's hungry . . ."

She heard his wife's laughter again as she sat at the edge of the bed and stared at the floor, uncertain how to handle this new turn of events.

Dreaming of his kisses, fantasizing about them, hadn't even come close to the pleasure that had engulfed her senses. A pleasure she wasn't going to forget anytime soon, if ever.

A pleasure she would never have imagined existed.

# • CHAPTER 7 •

Propped against the bar on the opposite side of the lobby, across from registration, Dane was still fighting his irritation at Graeme's interruption more than an hour later. His fingers still ached to take a punch at the arrogant Bengal for daring to interrupt one of the hottest sexual experiences of his life.

And he'd known a lot of them in the past decades. There was something about Katelyn that made it hotter, though, wilder. Made the pleasure more intense.

Maybe it was the restraint he'd always used around her. When he'd first considered seducing her all those years ago, he'd guessed her age to be over twenty-two or -three. When she admitted she'd just turned eighteen, he'd been shocked. Never, at any time, even when he was eighteen himself, had he desired a woman while she was so young. So innocent. So filled with fucking dreams that he swore he could almost see them playing across her expression.

He hadn't wanted to hurt her, and he hadn't been there to keep an eye on Harmony either. Katy drew him. Each time he came to town, he'd been unable to resist the need to check on her, make sure she was still there, ensure she had a bit of extra money for something other than what she just absolutely had to have.

He remembered the night he had stepped into her shack, the ache that struck his chest, his fury at her living conditions. The place had been spotlessly clean but threadbare and rough. And there she'd stood, enough pride for any Breed shining in her eyes as she fought the tears and her pain.

What had he done to her?

He'd changed her.

She wouldn't have been the first, he reminded himself. He was a hybrid Breed; he'd lived for over seven decades, and a man couldn't live that long and not hurt tender feelings. God knew he'd tried to confine his sexual trysts to the few Breed or hybrid females that still lived and worked in the secure Vanderale compound hidden in the Congo.

He'd met others, but still, they were few in number. He'd loved many women, but not in the ways he knew true love should be.

Harmony had been the closest he'd come, he imagined, but even that had slowly eased away at the knowledge that she wasn't his mate. And now they knew that hybrids did indeed mate.

So what did he do about Katelyn? So far, there were no signs of Mating Heat, but the few hybrids who had mated didn't always show Mating Heat as first-generation Breeds did. Lucky bastards—they knew what was going on immediately. But there should have been signs by now, if Mating Heat were possible.

He was going to end up in that big bed with her. He knew that;

there was no avoiding it. From the moment he'd met her eleven years before, he'd known the day would come when he'd have her beneath him. And he'd hoped to convince her they were friends, that friendships weren't thrown away when the sex was over. It wasn't true love or happily ever after. Instead, he'd broken her tender heart and contributed to the destruction of the girl he'd known as Katy.

Katelyn.

Graeme and Rhys were right, she was no longer Katy, though he could sense his Katy there, waiting for what he wasn't certain. Hiding, rarely letting herself be seen because the world was simply too harsh for her tender heart.

"Staring pensively into fine whisky is a crime, Vanderale," Graeme stated as he moved to the bar, edged Rhys back and gave the bartender his order.

"I'm going to kill you, Graeme," Dane muttered under his breath, knowing full well the Bengal could hear him.

"I'm of far too much use to kill," Graeme chuckled. "Before this little adventure of yours has finished, hopefully, you'll thank me."

"Is she my mate?" he asked, careful to keep others from hearing. "And don't give me one of your cryptic-assed answers."

He glanced at Graeme and saw the thoughtful frown on his face.

"Honestly, I'm not certain," he stated. "You hybrids are such an odd lot sometimes. I'm still working on it. Blood tests, yada yada, and you've yet to supply me with proper samples." Graeme smiled back at him benignly then. "Blood, saliva and semen always makes such tests so much easier."

The bastard had been after DNA material from him for years.

"You mean you haven't found a way to steal it yet?" Dane grunted.

"Well, there was the bloody clothing I managed to hijack after you got yourself shot a few months back, but you neglected to leave saliva and semen in your clothes." The Bengal sighed as though such things were normal.

"You're crazy." Dane lifted the whisky to his lips and consumed what was in the glass in a single gulp, knowing the Bengal would have those samples at the earliest opportunity.

"Well, of course I am," Graeme stated as though surprised Dane had just realized it. "I believe that last vivisection the scientists insisted on was just too much."

Dane grimaced.

Fuck, there were days he forgot the hell Graeme had endured, though he suspected the Bengal had never been sane to begin with.

According to his twin, Cullen Maverick, Graeme hadn't been right since the moment the scientists had created him.

Lifting his glass to his lips once more, he'd only started to take the drink when the elevator doors opened and she stepped out.

He swore he nearly swallowed his tongue with the whisky.

He straightened against the bar, aware of the other men around him taking immediate interest as well.

His eyes narrowed on the vision that strolled from the elevator. All that long, lush hair framing her face in finger-tempting curls, brown eyes gleaming with secrets. The bronze sheath whispered from her shoulders, over her breasts, the cut and tailoring ensuring it displayed those mounds perfectly before falling just below her thighs.

The summer tint of her flesh, the perfect, sun-kissed tan, was completely natural, covering her entire body, he knew. It emphasized the color of the bronze material covering her and drew the eye to her shapely legs and small feet, where they were encased in strappy heels. The kind of heels a man wanted to see his woman in just before she wrapped them around his hips.

She moved, neither in a hurry nor for effect, her hips swaying with natural, sensual grace. Her face was alluring, her lips parted just so, shimmering and kissable. There was something about her, an inner glow, some elusive, caged "something" he'd always sensed in her that was even closer to the surface now.

And he wasn't the only man who sensed it. Even the human males in the vicinity kept looking her way, trying to figure out what that something could be—bullshit, they were imagining her beneath them, head thrown back in passion, face flushed with pleasure, just as he was.

He wanted to kill them all.

As he watched, her assistant caught up with her, saying something as she handed Katelyn the tablet she carried. Katelyn paused, a frown marring her brow before she nodded and handed the device back to the other woman.

Graeme was right, he thought, she wasn't his Katy any longer. Katy had been innocent. She hadn't demanded her due. Hell, she hadn't even known what her "due" consisted of. This woman knew and she wouldn't just demand it, she would reach right out and take it, no matter who tried to hold it out of her reach.

"Fuck," he heard Rhys whisper as he moved to Dane's side. "What the hell . . ."

"What the hell" didn't even come close, he thought, watching as her bodyguard, Drew, stepped closer, eyes narrowing on Joel Santiago as he entered the lobby.

Obviously still dressed in work clothes, he moved to her with a steady, purpose-filled stride. He was a man on a mission.

And, of course, she smiled. Lush, gleaming lips curled in unconscious pleasure as the other man seemed to blink before he could actually speak.

"This is interesting," Graeme murmured behind Dane, his tone a bit more concerned than normal as Katelyn gestured to Joel's bruised face and swollen lip.

She frowned as he began speaking.

Drew folded his arms over his chest, the shadowed Bengal marks on his face seeming to darken as he flashed Graeme a hard, warning look.

Katelyn listened while Joel spoke, though he saw the frown, the compressed lips and her assistant's expression as disapproval crossed her face and she began speaking.

Katelyn simply lifted her hand, never looking at the other woman. The redhead backed off, though still tense as she waited for whatever was coming.

When Joel finished, Katelyn simply stared at him for long moments.

"This can't be good," Graeme murmured. "Katelyn makes decisions rather quickly. She doesn't normally run through the odds first."

Drew was saying something, but once again, Katelyn simply lifted her hand, bringing instant silence.

"She stomped his toes with the sharp heel of her shoe once when he ignored her," Graeme remarked. "One of her requirements in a bodyguard is that they wear normal wing tips, rather than steel-toed military boots just for that purpose. Several have actually quit before the first week working with her. For some reason, she only gets along with either Lion or Bengal Breeds when it comes to bodyguards. Most perplexing."

Dane shot Graeme a surprised look before turning back to whatever was going on. As he stared at her, she finally nodded sharply. A second later, Drew trailing like a chastised puppy and her assistant sticking close to her side, she followed Santiago to the other side of the lobby, then inside a small conference room.

Dane picked up the drink the bartender placed in front of him. "Shall we join them?" he asked Graeme and Rhys.

"Looks like business," Graeme drawled as though unconcerned. "I normally keep my nose out of her business dealings. We have a deal: I keep to what I know, she keeps to what she knows or she quits." He finished his drink. "I'd rather not have to find another managerial analyst, Dane. They're rather hard to come by."

"Stay here, then." Dane shrugged. "I don't like the looks of that little meeting."

Graeme actually glared at him in disapproval.

"Oh, do give her a minute first," Graeme suggested, motioning for the bartender to bring him another drink. "Drew and Santiago will keep her safe until we get there, and I have a feeling I'm going to need this drink."

"How many minutes?" Rhys asked curiously, amused.

"One . . ."

"Now Dane, I'm attempting to keep you from agitating the girl further," Graeme grumped in irritation. "Three minutes, not a second less. Otherwise, she'll rip our hides later. And the beast that lurks within me refuses to allow me to do more than hang my head in shame when she does. It's vaguely disconcerting. And my mate tends to laugh at me on those occasions."

Dane couldn't help but stare at Graeme in complete disbelief. He'd worked with the Bengal several times over the past decade, and never had anyone caused his beast to refuse to make an appearance.

He seemed to delight in letting the creature out to play.

The woman he'd just seen, though, didn't seem to be one that tolerated much in the way of interference. Come to think of it, she hadn't backed down an inch earlier when he'd invaded her bedroom.

No fear, no lack of confidence.

No, this definitely wasn't his Katy . . .

Three minutes later, not a second before, they stepped into the conference room, Graeme closing the door silently behind them as all eyes swung to them.

Katelyn's narrowed and her gaze met Dane's warningly.

"We're just here to reassure ourselves of your safety," Graeme drawled. "We'll be silent. I promise."

Her jaw tightened and she turned back to the four couples. The four men, the same three who had verbally assaulted her that morning as well as the bear of a man who had grabbed her, sat in chairs in front of one of the tables, with what appeared to be their wives behind them.

"Katy, this is Jan Mosely, Kim Jones, Samantha Weldon and Sherry Weldon," Joel introduced the women.

The last, Sherry, Dane noticed Katelyn tensed further before taking her hand as well and shaking it with a cordial nod of her head.

"At some point that woman has caused Katelyn great pain." Graeme's voice held a growl as he said the words in a bare breath of sound. "Perhaps when they were children."

"You'd know that how?" Dane sighed, as confused by the Breed as ever. Glancing up, he caught the slight roll of his eyes as his mate, Cat, simply watched what was going on quietly.

He could be right, though, Dane thought. He could sense her pain, uncertainty and the shadows of that lack of confidence she'd once possessed.

The women began speaking then, almost as though they were taking turns and adding to whatever the other said before her. Their expressions were sincere, with a hint of fear and desperation and love. The love a woman has for her man. For her heart. They were there to beg on their husbands' behalf? He wasn't going to allow it.

"Dane."

He paused as he moved to step forward, his gaze narrowing at Graeme, who now stood before him.

Weariness and sadness touched the amber glow that resonated in the Bengal's green gaze.

"Take this from her, or attempt to, and everything that child has held for you in her savaged little heart will become ashes. And you and I will forever be enemies. More to the point, you and my 'other' will clash."

It wasn't a threat. As Graeme stared at him, Dane glimpsed the "other," as he called the Primal, as it flashed in his oddly colored eyes. It wasn't a threat, it was a declaration of intent.

"Those women are here to play on her compassion," Dane snarled, glancing to the group again as Joel shot him a hard, assessing look. "I won't have it."

"You haven't a choice," Graeme reminded him, and seeing the odd flash of pain that crossed the Bengal's face had him pausing. "This is her world. She created it for herself, and trust me, she owns it. To attempt to take it will destroy what's left of the dreams she had of you. Is that truly what you want?"

Dane's teeth clenched. Anger tore at him, and he swore his Breed instincts were only seconds from jerking her out of there and risking whatever dire consequences Graeme was threatening.

But the other Breed was right. Dane had hurt her enough in the past. If he pushed her further where her hard-won independence was concerned, he'd definitely lose her.

Forever.

"They make a single move toward her, threatening or not, then all bets are off." He pushed the words past clenched teeth, fighting his need to protect her.

"They do that, and their lives will be forfeit before you can reach them. Now watch her," Graeme suggested. "See the woman your Katy has grown into. Sense her, my friend, and see how truly exceptional she has always been. She had only to grow into it . . ."

✦ ✦ ✦

Katelyn met Sherry's brown eyes and knew the other woman remembered that year so long ago, in the fifth grade, when she'd told Katelyn that she made her skin crawl. Because of it, Katelyn had kept the handshake as brief as possible before stepping back.

"We understand why you fired our husbands," the eldest, Jan, stated, her hazel eyes fraught with fear and pride. "That wasn't the man I know, Ms. Chavos . . ."

"You know my name, Jan," Katelyn reminded her. Jan had always been popular when they were younger but not cruel. "You can call me Katelyn."

The other woman nodded her head, her short brown hair framing her face in a neat little cap.

"Frank isn't normally like that," Samantha said then. "None of our husbands are. They're good men. They lashed out, not because they were angry with you but because they had simply been pushed too far."

Chet Jones moved to speak a second before his wife, Kim, tightened her hand on his shoulder. His parted lips snapped shut, and he lowered his head again, staring at where his hands were linking and unlinking nervously.

"I know it's hard to believe now"—Tank's wife, Sherry, a tiny blonde, barely five-three but her voice was firm, her expression determined. "But my husband has never laid a hand on any woman in violence. And I swear to you, Katelyn, he meant you no harm."

Katelyn breathed in slowly, deeply, determined to keep her promise to Joel and just listen. Her gaze met his, once again saw his bruised face and wondered if one of these men had been the cause of it.

"There's been a lot going on, since the men took that job. A lot they haven't told anyone but us about, and I think it needs to at least be cleared up," Sherry continued. "I won't have Tank's name trashed and have an arrest on his record without at least ensuring the truth is told."

Now this was beginning to get interesting. She always liked hearing the truth.

She stared at the four couples, weighing expressions, demeanors and the general feel of the room. There was no tension, no anger or violence, just determination, and it appeared these women obviously had a courage the men may lack. They were willing to discuss the problem rather than insult her.

She nodded to Jan. "I'll listen, Jan."

"With an open mind?" Sherry asked. "And no one can blame you for not wanting to."

"With an open mind, Sherry," she assured the other woman. "But I want to hear it from your husbands, not from you."

Frank's head lifted, his expression hangdog and filled with remorse, and began to speak. As he did so the story emerged. The others added when they felt needed, and what others might find confusing as the four men seemed to speak over each other at times, Katelyn followed easily.

For a week, every morning, they'd return to the job site to find what they'd done the day before was shifted, redone or just undone sometime after they'd left. Katelyn always arrived first thing, before they could fix anything, to find the shoddy work, and when she demanded explanations, they hadn't known what to say.

Joel hadn't shown up until the morning of the confrontation, so he hadn't known the extent of the problem and hadn't been told because Katelyn had once lived with his family, until Katelyn had shown up, demanding explanations.

As the problems continued, the men working beneath them would mutter among themselves and had come to the belief that Katelyn was behind the sabotage. They'd somehow learned she hadn't wanted to hire from town but bring in Tech-Corp people. They thought she wanted to destroy the four contractors to ensure the jobs went where she wanted them to go.

Many of them had learned about her foster parents, their refusal to adopt her and the cousins who had briefly let her sleep in their home until she moved in with the Santiagos. The old gossip surfaced, convincing those same workers that Katelyn was behind the deliberate destruction of the work done the days before.

"We can't blame you for hating all of us. We ignored what wasn't right in those days. Dumbass kids that we were . . . Even when we saw things that were wrong." Tank wiped his hand over his face as his wife, Sherry, stroked his shoulder. Then his gaze turned tormented, fierce. "I swear to you on everything I hold important in my life, I didn't mean to hurt you this morning." He stared at his hands, big, beefy weapons if he meant to use them as such. He dropped them to his knees and lifted his head again to stare at Katelyn, tormented. "I don't even discipline my kids 'cause of these hands. I just wanted you to not leave until we could try to explain, and everything got crazy . . ."

They were all silent then.

Katelyn didn't dare look at Dane or Graeme, she just prayed they stayed silent. Instead, she stared back at Joel.

"Who hit you?" she asked.

His arms went over his chest and a smile tugged at his swollen lips. "Not one of them," he grunted. "Don't worry, though, they're a hell of a lot worse."

"It was Charles Moran. He was the one who got some of the men riled up," Sherry spoke up. "Momma called me earlier and said Lisa called her momma, cryin' over it." She frowned when her husband glanced back at her. "We promised her the truth, Tank Weldon. No matter what." She looked back up at Katelyn then. "If Tank and the others lose these contracts, we lose everything, Katelyn. They were wrong. They knew they were wrong, and they let their anger run their mouths for them. We're not making excuses for them. But someone else set this up, someone who knew they could push our husbands to being stupid if they were mad enough and confused enough. I won't pretend to know why, but it could only be to hurt you."

Katelyn stared at Sherry then. She was finished with the men. She'd already made her decision before she knew they'd lose everything. But she did need to know one other thing.

"You told me once I was too 'different' for friends," Katelyn said softly. "That I made your skin crawl . . ."

"I didn't say that." Sherry shook her head quickly, her gaze rounding in surprise. "I said you made my skin feel funny."

"There's a difference?" Katelyn asked.

"There is," Frank answered for Sherry. "I always felt it too."

The others looked between Sherry and Frank, each showing obvious agreement.

"Katelyn," Sherry almost whispered. "It's like there's all this energy packed inside you that you keep caged up. It feels staticky around you. Like everything inside you is just so tightly wound." She stared at Katelyn in concern. "It makes people wary or something. What will happen to you if all that control breaks free and begins unwinding inside you? I'd be scared of the fallout, even now. It was bad enough watching how the adults treated you, but I was always worried that you'd do something worse to yourself."

"No, it was that she was always so smart and quiet," Frank disagreed. "Like she could see inside us and we worried what she saw. What she'd tell."

"I always felt like she was better than us," Chet breathed out wearily. "Not that I thought you felt that way, but I did. You were better than us . . ."

"We all knew what everyone said." Samantha sighed. "Marie, Lisa, Charles. Everyone but your foster father, John. The other three would get our parents all worked up. We were kids," she said softly. "What the hell did we know?"

"Joel?" she asked her friend, wondering if it was truth or exaggeration.

"You don't make me feel funny," he assured her with a little wink. "Not since you said I had knobby knees right after Mom and Dad brought you home."

"You did have knobby knees."

She sighed, but she had her answer. He believed them.

"Not anymore." He grinned. "But I'm sure that's not what you were asking."

"Frank fired you, correct? And Tech-Corp hired you," she stated.

His gaze turned somber. "Yes, ma'am, and I accepted the job. I stand by that."

Sherry's breath caught on a sob, the sound barely heard. But her husband heard it. He reached up, caught her hand in his overlarge one as he kept his head down and just shook it almost tiredly.

"Tech-Corp is your employer. It's your job to find out who's fucking with my goddamned construction site and put a stop to it. Your crew is your choice; your contractors are your choice. Their behavior is your responsibility. Is that understood?"

Surprise flashed across everyone's face as Katelyn stared at them, her gaze cold, her resolve icy.

"Yes, ma'am." Joel nodded, his expression firm, understanding. "Completely understood."

"Disagree with me all you want," she told the other men coldly. "But ever disrespect me again and I promise you, Tech-Corp will destroy you. If I don't beat them to it."

She turned on her heel and took a step to leave the room.

"Katelyn." Sherry moved quickly from behind her husband, her hand remaining on his shoulder. "Thank you."

"Why?" Katelyn asked her, turning back, making certain she saw nothing but the iron-strong will she allowed the other woman to see. "You didn't save their jobs. Neither did Joel. All they had to do was be honest and do their jobs. That's all I require." She looked at the four men watching her now, uncertain and almost disbelieving. "I check construction sites first thing. I won't change that. If there are problems, tell me. Don't excuse it, don't lie to me, just be willing to discuss it." She looked back at Joel. "A security team will contact you before Monday. I expect a report Monday night. I'll make certain all charges are dropped before morning."

Joel inclined his head in agreement at the order. Then before she could stop herself Katelyn turned to Dane, met the gold-and-green depths of his gaze, and in his eyes, she saw something she hadn't expected to see.

Approval. But more than that, acknowledgment.

"Portia." She motioned her assistant forward as she began walking to the doors, watching as Graeme, Cat, Rhys and Dane stepped aside for her. "I want Jonas contacted. See if we can get a Breed team on security; if not, get hold of Tech-Corp's head of security, John Canyon—he's at the home office this week—and see what you can do. I want a security team in place this weekend . . . and call the county attorney about those charges . . ."

# CHAPTER 8

Adrenaline pulsed in her body, barely contained, hovering at the edge of her senses and ready to flood her entire body. It was one of her strengths. When it gathered, she was actually able to push it back, to contain it. Doing so gave her a moment that she was certain she'd become light-headed. Her stomach would pitch, then she swore all that excess energy sparked straight to her brain.

She could see things so much clearer, tie actions, words and the expressions of others together and instantly form answers, impressions or coming trends.

Ross Monahan, Tech-Corp's CEO, had often stared at her in disbelief when she'd come to him, pitching an idea or a coming need for hardware that didn't exist.

The first time he'd overlooked her projection.

Six months later, programming chips in several satellites had begun failing completely where before reports had simply listed anomalies. If he'd been prepared, Tech-Corp could have made millions in that first rush to replace the faulty programming hardware.

Too bad she hadn't had that ability before she'd begun working with Tech-Corp. It would have made school so much easier for sure.

As she stood and watched the contractors for the office construction, she'd taken in the fact that their wives were behind them as they sat awaiting her. They were women who had seen something more than just four men who were being asses. These were women who had seen something happen to their men that they'd never seen before.

They hadn't blamed Katelyn. They'd demanded their husbands explain, make amends, do whatever it took to, first, reclaim their manhood, and second, save their livelihoods.

It had been those women who had gotten together after their husbands returned and admitted what happened and called Joel. They'd all gathered together at Kevin Mosely's home and convinced Joel there was far more behind the event than anyone was seeing.

It was they who were there each night their men returned home, heard the stories of the subtle sabotage, missing equipment and tools, accidents on the job site and the anger beginning to fill the men that worked for them. They were the ones that watched their husbands losing sleep night after night as they tried to figure out what was going on.

Convincing Joel of what they knew would do no more than possibly, just possibly, get them a few moments of Katelyn's time to explain.

Kevin Mosely's wife had told Joel that she couldn't believe the woman she'd worked with as a teenager at the Santiagos' diner wouldn't at least give them a short meeting.

Now, sitting at the dinner table with Graeme and Cat, Rhys and Portia and Dane, she had to fight back the release of that adrenaline for just a little while longer.

It zapped at her brain, sizzled and sparked and reminded her of what the couples had said about the energy that had poured through her when she was younger. It had been nothing like this, though.

Learning to control the energy and redirect it hadn't been an instant process. And it hadn't become so damned intense until after she'd graduated high school. It had been that year after she joined Tech-Corp, under Graeme's guidance, that he'd taught her how to make it work for her rather than against her.

Now Graeme sat back in his chair, an after-dinner drink in front of him as he kept an eye on her, watching her. He would know when it was simply too much, she hoped. But she was reaching that limit.

Her brain was in overdrive. She could feel it. Everywhere her gaze touched she saw shadows, tangled webs, interconnections and fears. She swore she could feel that energy crackling in her brain.

"Dane, I heard your father's meeting with the Lion Breed Prime, Callan Lyons, to discuss the possibility of creating an independent infrastructure within Sanctuary. Energy grid, water supply and so forth. Is there any truth to it?" Graeme kept his voice low, carrying no farther than the table, as he broached the question.

"They've discussed the possibility of it," Dane agreed with a nod and comfortable smile. "The meetings are for more than that, though. Father likes to visit. The Prime allows him to play with many of the toys Vanderale's weapons R&D sends them."

She could sense a fondness in Dane's voice when he spoke of the feline Prime. She doubted others heard it, it was so subtle, but it was there.

"I hear R&D sends those weapons to Sanctuary often before your father even sees them. Are they still working closely with the Breeds weapons experts there?" Graeme asked him in interest.

Leo Vanderale did visit often. With his wife, Dane's mother, and their daughters. Dane and Rhys often joined them as well. It was also rumored they'd spent nearly every Christmas there for the past five years or more.

She slid her gaze to Dane, remembering that the tabloids often speculated that the Vanderales could be Breeds, or, at the least, Callan Lyons had a genetic blood tie to the family. But they weren't the only influential family the tabloids liked to link to the Breeds.

She shook the thought away mentally. That was a rabbit hole she was not going down.

She took another sip of her wine, let her gaze travel over the room again, wondering at the direction she seemed drawn to. She glanced at the Breeds she suspected were there as private security for Dane. The Bureau took Dane's protection very seriously when he was in the area. Vanderale Industries was a major patron to the Breed community.

At another table, three men, obviously brothers, were having dinner together. They were odd enough, for brothers. Enough so that they stood out in their surface differences. From business casual, to deliberate slouch, to absentmindedly messy, she thought with an edge of amusement. There was something oddly familiar about them, though she couldn't quite put her finger on why.

At another table, a father and three grown sons. The sons looked hard, likely military, the father intent on whatever one was saying.

There was a family, obviously on vacation. The excitement that filled the table almost sparkled like pixie dust in the air. The youngest, a girl in pigtails, watched her father with a little girl's adoration, and her mother with love.

Katelyn had never had that, she thought in regret. She'd thought by now she'd have her own children, know their love, their father's love. But it had never happened, and there were days that she ached for it.

A child's love was unconditional, without artifice and freely given to their parents, far longer than it was deserved in some cases.

She would have been a good mother, Katelyn thought, her gaze moving to her lap where she played with the napkin lying against her skirt. She wouldn't have traveled. A career wouldn't have mattered, just a good job that would provide everything a child needed.

There were nights she imagined what it would be like to hold a baby close to her breast, to feel a child's love staring up at her.

Dane's child. It had always been Dane's child she'd imagined, but if the father hadn't been Dane, she would have loved her child just as much. Completely. With all her soul.

Her gaze turned back to Dane then. He was watching Graeme with a thoughtful frown as they discussed caves on the Feline Breeds compound Sanctuary.

He was hiding his tension, she realized. But she'd learned that was normal after the past week in his company.

"Those caves are a hazard," Dane said as she pulled her attention back to the discussion. "Callan's considering just filling the entrances with explosives and closing them down . . ."

"I wouldn't," Katelyn said, keeping her own voice low as she stared at the wine in her glass now, frowning.

Red wine. The color of blood. She glanced back at the three tables she'd noticed before wondering why she would think of blood.

"Callan fears a child or teenager wandering inside them and triggering an explosion," Dane told her, watching her with narrowed eyes.

She forgot the other customers, everything around her drifting away as he suddenly claimed her entire focus.

God, she wanted him.

She wanted to scratch his back as he rode her furiously, pounding into her and sending her senses exploding.

She lifted her gaze in time to see him shift in his chair, his jaw tightening as his gaze leveled on her. Rhys was sipping at the whisky he'd ordered, his gaze amused as it flicked to Graeme.

"Why shouldn't they close the caves?" Graeme asked her, his voice almost a smooth drawl.

"The scientists nor the soldiers would have explored those caves." She shrugged. "The explosives likely haven't been placed more than a quarter to half mile inside them. The minerals that compose them are impossible for ground-penetrating radar or satellites to see into. They may never have the technology to do more than penetrate the first or second level. They could be a defensive and strategic escape should the worst happen."

Graeme would know that, of course. He owned his own rather secret cave system in the desert that had never been detected by satellites, ground-penetrating radar or other mineralogical means of prying.

"The caves in that area aren't known to extend to that depth or length to make them a possible defensive or strategic area," Dane pointed out.

Katelyn lifted her shoulders in a slow shrug. "Location and the inability to use radar to measure or track the direction they extend to or where they exit still leaves questions and possibilities." She wasn't well versed in geographic areas, but it interested her. She often read articles geared to the subject.

Her gaze slid to the three apparent brothers across the room as well as the Breeds positioned around them.

"Katelyn?" Dane questioned her seeming distraction.

Her gaze returned to him, meeting the green-and-gold depths as she felt her body responding to him again.

She was warm, flushed.

For a minute she was twenty, it was two in the morning at the

Santiago Diner and they were alone but for the cook sleeping in the office in the back. Dane was helping her drag the large bags of garbage out the back door and she'd tripped.

Suddenly, she'd found herself against his body, his arm holding her to him, and she felt his erection, ironhard beneath the slacks he wore as she stared up at him.

Those eyes had stared down at her, seeming to glow in the dark as her lips parted, needing his kiss, aching for it. And he'd ached to kiss her. It had been in his face, his hooded gaze and the lust that she swore she could feel wrapping around her.

She forced herself to look away, blinking, her tongue itching, her thighs clenched, her pussy aching. It had been years since she'd had sex. The two lovers she'd taken had failed to help her achieve the release she needed for satisfaction, and she'd grown tired of reaching for something that never existed.

She pushed her wine back slowly.

"I think I'm going to have to excuse myself for the night," she murmured, giving them all an apologetic smile. "I'm tired, and it's well past my bedtime."

"The night's young," Graeme assured her. "And we still need to discuss the appointment you have with the Bureau's medical facility and Rule Breaker's office for the security clearances for Tech-Corp employees."

Katelyn shook her head. "The medical facility contacted me earlier," she told him. "Rather than attempting to schedule as one or two of our people come in, they prefer to wait until the offices are complete and the employees begin coming in, to get started. I agreed that would be best. Other than myself and Portia." She nodded to her assistant. "We're scheduled for Monday so our security can be upgraded to allow us to work with their PR and security departments."

"I'm going to start feeling like a guinea pig." Portia gave a low little laugh. "Two different testing phases in two weeks' time, same samples and multiple meetings with Breed interrogators. I'll need a vacation when I'm finished." She shot Katelyn a little arch of her brow.

"Only when I get one." Katelyn snorted, finishing her wine after all, then turning to Graeme again. "I am definitely finished for the night," she told him firmly. He'd keep them there talking until dawn if she allowed it. "I'll see you sometime tomorrow if you have any other questions. But I'm rather looking forward to a quiet weekend."

She had files to go over, security dossiers waiting for her from the head office for potential transfers to the new offices.

"When will Sabra and Catherine be joining you?" Graeme asked, watching as Dane slid from his chair and moved behind Katelyn's.

"Week or two," she murmured, distracted now.

She swore she could smell the scent of saffron and lust surrounding her as Dane helped her from her chair, one hand lightly gripping hers until she stood next to it. "Good night, Graeme."

"I'll see you up," Dane murmured.

"That's why Drew gets paid those big bucks," she assured him, feeling the desperation rising inside her.

All that adrenaline was going to begin spilling from her brain to her body with a suddenness that would be uncontrollable. There would be no holding it off much longer.

As she stood, Graeme and Rhys rose to their feet as well and Portia began to rise to follow her.

"There's no need to come up, Portia," she assured her friend. "I'm done for the night. I just want to shower and sleep."

Toss and turn, ache with arousal, and, with any luck, use the vibrator she'd brought, hidden in her luggage. She needed that desperately.

"I'll be up in a bit," Dane told her as Drew stepped forward, close enough to protect her but giving her space as well.

"Why, take your time, Dane. I'm certain I won't even know when you've arrived."

He refused to take the spare room in Rhys's suite and had forced Portia to stay there instead.

She looked around the table. "Good night, everyone."

Holding the small purse that matched her dress, she moved ahead of Drew, feeling more than just the eyes on her from those she knew. Centered at the back of her head, she could feel eyes watching, tracking every move, every shift of her body.

What Drew felt, she wasn't certain, but in the next second his body completely blocked the sight of her from anyone behind them.

She strode quickly, hoping she didn't appear to be rushing, to the lobby and the elevator that would move her quickly to her floor, and her room.

Her skin prickled as they entered the elevator, and as she looked from the cubicle to the restaurant entrance, she glimpsed one of the brothers, business casual, from the table her gaze kept being drawn to, stepping into the lobby, his eyes going to her instantly before the doors closed.

"You're on edge," Drew commented as the elevator began moving up.

"Long day," she said quietly, fighting the effects of the rush of energy. "Long week. Maybe Portia's right about a vacation. Maybe I should give all three of us a month off once this is completed, before we head to the next job."

Tech-Corp hired her out often to various businesses and government offices to streamline their managerial departments. She was hoping her request for a permanent home base would be considered before she was done here. She'd like to oversee a single company, both managerial as well as employee. She'd stayed on the move after her first year at Tech-Corp, and she could feel the toll with each job.

The elevator stopped at the top floor, and Drew stepped out ahead of her before giving her a nod to follow him. Within seconds she was entering the blessed silence of the suite, then the privacy of her own room.

The second the doors closed behind her, a low, desperate moan left her lips and she felt a sudden, gnawing heat, much more intense than it had ever been suddenly suffusing her body.

She shuddered, stumbled to her bed and didn't even try for the shower. Curling into a fetal position, she whimpered at the arousal that tore through her, rushing to her breasts, her already slick pussy.

Oh God. It was bad this time. Why was it so much worse, hotter, the aching need slamming inside her rather than washing over her as it normally did?

This time, it was like hard, wicked bolts of sexual intensity hitting her womb. Her breasts were swollen, nipples spike hard as her clitoris throbbed in desperation.

It wouldn't be a night for her vibrator after all, she thought, whimpering. She didn't dare try to use it with anyone in the other room, especially Dane. She would moan and she knew it. It had never been this bad before, but there were times it had been worse than normal. She could fight for hours for release with the erotic toy she owned and never find the right touch, that certain caress at the proper time that would send her peaking.

At best, she only found relief when it was just the normal flood of sensation. This wasn't normal. This was like the difference between a pinch and a broken bone.

She moaned again, praying Dane stayed away until she got a handle on the worst of it and managed to adapt to the waves of excruciating need.

It would be gone by morning. It always was.

Her thighs clenched on the sudden wave that attacked her clit, the desperately clenched channel of her vagina.

"Oh God, Dane," she whispered.

She always whispered his name.

It was always Dane she imagined joining her wherever the fallout hit and fucking her until she was mindless, until she was screaming out her release and still begging him for more.

It was always Dane.

But he was never there. And never would be, she told herself. By the time he entered the suite she promised herself she'd have a handle on it.

She would not beg him to take her like the animal she sometimes felt the hunger turned her into. She wouldn't, couldn't let him see her like this.

The whore's daughter.

She bit her lip, fought the tear that escaped the corner of her eye at the memory of what Marie Moran had always called her.

The whore's daughter.

If her mother had known the desperate need for touch, to be taken, anything like Katelyn did, even when it wasn't this bad, then who could have blamed her? Katelyn never allowed herself to be around anyone when she knew it was coming. Too frightened the temptation would be more than she could fight.

But it wasn't just anyone, she thought as her body bowed at another hard, burning wave of lust. It was never just any man she needed.

It was Dane.

It was always Dane.

# CHAPTER 9

"Give her a bit, Dane," Graeme murmured as Katy and Drew left the restaurant and disappeared from sight. "This evening's been hard on her."

Dane stared back at the somber Breed, feeling the strange disquiet moving inside him as Graeme actually seemed to avoid his gaze for a moment.

"I think I'll turn in as well." Portia rose to her feet as the tension at the table thickened.

"See the girl to her suite, Rhys." Graeme flicked the bodyguard a glance.

"I'll be fine," Portia declined, gathering her large bag as Rhys moved her chair back for her.

"Nonsense," Rhys assured her softly before turning back to Dane with a questioning look.

"I'll be coming up soon," Dane assured him. "I'll have one of the others watch my back." His lips quirked mockingly. "I'm certain they can keep me alive that long."

Rhys grunted at the comment. "With the people you piss off? These days I wonder . . ."

He turned back to Portia and extended his arm in invitation. "Please tell me you don't have murderous friends."

"Only a few, but I'm certain you can handle them." The droll answer had Rhys chuckling as he followed her.

"You knew what was going on when she was a teenager, didn't you?" Dane asked the other Breed as they resumed their seats.

It would have been hard to miss, Dane thought. She'd been ostracized, pushed away and distrusted. When he was in town, Dane had tried to give her laughter, but he'd only ended up hurting her.

Graeme leaned forward a bit, picked up his drink and finished it before motioning to the server for more.

"Let's say, the 'other' me knew." He sighed then. "The monster would retreat occasionally, sometimes I remembered. When I did, I checked on her. But I remember very little beyond those last weeks before I watched you destroy her."

That part still had the power to piss him off, Dane thought, glaring at Graeme.

"You left," Graeme hissed, leaning closer, flashing the wicked incisors at the side of his mouth. "You left her, Vanderale, to their less-than-tender mercies. You've no right to stink of self-righteous anger that you didn't know where she had gone."

Yeah, that part pissed him the fuck off too. But Graeme's anger, his protectiveness where Katy was concerned and his obvious affection were confusing as fuck. This wasn't Graeme. He normally didn't give a damn.

"I'm just curious why you took her under your wing," Dane

informed him suspiciously. "I know you, Graeme. I knew you then. As you are and as the 'other.' You don't take humans under your protection without a damned good reason."

Graeme's eyes widened in patently false disbelief as he turned to his mate, who had remained quiet, sipping her wine and watching them in interest. "Cat, do you hear how he's maligning me?"

A little smile tugged at her lips. "I do, dear," she assured him. "I'll soothe your ruffled fur when we get home so you don't have nightmares over it."

She reached up and rubbed his shoulder consolingly.

"You're a bad girl," he only chuckled, turning back to Dane. "Tell me, Vanderale, have you found yours yet?"

"My what?" Dane could feel his teeth getting ready to clench.

"Your woman, of course," he drawled.

His mate. Dane knew what the hell he meant.

"You're irritating me, Graeme," he told the other Breed. "Excessively so. You promised to stay out of my dealings with Katy while she's here, so once again, I'm heading up." He turned to Cat. "Good night, Cat."

"Dane?" It was Cat who stopped him this time, and he was damned if he could be rude to her.

"You're going to break her heart again if she's not yours."

And Dane knew what she meant.

They were in public, and as far as the world knew, Dane was fully human.

He could only stare at her.

"Is she, Dane?" She mouthed the question more than vocalizing it. "Is she yours?"

"I don't know, Cat," he answered her, rising from his chair and staring down at her. "I just don't know. I do know I pray to God she's not."

✦ ✦ ✦

As he walked away, Graeme looked down at the table, making certain to hide the pain and fear he felt just in case Dane looked back.

Not that he expected him to.

The little fucker prayed Katelyn wasn't his mate? Dane wasn't just going to destroy Katelyn's heart with that attitude, but something far more important if he didn't heed the instinct warning him that Katelyn was indeed his mate.

He could feel his "other" raging inside him, clawing at him. Katelyn's time with them was coming to an end, he could feel it. His "other" could sense it. And when that time came, it would destroy him as well as the maddened creature that was the other part of him.

"Tell me, my dear," he asked his mate, turning his head to look at her from beneath his lashes, "did you smell chili peppers and honey?"

"While she was here," she answered, glancing around to be certain no one could overhear. "But she was sitting right beside me. After she left, so did the scent."

His lips tightened, fighting the fear that the mating he knew should already be flaming between them might not arrive in time.

God, it had to arrive in time.

"How much longer before it's a problem?" she asked him, the concern in her almost matching his own.

"I can sense the heat just out of reach." He shook his head. "I can feel both of them fighting it. Not just that stupid hybrid Lion, but Katelyn as well. All it would take is the right spark, or for one of them to accept the truth. We should have time." He breathed out heavily. "I don't feel the Flaming yet, I feel the Heat. They'll surely not be able to fight it much longer."

"And if they do?" Cat asked him worriedly. "If it doesn't happen. How much time does she have?"

He stared down at his drink, feeling the "other," a mournful haunted silent cry echoing inside his head that such a thing should happen.

"A year," he finally said, his voice low. "Perhaps a bit longer. She's still channeling the adrenal hormone to her brain. It hasn't become excessive yet, and I haven't yet detected it escaping to her musculature or internal organs. Once that begins . . ." He finished his drink. "Once that begins it will only be a matter of months or weeks. Or perhaps some catastrophic event before if it builds to the point that it floods her entire system. Then . . ." He swallowed tightly. "Then, perhaps, forty-eight hours."

Once the Genetic Flaming took hold of her it was just a matter of time before her Breed genetics flooded her system.

And that was the part that both Graeme and his "other" feared. If she wasn't mated when that happened, then those genetics would destroy her from the inside out in such a cruel and inhumane manner that Graeme knew he couldn't allow her to survive till death came naturally. He couldn't bear knowing he'd allowed her to experience such a fate.

Had he waited too long? he wondered. Kept them apart too many years? The "other" that helped guide his actions assured him he hadn't. The instinctive knowledge he had of her unique genetics as well as Dane's assured him that he had actually brought them together too soon. But he couldn't wait longer, and he knew it.

He'd tried to give Katelyn time. Interfered when he knew she and Dane were close to having sex, hoping Dane's Breed instincts would react and release the mating hormone, but it hadn't happened.

Even the minute amount Katelyn had released hadn't brought Dane's beast out of hiding.

Going to them with the truth would only cause each of them to reject it, and he was certain of that. His sense of future events screamed in denial each time he considered it.

If they didn't mate soon, though . . .

Grief tore at him, clenched in his chest and tempted the "other" to tear free of his control.

Taking her life to spare her the agony he knew that he could never allow her to experience would destroy a part of him.

And it just may cause him to destroy Dane as well . . .

# • CHAPTER 10 •

Dane didn't go straight to the suite he shared with Katy. Hell, he doubted he'd have the self-control to not touch her if he did. Instead, he invited the bodyguard trailing him for one of the slender cigars Vanderale Industries created just for the Breeds. The rich tobacco soothed Breed senses and helped calm the often irritable animal senses.

Burke Morrow was one of the Breeds Leo normally kept on the Congo compound for security. He was a damned good security specialist. One of the best Leo possessed. But his Breed senses were often agitated by the influx of human emotions that he seemed sensitive to.

Burke didn't talk overly much, just enjoyed the fragrant tobacco and, when Dane was ready to go, followed silently. A shadow waiting, watching for any hint of danger.

When they reached the outside of the suite, the Breed turned and entered the open waiting area that hotel staff kept supplied with hot coffee and snacks. Three other Breeds were already there, their voices quiet as they discussed some new security gadget.

It wasn't a conversation he was interested in, not when he was so damned close to Katy, he swore he could smell her sweet scent.

Letting himself into the room, he secured the dead-bolt lock and attached an electronic alarm he carried in his evening jacket. Just to be on the safe side.

Pushing his fingers wearily through his hair, he glanced at her closed door, grimaced, then stepped farther into the suite to head to the bar and a drink. Only to come to a hard standstill.

She caught sight of him about the same time she made her way from the bar, a half-filled glass in the hand she'd just lowered. She stopped, staring back at him, her eyes wide, the whisky brown picking up the dim light in the room and gleaming with a hint of amber in the depths.

Dane forced himself to swallow, to breathe. God help him, but she was the most beautiful creature he'd ever laid his eyes on. Dressed in nothing but lacy white boy shorts and a matching snug tank top, she looked sensual, as erotic as the hottest sex dream.

Her breasts were swollen, pushing against the top, her nipples hard and pressing at the material, seeking attention. Sleek tan-toned flesh gleamed in the low light against the white material while her thick, wavy dark hair flowed around her shoulders, untamed, tempting his fingers.

He could feel her emotions wrapping around him, and his chest clenched at the sensation. Because he knew the scent of the emotion that sank into his chest and clenched his heart with desperate fingers. She loved.

As much as he hated the knowledge that no matter what he did, he was going to hurt her, he knew he couldn't walk away. At some point, both their hearts would break. She would age; he wouldn't. He was going to lose her no matter what he did.

He glanced at the glass again as he stepped slowly across the room, his already erect cock seeming to harden further as he watched her breath catch.

Stopping in front of her, he took the glass from her hand, finished the drink, then placed it on the table next to the sofa.

"That your first one?" he asked, keeping his voice soft.

She looked at the glass and sighed.

"Yeah." The breathy little catch to her voice had the arousal pounding in his body, quickening. "Maybe I should have started sooner."

"Maybe it wouldn't have mattered." Dane reached up and cupped her cheek, his thumb caressing the reddened mark on her cheek. Proof of the tears she'd shed because of him.

Proof of the love she'd felt for him.

Her lashes fluttered against her flushed cheeks. Dane could see her breaths quickening, the pulse beating at her throat. When her gaze lifted to him, the gold in her whisky-colored eyes was more apparent, and her expression was hungry, filled with all the need she'd tried so hard to convince him no longer existed.

"Why can't I let you go?" she whispered then, tormented.

"I don't know, baby," he answered her. "When you have an answer for that, then find the reason that I can't stay away from you."

His arms went around her, his lips settling over hers as his tongue parted them and slipped inside the spicy heat of her mouth. It was whisky burn and just as intoxicating.

He swore if Graeme interrupted them this time, then he was killing the bastard.

Her flesh was like hot silk, her hands stroking over his shoulders, nails pricking his flesh, sharp little bites of heat that had him throttling a growl as he lifted her to him. It was a hell of a long way to the bedroom, or just a few steps to that damned counter between the kitchenette and the sitting area. Dane chose the counter until he could get his senses together, get a taste of her, before he made that trek to the bed.

Hell, he might just end up fucking her on the floor at the rate he could feel his control slipping.

Sitting her on the counter in front of him, his lips and tongue still locked with hers, tangling, battling for supremacy of the kiss. It wasn't that no woman had ever dared him in a kiss before, it was that no other woman had ever meant it until Katy.

And he knew she meant it.

She twisted against him, her nails raking over his shoulders, his back, as lost in the need for his taste as he was for hers.

He wanted more than that hot little kiss, though, and the hint of spice he could taste in it.

His hands gripped the hem of her little undershirt and drew it quickly upward as he pulled back from her. And in the dim light from the kitchenette he gazed on those pretty breasts again. Sweet dark pink nipples, hard and tempting him to taste.

Tempting nothing. They were just waiting for him. He knew he was going to feast on those ripe little points before there was a chance of going further.

He cupped the swollen curves, his thumbs finding the hot little peaks as he lowered his head, his gaze holding hers, watching as her lashes lowered, the color of whisky staring back at him from that fragile shield.

Filled with a hunger for him that he swore he'd never seen in another's face, the little temptress licked her swollen lips and slid one hand into the hair at the back of his head.

"Stop teasing me," she whispered, trying to pull his head to her as he held back, letting his breath caress the tight little points.

"What do you want, baby?" he crooned, turning his head to brush his cheek over a sensitive tip. "Tell me what you want me to do."

"Suck my nipples," she whispered, no fear, no shyness, just a woman's need. "Suck them hard."

Fuck!

She wasn't supposed to say that. Wasn't supposed to demand exactly what he wanted.

He turned his head back to her, caught her nipple between his lips and raked his tongue over it. The tight, silken feel of her flesh against his tongue had him biting back a moan. Holding the sweet flesh in his hand, he drew on her, tasting her, feeding from her pleasure and her need until she was shaking from it.

The feel of her hands in his hair, tugging at it, holding him to her as her body bowed, pushing her nipple deeper between his lips, was exquisite. The way her legs gripped his thighs, the feel of her damp, hot pussy as she rubbed against the cloth-covered erection pressing against it, was nearly his undoing.

He swore he could feel those slick juices through his pants and her thin silk-and-lace panties. And the scent of her. That hint of vanilla she used in her shower, fragrant against her flesh, and the smell of feminine need and lust. He couldn't actually smell it, he told himself. His Breed senses were more recessed, less refined than other Breeds unless he deliberately pulled them free. Which he hadn't done. But that hint of chilis and honey, he swore, was mixed with the unmistakable scent of sweet, feminine arousal.

He didn't have to be a Breed to smell that. It was a barely there scent, but where a hint of heat and musk normally flavored the air, it was different for this woman.

And he was hungry for the taste of it.

His hands moved from her breasts, caressed her back and sides, came back and moved to her thighs. The muscles were taut, clenched on his outer legs as he ground the hardened length of his cock against her.

He could feel the pleasure spiraling out of control for both of them, and he was damned if he was going to fuck her on a counter. Not this first time.

Pulling back, releasing the swollen, reddened peak from his mouth, he stripped his shirt from his shoulders, intending to pick her up in his arms and hurry them both to the bedroom. Before he could reach for her, she slid from the counter, her nails running down his chest to his abs then to the belt of his slacks.

◆ ◆ ◆

She'd dreamed of him for so long. Katelyn was desperate for more now that he was touching her, that everything she'd imagined in every fantasy was there at her fingertips. And he wanted her. He was there, touching her, his groans echoing around her, his pleasure whispering over her senses as she touched him.

She needed this. Needed him and the memories this night would bring her when he walked away again. And he would walk away. Just as he had before.

She didn't fit in his world, in whatever vision he had of his future. But for this one night at least, she was the vision he wanted in his bed.

Releasing his belt then his slacks with shaking fingers, she didn't have to worry about working his hard cock from underwear, because he obviously didn't wear them.

"Hmm. Commando . . . ," she whispered, palming the tight sack of his scrotum as she stroked her other hand from the bloated crest to the base of the stiff erection.

It took a special kind of hedonist to go commando, she'd always heard.

Stroking the shaft again, she leaned forward, balanced on the balls of her feet, the throbbing, plum-shaped crest touching her lips as his hands threaded into her hair.

She ran her tongue over the head and moaned when a droplet of pre-cum touched her taste buds. *Saffron*, she thought. There was a subtle, erotic hint of saffron and salt there, and she wanted more.

As she rubbed her tongue over and around the swollen crest, the little itch she'd had under her tongue eased, but her hunger for him increased.

How odd, she thought, wondering if she would remember it later.

"Who's teasing now, baby," his voice rasped in the dark as his hands clenched tighter in her hair, holding her still as he pressed deeper inside her mouth. "Suck it, darlin'. Take what you want."

Take what she wanted.

Him. All of him.

A barely smothered cry slipped free as she closed her lips on the heated, steel-hard flesh, feeling the blood pulse and pound beneath his skin. He was her hunger, her fantasy, and for tonight at least, he would be her lover.

Dane clenched his teeth, staring down at his Katy, certain he was losing his mind as her mouth moved on his cock.

"Sweet Jesus . . . ," he groaned.

His body jerked involuntarily, pleasure whipping through his senses. She filled her mouth with him, sucking him deep. Feminine hunger filled her features as her mouth worked over his cock head, her tongue licking and rubbing the sensitive flesh underneath.

"Ah God. Baby . . ." Her name was on the tip of his tongue, his Katy, but he was damned if he was about to ruin this. He didn't dare. It was too fucking good. Too hot.

She knelt in front of him, those beautiful breasts and hard-tipped nipples that he caught teasing glimpses of as her mouth moved on him, nearly making him insane.

Her mouth was hungry rather than experienced but no less effective in shattering his illusion of control where she was concerned. Pouty lips stretched over his engorged erection as slender fingers stroked the hardened shaft, palmed the tightened sack of his balls. She licked and stroked and tasted him like a woman who had dreamed of nothing else.

"There you go, love," he groaned. "Fuck, your mouth is sweet."

Her tongue licked over the small slit as she drew back, just in time to catch a pulse of pre-cum that escaped. And she moaned. Fuck, moaned like she loved it, like she needed more. And she was determined to have more.

The moist sounds of her suckling mouth filled his head as the sight of her taking him, those pretty, swollen lips tightening, the feel of her drawing him to her throat, swallowing. Her expression was tight with her own pleasure. She had his body strung like a bow, and knew when he came, it was going to blow his mind.

Holding back had sweat popping out on his forehead, his cock pounding with the need for release. When she added rubbing little caresses of her tongue beneath the engorged crest once again, it was nearly destructive.

And, fuck, she was beautiful. His Katy. Kneeling before him as he thrust past her lips, fucking her mouth with short, desperate strokes.

If he didn't pull free soon, then it wasn't going to happen. He could feel the haze of pending release beginning to fill his senses, tightening through his body.

Not like this.

When he came, he was going to be buried inside her, marking her senses and her body until she knew, all the way to her soul, that there was no running from him again.

Pulling back took everything Dane possessed. The sight of his cock slipping from her mouth, damp from her hold on it as her tongue licked over the tip, almost had him coming then and there.

"Witch," he groaned, pulling her to her feet before he lifted her against him as he took her lips in another of those deep, tongue-twining kisses that burned through his senses.

# CHAPTER II

Katelyn wrapped her legs around Dane's hips as he lifted her to him, his kiss holding her almost spellbound. The taste of him she'd never forget.

Whisky but every so often a hint of saffron and spice as his tongue twined with hers, dominating the caress.

She could feel moisture spilling between her legs, dampening her panties further as the feverishness she'd felt earlier began to dissipate. Another heat filled her now. The heated lash of pleasure and a need unlike anything she'd known before as he carried her to her bedroom.

The two lovers she'd had in the past, she'd never taken to her own bed. She hadn't wanted to smell them in her room later. She'd cared for them, genuinely liked them, but not to the extent that she wanted to smell them on her bed later.

Dane was different.

She wanted to smell him all over her, a scent she'd never be able to rid herself of. She wanted to not just feel his mark on her once he left her bed but wrap herself in it when he wasn't there.

When he reached her bed, he placed her on it and seconds later toed his shoes off as he shrugged from the shirt, then his slacks.

Gloriously naked.

All tanned, cut muscle and powerful strength. His cock stood out from his body, the crest dark, plum-shaped and imposing as it throbbed in lust.

"Lie back," he demanded as he placed one knee on the bed. "Let me taste that sweet pussy, love."

That hint of an accent, all arrogant and precise, had her stomach clenching in added arousal because the hoarse, almost broken tone wasn't so arrogant and precise.

She lay back, almost whimpering with need as he pushed her thighs apart and came between them.

"The perfect sweet," he rasped, his head lowering, his breath caressing her first. "My perfect sweet."

Then his tongue swiped through the slick, sensitive folds of her pussy to the desperately aching bud of her clit.

Katelyn arched, her hips nearly coming off the bed at the pleasure tearing through her senses. Waves of sensation raced across her body, through it, filled every part of her and built when it shouldn't be possible to build.

She cried out, her hands clenching in the blankets beneath her as he anchored her hips by placing one arm over them, holding her in place as he used his lips and tongue to torture her with mindless pleasure.

The burning eroticism of what he was doing to her combined with the pleasure racing through her system, destroying any concept she'd once had of sex with him. Heat built through her senses, burning out of control as his tongue flicked through the narrow slit, circled her clit, moved lower and teased the entrance to her vagina.

His groan echoed against her flesh as she felt yet more slick moisture spilling to his tongue.

"There now, love," he crooned as a ragged cry escaped her. "Just let me taste you a minute. You have the sweetest little pussy . . ."

Katelyn panted for breath, unable to stop the whimpers of need as his tongue traveled back to her clit, circled and stroked around it. Each stroke sent heat blazing through her sense. Her vagina wept with need, clenching as shards of piercing want attacked her womb.

He was licking at her, his fingers stroking, pressing. Katelyn whimpered, fighting to still the undulations of her hips against his restraining arm as the need to get closer to his wicked tongue nearly overwhelmed her.

"Dane . . . Please . . . ," she panted, gasping, the need to be filled, to be taken, clenching her inner muscles, the spill of moisture dampening her thighs.

She was burning hot. Her body had never been strung so tight, so desperate for release. She was hovering so close to the edge that if he didn't do something, didn't ease the flames licking through, burning her senses, her body . . .

His lips surrounded the swollen bud of her clit as two fingers thrust inside the clenched, slick tissue, parting them in a single, hard stroke. He was filling her, stroking and rubbing as he worked them inside her, finding the most incredible spot . . .

She exploded. Detonated in a pleasure so intense, so chaotic she was certain she was dying. Jerking, shuddering in his grip, piercing forks of ecstasy raked over her clit, spread through her pussy and coalesced in a fireball of heat that spread through her womb.

The rush of pure, naked sexual release was like nothing she'd known before, so intense and destructive that she knew she'd never be the same again. It just wasn't possible.

She was fighting to catch her breath, to make sense within the chaos as the waves of rapture begin easing and she felt him move. He came to his knees, pulling her with him, then turning her until her back was to him and a hand at her shoulder blades exerted enough pressure to have her bending in front of him.

"Just like that, baby," he crooned, the wicked, sexual tone of his gravelly now.

With his knees, he pressed her legs farther apart, angled her hips and tilted them. She was open to him now, exposed in a way she had never been to another man.

"Dane . . . wait . . ." But he was already there, the ironhard flesh beginning to penetrate the still clenched, overly sensitive entrance of her pussy.

"Wait?" He paused.

His hands gripped her hips as the broad cock head throbbed, barely parting the snug entrance. "Should I stop, love?"

Should he stop? She whimpered, feeling far too vulnerable, too feminine as she knelt before him. Her hips were lifted to him, open as she had never been to another man, her senses becoming far too acute.

She had never allowed herself to be taken this way. Had never considered it.

"Ahh, you feel it, don't you, baby?" he whispered, moving behind her, working the stiff flesh deeper inside her by slow increments. "So independent and fierce." He came over her further, bending to her, one hand at her hip holding her in place. "Never allowed a man to take you like this, have you?"

Katelyn gasped as he pressed in farther, not enough, the wide crest teasing her until the desperation for more was stealing her breath. And Dane was stealing her control.

"Answer me, love," he demanded, his voice so graveled it was nearly a rasp. "Did they take you like this? Make you feel them with all your senses as they controlled your pleasure?"

His teeth raked her shoulder, drawing another mewling little cry from her as the little pain from his teeth had her pressing back, aching for more.

"Dane," she whispered his name on a broken sob. "I can't . . ."

Her breath caught as he pulled back, nearly retreating fully before returning. No more than the crest was buried inside her, throbbing, inciting the desperate, furious clench of her vagina to keep him in place.

"Can't what? Can't take me like this, love?" he crooned at her ear. "You can, Katy. Just like this, or we stop." He stilled, no longer moving, the head of his cock pulsing inside her, driving her crazy with the need to be taken. Hard. Taken until she was screaming with her release.

Stop? The words finally penetrated her dazed senses.

This way or stop?

And he was calling her Katy. She should protest, something, but, God, what if he really did stop?

She fought to breathe, feeling not just the pleasure but that "something" she'd felt when she'd first entered her room. That clawing need she knew she shouldn't let free. And by taking her like this, he was tempting it to escape.

"No. Don't stop," she cried out, pushing back when he would have pulled free of her. "Please, Dane . . . Don't stop . . ."

If he stopped, there would be no way to stop the wild, clawing sensation tearing at her.

"Sure, baby?" He came over her again. "If I fuck you like this, I'm going to bite you too, Katy," he growled. "I'm going to be so deep inside you that when I come, you'll feel me. You'll feel every drop of my come shooting inside you. So deep and hot you'll never forget the feel of it. Never forget me taking you."

She shuddered, her pussy clenching around the throbbing head, ready to beg for just that.

"Can I have you like this, Katy?" His teeth raked her neck. "All of you? Are you going to give yourself to me?" He pushed deeper inside her, a hard, forceful thrust, a second of sheer rapture, before he stopped again.

Hadn't she already given herself? she thought, dazed. So long ago, she had given him all but her body. Given him all of herself.

"Don't stop," she cried out. "Dane . . . Please . . ." She was suspended on a rack of pure sensation, deep white pulses of exquisite agony and ecstasy, so intense she didn't know if it was pleasure or pain.

"My Katy," he groaned, eased back, rasping the sensitive inner flesh of her pussy, creating a vortex of sensation. "Take me now, Katy."

The hand at her hip tightened as the other clenched in her hair, his elbow braced on the bed. When he moved, Katelyn felt the world dissolve around her. The hard, powerful thrusts impaled the steely flesh inside her, thrust after thrust, as he buried to the hilt. Then what he did to her destroyed her senses.

His teeth bit into her shoulder, holding her in place as he moved. Hard, blinding strokes stretched her, sensitized her. The friction sent burning waves of pleasure/pain rushing through her. The conflicting, addicting rush of sensations mixed with the adrenaline sweeping through her as she lost control of it, amplifying the intensity, increasing every nuance of feeling until it flung her into a twisting, exploding kaleidoscope of sizzling ecstasy.

The orgasm encompassed her entire body.

She felt as though she were flying, lost in clouds of rapture made hotter, bright, when he thrust inside her a final time, stilled then tightened his teeth at her shoulder and did just as he'd promised.

His release shot inside her in forceful pulses so hard she felt each one. Felt them push her higher, expanding the ecstasy cascading through her until she knew she must have died.

She had to have died.

Surely there was no way to have survived it.

✦ ✦ ✦

Dane lay in the cool darkness of Katy's bed hours later, glaring at the ceiling as he tried to figure out just what the fuck he was doing. From the moment Katy turned and stared at him in the connecting room, everything had seemed off-balance, out of kilter in some way, and he couldn't make sense of it.

If she were his mate, then he could understand it. Mating Heat, the extreme hungers, amplified sexual needs and emotional roller coaster was hard for both mates. He'd heard Breed mates describe it as both the most natural thing in the world to them, to sheer hell, according to who the Breed was.

There were those he knew who had fought the emotional implications. Having nothing or no one that was theirs, even a parent or sibling, then it would be a shade unfamiliar, he reasoned. Those who had accepted what their mate was to them, longed for that connection and bonding, they swore even the heat was one of the most incredible experiences of their lives.

Over the years, he'd made a point to question mates, to try to understand what they felt and sensed when Mating Heat overtook them. Because despite the hellish knowledge that he'd have to walk away if he suspected Mating Heat was beginning, there was a part of him that wondered. That ached at the knowledge that if a mate did exist for him, then it was something he could never have.

If the world ever learned Leo Vanderale was the first Leo, and that the multinational playboy and heir Dane Vanderale was more than seventy years old, then the blood frenzy would destroy all Breeds. As well as their mates.

The world wasn't ready for the knowledge of Mating Heat, the age delay or any of the other secrets Breeds kept carefully under wraps. And some of those secrets, even the Breeds weren't aware of. There were things only Leo knew, and there were few of those secrets that he shared with Dane.

If Dane didn't know, then he couldn't be tortured for the information, his father had once told him heavily. It was for his protection that he didn't reveal secrets that had no bearing on the Breeds today, other than as a weapon that could be used against them.

As he lay there, the erection that hadn't abated, even after he'd taken Katelyn the second time, was as confusing as anything else that happened in the last week. He should be exhausted, physically drained and ready to sleep for at least a few hours. Instead, he was lying there, telling himself he couldn't take her again, that he had to allow her to sleep. Meanwhile his cock was still erect, and beneath the head, he could feel a sensation, rather like a band surrounding it. Something he'd never felt before and had never heard of anyone feeling in Mating Heat.

Thank God.

A part of him had been terrified when he'd first seen her again. That scent of chilis and honey, so subtle that even during those times that his Breed instincts woke, he barely sensed it.

Unlike most recessed Breeds, Dane could awaken his senses or turn them off completely at will. When away from the Vanderale compound, he kept them buried, bringing them out only when necessary. During the times he'd had trouble controlling them, he'd taken one of the scent blockers his mother had created years ago. It blocked the Breed scent, leaving only the human scent. Take enough, and it blocked all scent, period.

The cigars he and his father had created helped as well in shielding the Breed scent if the right hormonal mixes were used. *Different recipes for different problems*, he thought with a sigh. Staying safe had often meant staying hidden from any Breed but those raised on the Vanderale compound in the Congo. At that time, Breeds were under Council control, and it was just too dangerous to trust them without safeguards in place.

Now, only he and Leo were tied to that need for secrecy, and Dane's mother, Elizabeth, as Leo's mate. Being the first Breed created and having escaped to boot nearly one hundred and fifty years before, both humans and some Breeds would see him as a threat.

To know that his son hadn't aged after his thirtieth year, was still in his prime as well without mating, made him even more valuable in some ways. Knowledge of who and what they were would destroy them.

And now there was Katy and that streak of dominance he'd used when he'd taken her. That, alone with the perverse insistence of taking her with no condom, would have been impossible to deny if he'd realized at the time how unusual it was.

Why the hell had her submission been so important that he'd been unable to still that impulse? What was it about her that made him so determined to hold her to him, even eight years ago?

As Katy rolled closer to him, Dane tightened his arms around her, a wave of almost gentleness easing through him.

Hell.

What the hell was he going to do about her?

# CHAPTER 12

Dane was gone when Katelyn awoke. She knew he was gone. Whenever he was anywhere close, the aloneness she normally felt around her was absent. As though his presence in the vicinity had the power to wrap her in a shield that ensured she never felt alone.

She'd felt that when she was younger, she realized as she rolled over and buried her head in the pillow where he'd slept. His scent was there, filling her senses and bringing a warm glow to her.

Her body was sensitive, sore. She smiled at that realization. How many times had he taken her the night before? At least three. And they hadn't been quick, hurried instances. He'd played with her body, sensitized it, made her mindless for him before he'd ever given her what she needed.

As a lover, he was extraordinary. Selfless in the time and care he took to ensure she found more pleasure than she'd thought possible before he found his own. And now he was her lover.

She breathed in deeply at the thought and forced herself to leave the bed. She had no illusions that she could possibly be his last lover. Dane didn't form relationships, nor did he go for attachments. Some women lasted a night, some a few weeks. None more than a month. He wasn't a man that made commitments to his lovers, or encouraged them to make any to him.

But last night, he'd demanded that she belong to him. That she give him all of herself, a small voice reminded her. She reached up and felt the small mark on her shoulder where he'd bitten her. It was tingly, sensitive and hot.

He never left marks on his women either. If he did, they were never left in an area impossible to hide without clothing that covered the neck nearly to the throat.

Standing naked in front of the mirror, she tilted her head to the side and stared at the small, almost-purple wound. A bruise with the imprint of two teeth, barely detectable. Nothing like a mating mark, she thought in amusement, but the mark of a man claiming his woman.

Just a man.

He'd left this mark, and he'd left it where it could be seen. She brushed her fingers over it again, almost shivering at the pleasure that raced over her flesh, then forced herself into the shower.

An hour later, dressed in tailored black slacks and a white chiffon blouse with moderate heels, she dried her hair before pulling it up and looping it into a loose, messy bun and calling it done. Minimal makeup, and she was ready for whatever the day may bring, she hoped. It seemed that lately life had decided to throw a few curveballs that she was still adapting to.

She called Portia to find out she was already in the lobby waiting for her and that Graeme had already gone into the restaurant for coffee as he waited for them.

"It's Saturday," Katelyn muttered.

Portia only laughed at the statement. "I don't think he recognizes weekends."

And wasn't that the truth.

Disconnecting the call, she picked up her bag, checked it for her epad and needed items, along with the files she'd need, and stepped from the suite.

Drew was waiting for her, watching the morning news with several other Breeds as they drank coffee. He came to his feet instantly, buttoned his neat suit jacket and, without seeming to hurry, was at her side in seconds and moved a few steps ahead of her.

"Mr. Vanderale asked that I inform you that he'll return this evening," he told her as they reached the elevator. "He left just before daybreak."

She looked up at him, grinning. "Do you ever sleep, Drew?"

"Sometimes." He looked at her, surprised, though she caught the amusement in his gaze. "I nap a lot, though."

She rolled her eyes. It was the same response Graeme often gave her. Unfortunately, she understood the statement. She was prone to nap more than actually sleep. A result of the two years after her foster parents had died that she'd been forced to stay with Charles and Lisa Moran.

Both had the disturbing habit of slipping into her room while she was sleeping and attempting to steal whatever cash she'd made working odd jobs. She'd learned to sleep light if she wanted to eat, because meals were not free at the Moran house.

Stepping into the lobby, she glimpsed the three men she'd seen in the dining area the night before enjoying coffee together in the more casual seating area off the bar. They didn't look up as she met Portia, but she had a feeling they knew she was there.

"Guess what?" Portia's smile was bright and filled with anticipation.

"Okay, what?" Katelyn asked, hiding her smile at her assistant's obvious pleasure.

"The house is almost ready. The rental agent called about an hour ago and asked that you come by to approve the changes they made, then it's just a matter of cleaning and moving the furniture in for you."

And that was good news.

"You won't have to share a suite anymore," Portia tacked on.

Katelyn almost laughed at that. "And perhaps Rhys and Dane will share a suite and let you have your solitude?" she asked her assistant.

"I do rather like my solitude," Portia agreed with mock seriousness. "And men do rather tend to disturb it."

"Then it's a good thing that Graeme and Ross agreed to the apartment lease close to the house that I requested for you," Katelyn told her, grinning at Portia's surprise. "The email was waiting this morning when I checked my messages. Looks like you get to go apartment hunting."

"Yes!" Portia barely restrained herself. The tone wasn't a squeal, but it came close as she all but danced in the middle of the lobby.

"I wasn't going to leave you in the hotel for the next year." Katelyn shook her head in amusement as they headed for the restaurant entrance. "You'd have disowned me."

"Or found my own apartment," Portia pointed out, her green eyes alight with pleasure. "Which I was going to do. But if Tech-Corp's willing to help out with that, I'm more than happy to let them."

The Broken Butte project was Tech-Corp and Katelyn's baby.

Normally, she and Portia weren't out of their home territory for more than a few weeks per project. Most of the work they did from the main office in San Francisco with weekly videoconferencing. The final stage of a project was when Katelyn and Portia made the trip to the client, usually a two- to three-week stay to implement the changes.

"I hear someone will be apartment hunting" was Graeme's greeting as Katelyn and Portia took their seats at the table he kept reserved in the dining room.

"Thank you, Graeme." Portia's pleasure was apparent.

"My dear, I'd never allow one of my favorite girls to be less than comfortable on a Tech-Corp job," he assured her with a smile. "Once Catherine and Sabra arrive, you'll all be together once again. My favorite little coffee club."

That was what he'd called them since he'd brought them together and arrived at the training center to find them all parked in the coffee hall, each with a cup of rich black coffee as they discussed all the reasons why sugar, cream or flavorings just were not needed and just wouldn't do. To which he'd agreed wholeheartedly.

They'd all come from different, difficult pasts and traumas, and found themselves at Tech-Corp's main offices in one of the most sought-after programs in business restructuring.

Once breakfast was out of the way and a fresh pot of coffee on the table, they got down to business. New applications, security checks and all the various decisions on the table as well as those they projected to be upcoming and the various firms involved in the project being developed within and around Broken Butte.

By the time they finished, they went through lunch and another pot of coffee before Portia turned to Katelyn.

"The Realtor will be at the house in an hour," she told her. "Should we reschedule?"

Katelyn shook her head decisively. "Let Drew know we're ready and where we're going."

As Portia sent the message, Katelyn turned back to Graeme. "We can continue this later if you like, but I think we have everything for today."

He nodded back at her with a hint of a smile. "I have plans upcoming as well, my dear," he assured her. "And Cat is expecting me at home."

"I haven't seen Desalvo and Vanderale," Portia said, looking around.

"Dane was called to the Bureau this morning to meet with his parents about one of their own projects, I do believe," Graeme answered her. "They're dealing with several irate board members at the moment and are deciding if they should soothe ruffled feathers."

Katelyn remained quiet. The thought that Dane hadn't mentioned any business concerns in the area shouldn't have been surprising, she guessed. She'd asked him several times if he didn't have to return to business at some point, and he'd given her some neutral reply that didn't really answer the question.

"And here's Drew," Portia announced as the bodyguard entered the dining room, along with another security member, Steven Revin. Steven wasn't a Breed, but his qualifications were excellent. Former military, Breed trained and several years' experience under Dash Sinclair, a prominent Wolf Breed alpha.

"Why do I have additional security, Graeme?" she asked her mentor and employer suspiciously.

Graeme met her gaze squarely, his expression bland. "Because I've seen far too many unfamiliar faces of late," he told her, reminding her of those she'd noticed the night before as well. "Better safe than sorry, my dear."

She glanced at Drew and Steven. "I won't have bodyguards living with me," she warned him.

He merely shrugged. "Drew doesn't mind sleeping in the vehicle, do you, Drew?"

"Better than some places I've slept," Drew agreed quietly. "And it's a comfortable SUV."

Katelyn rose to her feet, giving Graeme a hard, warning look. "We'll discuss this when I return . . ."

"Hmm, Cat has plans for us today," he told her, his tone rather droll. "Have Portia schedule time for tomorrow. Or perhaps Monday. It is a weekend, my dear."

He lifted his coffee cup as though the matter was of little or no importance.

"It is a weekend." She looked at Portia, who was so obviously holding back her laughter. "Yet we've been working since seven this morning. Explain that one."

"She isn't yet a genius." Graeme sighed, his expression pitying as he glanced at Portia. "She wouldn't understand."

"I'm not a genius *yet*," the redhead told Katelyn. "There's hope for me."

"Work hard, my dear," he stated before Katelyn could form a comeback. "Work hard and all things are possible."

The look he shot Katelyn was filled with laughter; the gold in his eyes actually seemed to twinkle with it.

"I'm telling Cat on you." She shook her finger at him, trying to hold back her own laughter. "You're being mean to us. I haven't figured out how yet. But I will."

He chuckled at that. "When you figure it out, my dear, be sure to let me know as well."

Shaking her head at the Bengal Breed, she followed Drew through the restaurant as Steven took up the rear. And she had to admit to a bit of unease at the knowledge that for whatever reason, Graeme had felt the need to add another security member to her. She'd thought Drew was overkill, personally. She rarely had any problems with any of her projects. Even irate managers were few and far between.

But this was Broken Butte. She'd learned long, long ago that when it came to her hometown, all bets were off. At least where she seemed to be concerned.

✦ ✦ ✦

The house was perfect.

Katelyn did a walk-through with Portia, ordering Drew and Steven to remain on the porch. She didn't need them making the rental agent nervous; that would just make her nervous as well.

There was a nice fenced-in backyard, the grassless area thick with decorative pebbles. A fire pit sat in the middle of it with comfortable, padded chairs surrounding it and a portico covering it.

The roofed back patio held a porch swing, table and chairs and a modest grill station just as she'd asked. The gray porch stones were smooth and looked cool, sheltered as they were from the hot overhead sun.

The two-story house held four bedrooms with attached baths upstairs. A guest bathroom downstairs off the laundry room. A wonderfully large chef's kitchen, dining room and open living area. Plenty of room for entertaining, with large overhead fans and wide French doors that opened to allow the cooler evening air to filter into the house.

Katelyn enjoyed allowing the evening air in when she was home, and with the move to Broken Butte, there would be fewer trips to the office and more videoconferencing, which would allow her to enjoy the house. That part she was looking forward to.

Another week and the furniture she'd chosen to have shipped from Phoenix would arrive, along with rugs and decorations. Everything would be ready to move in within ten days, the Realtor assured her.

Portia would be staying in the house with her until she found a suitable apartment and needed furnishings.

Leaving the house, she stopped at the end of the walk leading to the house and stared around the residential street. She could hear children playing in backyards. Several houses up, a pair of teenagers sat on a shaded porch with mobile devices in hand. Across the street, three houses up, two men stood next to a car, talking to the one that sat behind the wheel.

Friends, she assumed as she heard their laughter. There weren't a lot of vehicles parked at the side of the street for a Saturday afternoon. But many couples took care of errands, groceries and other assorted things that couldn't be done through the week.

Saturdays and Sundays had been the diner's busiest days when it had been open, she remembered.

Her gaze was drawn up once again. Most homes were single-story; there were only a few two-story homes along the street. Everything appeared neat and peaceful, but something just felt "off." Or maybe *she* just felt off, she thought.

She had to admit Graeme had roused her own suspicions by the addition of Steven to her security. But she also knew how protective Graeme could be of her and the other "coffee club" girls, as he so fondly called them.

"Ms. Chavos?" Steven stepped to her from where he and Drew waited beside the car. "Everything okay?"

Portia was already in the back seat, watching her curiously, and Katelyn realized a fine sheen of perspiration had begun covering her skin, though she didn't feel warm. She was actually a bit chilled and had felt that way all day.

"Of course." She smiled back at the bodyguard and allowed him to escort her to the vehicle. "Drew, I'd like to stop at the construction site, please. I believe they're working today."

"Yes, ma'am," he answered, putting the vehicle in gear and pulling away from the parking spot.

Katelyn had to force herself to not look back. Everything was fine, she told herself. It had to just be her.

They stopped at the construction site, meeting with Joel and Frank Mosely for a tour of the work completed since she'd been there two days before.

There were rumors that a local Breed opposition group was behind the sabatoge, and the investigation was proving the theory.

No problems so far, though, she was assured. Everything was ahead of schedule and looking good.

As she stepped from the building, she paused, looking around once again, but rather than staring around at the site yard, her gaze lifted instead, going over the rooftops of the surrounding buildings.

Several had small patios atop them and potted miniature trees that could tolerate the heat and dry conditions. Chairs sat neatly beneath tables and appeared serene and peaceful. Yet she kept scanning, wondering what drew her attention.

"Ready?" Portia stepped beside her, her gaze going up as well, as though searching for whatever had caught Katelyn's attention. "Are you okay, Katelyn?"

Maybe she wasn't, she thought. A chill seemed to have settled beneath her skin, while at the same time, she felt feverish, off-center. It wasn't an unknown feeling for her, just not a common one.

"I was just admiring the view," she assured her friend, aware that Drew and Steven appeared on guard once again.

"Mr. Parker asked that we return to the hotel now," Drew told her as they were moving away from the site. "He said to tell you some potential clients were in town."

She nodded at the information. "I was finished, Drew. We can return now."

As they left the city limits and headed along the ten-minute drive to the hotel and entertainment section of the small county, she kept her gaze on the surrounding area, with no idea why.

Halfway between Broken Butte and the hotel she felt that odd surge of energy burst through her bloodstream. As it began spiking, it refused to detour to her brain as normal, rushing through her blood, along her nervous system instead. She could feel the heat moving through vital organs, joints, bones. And it was damned scary.

"Something's wrong." She straightened in her seat, craning her neck to see outside as Drew punched the accelerator. "Do you see anything?"

"Nothing," Steven answered, shifting in his seat as Portia did the same to catch a glimpse of whatever might be coming.

A sudden alarm sounded from the vehicle's defense systems, shrill, piercing.

"Impact imminent. Evasive maneuvers," the computer announced as Drew cursed and Steven braced his arms against the fortified frame.

"Impact imminent," it announced again.

"Where is it?!" Drew demanded as the vehicle shot along the deserted highway. "Find it."

"No sight," Steven yelled out, obviously unable to catch sight of whatever the defense system was tracking.

"Notify base!" Drew demanded.

"Base notified. Help inbound. Evade . . . Evade . . ." The computer's strident summons was still giving the imperative order when something hit the SUV with a force that sent it heaving into the air.

"God, no . . . ," Portia whispered, holding desperately to the seat as Katelyn felt the vehicle suddenly hit the ground sideways, the force on her side of the frame, throwing her against the restraints as airbags suddenly inflated, only to deflate just as quickly.

The force of the blow had her ears ringing, her senses becoming scattered as she opened her eyes and found herself staring through the shattered window, where Portia hung in her restraint, unconscious, blood marring her forehead.

And she saw the strangest thing. The very air seemed to shimmer above the busted window of the SUV. As though the air were alive, energized. Blue rays flashed from it with a suddenness that had her flinching, certain she had to be hallucinating. It wouldn't be the first time, but never to this extreme. The muted sound of explosions in the distance drew her attention then. From the portion of the front windshield, she could glimpse a flash of flames and black smoke on a small rise far enough away that she couldn't make out details, and then an eerie silence.

So eerie it felt heavy, oppressive.

Unnatural.

"Portia," she whispered her friend's name as she fumbled with the restraints holding her in her own seat.

Releasing it, she forced herself to slide until she was kneeling on the door, wedging herself between the seats.

Drew, like Portia, was hanging in his seat, blood dripping from his forehead, possibly his shoulder as well. Steven was still, silent, his window shattered, and it appeared his airbags hadn't deployed.

A sob broke from her as she fought to breathe, reaching for his neck to check for a pulse.

It was there. Faint, but he was alive.

Feeling for Drew's, she found his pulse slightly better, and Portia's, like Steven's, was faint and thready but there.

She didn't dare try to release either her friend or Drew from the restraints. The full torso cross belts ensured they were held in the safest position possible until help arrived.

Instead, she fumbled for her bag, found it lodged beneath Steven's seat and dragged it free, cursing her own weakness.

Her hands were shaking, shock and reaction setting in fast as she gripped her phone and activated it. She hit the first number she came to, unable to see or to read whose it was.

Someone answered; she wasn't certain who.

"Dane . . . Dane . . ." She whispered his name.

What were they saying? She could hear someone talking, yelling, she had no idea what they were saying.

"Dane, please . . . ," she whispered on a sob. "Please . . ."

The phone fell out of her hand as adrenaline suddenly rushed through her body again. This time it was stronger, burning hot and blinding her with a wave of pain that rushed through her body. It didn't pour into her head, but through her system once again. Blood, muscles, her lungs. She could feel every bruise, every scratch, even the slice at her leg from the glass.

She thought for certain she'd black out.

She wasn't nearly that lucky . . .

# CHAPTER 13

Katelyn sat in the sitting area of her hotel suite, her head lowered in her hands, her leg aching where an adhesive bandage closed the wound broken glass had made, and her head throbbing.

It had been years since she'd had a migraine, but she definitely had one now.

"The missile would have killed all of you if Drew hadn't reacted and swerved as he had," Rule Breaker, the director of the Western Bureau of Breed Affairs, reported. "He and Steven are fine and being released this evening. Portia Connor is currently in stable condition in the Bureau's medical facility and expected to be released tomorrow sometime."

Katelyn had managed to remain conscious until Graeme had arrived, the desert vehicle he'd driven sliding sideways when he brought it to a stop. He'd jumped from it, the "other" fully in control as a roar ripped through the desert.

Behind him had been two heli-jets landing, and she remembered hearing Dane yelling her name. She'd been just fine, conscious and dealing with the whole event rather rationally, she'd thought. Until something had struck the back of the vehicle, causing it to heave and throw her against the frame with enough force to crack her head against it.

She didn't remember much of anything after that until she woke in the Bureau of Breed Affairs medical facility, disoriented and, at first, uncertain what had happened.

She remembered a cat hissing, a dangerous, warning sound, dark with the threat of violence. After she'd awakened, the tests they'd run had been crazy. She had been there long enough to have most of her blood drawn out, her tongue swabbed dry and vaginal swabs taken. Her pits had been swabbed, and she was surprised the techs there hadn't examined her damned ears. Then they'd slapped a Band-Aid on her leg and sent her on her way.

Why hadn't they needed to keep her as well?

She remembered that rush of energy as it refused to detour to her brain as normal. She remembered things she shouldn't. Things she couldn't have possibly seen, felt, scented.

"The front of the vehicle took the hit." Rule's brother Lawe stepped in. "The reinforced frame distributed the force, but it was still powerful. The second hit to the back of the vehicle was caused by the faulty missile that struck it. The ignition module backfired after failing to explode. The only reason any of you lived is sheer luck."

She remembered feeling the vibrations of the impact racing through the vehicle and being helpless to stop it.

"A desert dragoon was found on a little rise about a mile away with a direct view to the road. We found four human mercenaries, dead. We don't know who took them out," Rule finished.

She could hear a question in the statement, feel the eyes trained on her. Too many eyes.

She shook her head.

"The dragoon showed it had taken laser fire," Rule pressed. "Did you see laser fire? Anything that could explain what happened?"

She lifted her head, but it wasn't Rule; Lawe; the Bureau of Breed Affairs director, Jonas Wyatt; Graeme or Leo whose gaze she sought. She turned her head to where Dane sat beside her, watching her silently. He held her against him with one arm, turned slightly to her so he could watch her face.

He was so warm, and she felt so cold. She wanted to bury inside his warmth for just a second, just long enough to ease the body aches she could feel burning in each joint.

"I don't know what I saw," she whispered, and watched his gaze sharpen.

"What did it look like?" he asked her, his voice gentle as he laid his hand over where hers lay on her lap. "Describe it as best you can."

As best she could?

She remembered the adrenaline spiking through her system and refusing to detour to her brain. The way it seemed to fill her blood, muscles, pumping through her, ensuring she stayed awake, stayed aware.

She'd been aware of the fear racing through her too, the horrible feeling that Drew, Steven and Portia may not wake up. That they were going to die there beneath the blazing sun and there was nothing she could do about it.

Nothing but possibly be able to see something, someone, that would help Dane and Graeme find the ones responsible if she did survive. But what she'd seen didn't make sense to her then, or now. And she hated it when things didn't make sense, when she couldn't grasp what she was seeing or what she was feeling when she knew she needed to.

She inhaled deeply and shook her head, knowing what she was about to say would sound crazy. "It looked like something coming from the air itself. Like the air was alive, then blue bolts shot from it and slammed into that rise. Like the air was charged and striking and when it hit, there was just black smoke."

She shook her head. It sounded crazy, but she had no other way of explaining it.

"Keenan?" she heard Jonas ask, and turned in time to see him throw a sharp look at Graeme.

"He and his groups are in South America," Graeme answered, the stripes across his arms and face still apparent, his green eyes glowing neon as the Primal refused to fully retreat. "I'll get a message to him immediately and confirm it, though."

"No one else has that technology, do they?" Rule snapped. "Surely we'd know if they did."

"I would know if they did," Graeme growled. "None do. At least not my version of it."

He turned to Katelyn with a grimace. "Cloaking tech," he answered her silent question. "I was working on the design some years back, remember?"

She remembered walking into the R&D's underground work area to see it deserted but for Graeme as he worked on a mannequin outfitted in a black suit with what appeared to be wings. It had kept throwing off sparks, and the sizzle that hissed through it had sounded rather dangerous at the time.

In Primal form, he'd growled and muttered, his claws pricking at the threads of the suit, and he seemed to be tracing a particle thread.

"You didn't mention you'd perfected it." She sighed with a shake of her head.

God, that had been a lot of years ago. The cloaking tech Graeme had been working on was a suit of some kind, worn by a single person or even one wearing some sort of personal flight apparatus.

"It was completed not long after you found me in the lab," he grumped. "Works rather well. Could that have been what you saw?"

She considered that for a moment, then shook her head.

"The laser fire I saw was too big to come from an individual weapon," she told them. "I heard a hum as well, similar to the heli-jet. It was a craft of some kind, but I would say much smaller than a heli-jet. Low-flying, single-person." She frowned, fighting to remember everything now that the most confusing part may have an explanation. "I just saw it for a moment, and I thought I must be hallucinating. There was a shimmer in the air just before it fired. A very streamlined shimmer." She shook her head. "Graeme's design allowed for an individual wearing wings of some type. That's not the form the shimmer appeared to be."

"A personal heli-jet of some kind?" Rhys asked then. "There are only a few companies working on such a design."

"Whoever it was seems more friend than enemy anyway . . . ," Rule began.

"I think it was following us," she stated, remembering how she kept being bothered by something above them. "After I came out of the house, I was bothered by something. I kept searching for it, looking up . . ." She breathed out heavily. "I don't know. It was a pretty day. Maybe that was all I was seeing . . ."

But it wasn't, and she knew it. Whatever had disabled the dragoon and killed those men had been all but invisible, and she'd known they were being followed by it. She'd sensed it. Felt it. But how, she wasn't certain.

"You need to rest," Graeme growled, clearly still concerned. "Since you refused to agree to continued medical care, would you do that at least?"

Continued medical care. She wanted to roll her eyes. Poked and prodded at and awakened every hour on the hour? No, thank you.

"She'll rest," Dane assured him. "You find out who the hell has managed to obtain that cloaking tech, I'll take care of Katelyn."

She was capable of taking care of herself, in most cases.

"Graeme, I want a personal weapon." She looked at the Bengal, knowing he would be the one to agree to her request before the others did.

He stared back at her a long moment before finally giving her a short, quick nod. It would be taken care of.

He'd made certain she, as well as the other three women he'd taken under his wing, knew how to defend themselves in normal circumstances. Then he'd made sure they had a fighting chance in less-than-normal circumstances, and just to be certain, he'd told them more than once.

She rubbed at her temple again, wishing the damned headache would go away. EMS was certain there was no concussion, and even the Breed doctor at the medical facility had agreed to her release when she'd demanded it. But the headache wouldn't stop.

She felt off-balance, feverish again, and not quite herself.

"Come on, you need to lie down." Dane came quickly to his feet and, before she could do more than gasp, lifted her into his arms and carried her to the bedroom.

The bed had been turned down, the sheets looking cool, the pillows soft and inviting.

He helped her undress, removing her slacks and blouse and, more slowly, the lacy bra before slipping her silk top over her head.

She didn't bother with the pants. Before he reached for them, she lay back on the pillows he'd slept on the night before and buried her head in them, breathing in his scent.

"Just for a little while," she told him on a sigh. "An hour."

"Till you wake," he growled, and the sound had her smiling.

He was spending too much time with Graeme, she thought; he was even beginning to sound like him.

The blankets came over her, soft as a cloud and she let herself relax, knowing he was there. She could sleep, certain nothing or no one else could touch her, because Dane would never allow it.

Dane stepped back into the sitting area. Rule and Lawe had left and were likely on their way back to the Bureau. Graeme stood in front of the balcony doors, claws retracted. Leo sat silently in the corner of the room. His amber gaze had been assessing, watching Katelyn with an intensity that made Dane uncomfortable but hadn't seemed to faze her.

Jonas stood leaning into the kitchenette counter, a drink in hand, his eerie, quicksilver eyes like mercury, nearly obliterating the whites.

They were all monsters in some way, him included. They weren't human, even though they tried to convince the world they were in their fight to survive.

"Graeme," Dane addressed the Bengal, feeling the anger he normally tried to keep restrained, tightening through his body. "What the bloody fuck is going on here? What have you involved Katelyn in?"

The Bengal was a genius in normal form. A mad scientist with a gift for genetics that was completely astounding. In Primal form, he was terrifyingly so far past genius that there wasn't a word for it. He could smell genetics, taste them in the air, look into the eyes of a babe and predict habits and characteristics that child would have with no clue to how he obtained that knowledge.

Manipulating, calculating and with little care as to who he involved in his games. Usually.

He was shaking his head as he turned slowly, the Primal still aware, and gazed at him solemnly.

"Katelyn, Portia, Catherine and Sabra are the same to me as my brother, perhaps in ways more," he stated in that ruined voice, not animal but not human either. It was a mix of the two that could terrify grown men. "To the Primal, they are as a much-loved child and to be protected. Never, Dane, would I involve one of those women in any sort of game. Especially not one where you were concerned." His gaze flicked to Leo. "Some enemies even I would hesitate to make."

Leo grunted at that but didn't speak, he just watched Dane in that disconcerting way he had.

"Why?" Dane asked him then. "Why does she mean so much to you? Why did you take her out of Broken Butte as you did, ensure she was hidden for years in a training program guaranteed to keep her as isolated as possible?"

"Because you wouldn't," he snapped, his lips drawing back from his incisors in latent fury. "You left her here after breaking her. I heard it. I felt the agonizing cries she refused to voice when you broke her tender heart and walked away from her. I heard, and I saw how she was treated. How the people of this town would cut into her because she had no one to defend her. No one to care if she cried into the darkness late into the night."

And the words cut into him, just as they were intended to, Dane acknowledged, but it didn't answer the full question.

"Bullshit," he enunciated clearly, aware his accent was slipping. "If that were all it was, you would have made a few visits as the monster, caused grown men to piss themselves in terror and warn them to never disrespect her again."

It wouldn't have been the first time he'd done such a thing.

Graeme's lips kicked up in a savage grin, a hint of agreement.

"Have you paid attention to her?" There was almost a note of reverence in his tone. "She has a gift unlike any I've known. I can watch all this incredible energy building in her, zapping into that smart little brain of hers, and suddenly she sees things, threads and ties and the oddest facts that she draws together. Like a puzzle master who needs no picture to complete the pieces."

A monster waxing poetic. What the fuck was going to happen next?

"So you used her?" he demanded furiously.

"Oh, get off your high horse, Dane. You're beginning to remind me of your father. And here I had such high hopes you'd evolve above him," Graeme snarled.

A warning growl came from Leo's throat, but unfortunately it didn't seem to faze the creature.

"There's something else there." It was Jonas who gave voice to what Dane sensed Graeme wasn't saying.

"What?" the Bengal asked before Dane could with a curiosity that could almost have been genuine.

"I agree." Leo sat back in his chair, watching Graeme now, just as Jonas was watching him. "It's not always there; sometimes it's just a flash of scent or an awareness. Here, then gone. Is she a Breed of some sort?"

Graeme rolled his eyes. "Every time one shows a hint of uniqueness, you're convinced they're Breeds," he scoffed. "Does she smell like one? Act like one?"

She didn't, and Dane knew it.

"Have you mated her?" Graeme snarled at Dane then. "Trust me, if that child possessed Breed genetics, her love for you alone would have sparked the Heat. Rather than just this lust you're going to destroy her with."

"Don't push me, Graeme," he warned the Breed. "Not on this. Not right now."

The sheer terror he'd felt when his mother had received that call had caused the animal he kept carefully reined to surge free in protection.

Graeme gazed back at him with a hint of sadness now. "Caring for her isn't enough. The day will come when the animal will find its other half and you'll be unable to resist the mating, Dane. What will that do to her?"

"I'm not a normal hybrid," he reminded the Bengal. "Mating Heat may be something I'll never know. Living my life alone on a chance of Mating Heat would be foolish."

Or so he tried to convince himself.

"*Basilicus humanus rapax hybrida*," Graeme murmured, the Latin words rolling off his tongue.

Very roughly translated: Royal human predator hybrid.

Dane frowned at him, wondering what the hell he was talking about.

"Enough, Graeme," Leo growled with a dangerous rumble, rising to his feet, his still-powerful body in prime shape.

A mocking smile twisted Graeme's lips.

"I'll have the Bureau eyes and ears in town brought in, see if they can learn anything." Jonas straightened, finished his drink and placed the glass in the sink. "Until then, Graeme, why don't you use all those Primal genetics you like to throw around for something other than causing mayhem and madness and see if you can't figure out who's threatening her and why."

Graeme nodded, but there was a gleam in those green eyes that Dane found himself a bit wary of.

"If you need us, Dane," his father said, turning to him, his expression softening from its normally austere lines for just a second, "you know you have only to call."

When the door closed behind Leo and Jonas, Dane turned back to Graeme.

"*Basilicus humanus rapax hybrida.* Royal human predator hybrid," he repeated the words. "*Humanus hybrida.* Hybrid of a humanlike predator. You wouldn't have said the words if they didn't mean something."

Graeme snorted at the accusation. "I'm not a font of information for whatever questions Breeds have," he growled. "You want answers, find them."

"And Katelyn?" Dane snarled. "What does it have to do with her? I already know what I am: an abomination should the world ever learn it. Why point out the obvious? Unless it applies to more than the obvious?"

Graeme could be extremely helpful or extremely confusing, according to his mood. He was rarely anything in between, and at the moment, Dane needed information. He needed whatever Graeme was hiding, and he knew it.

"Or perhaps the obvious just *thinks* he knows what it means," Graeme snapped, stalking past him to follow the others from the room. "Do your research, boy. It's what you should have already done. I have far too many things to do to play teacher to you."

Before he could leave the room Dane found himself in the Bengal's face, a low, warning snarl vibrating from his chest, the instincts he kept under strict control surging from him in one brutal wave he did nothing to stop.

Graeme blinked back at him in surprise before a knowing smile twisted his lips. "You're stronger than I believed. Impressive."

"Don't fuck with me," Dane rasped.

The other Breed merely shook his head. "Would I dare? But it changes nothing. Some information isn't mine to give, but yours to learn. I pray the day never comes that you realize the reasons why, only to learn it was far too late."

✦ ✦ ✦

And of course Leo was waiting for him, Graeme thought as he stepped into the suite he'd taken in case he needed to stay at the hotel rather than return home.

The Breed sat in the corner of the room as he had in Katelyn's seating area, a drink of Graeme's finest whisky in his hand and the animal he kept leashed fully present and accounted for.

Primal. One of the strongest. One of the most fierce.

*Basilicus humanus rapax. Non-hybrid type*, Graeme thought in silent amusement. He could control his genetics at will, and the creature inside him was as much a part of him as the human appearance.

Unlike the spotted or striped Breed genetics, Lion Breeds had no outer markings to show the increased animal genetics. And the *basilicus humanus rapax* was more animal than human to begin with.

"To what do I owe the pleasure, Leo?" He sighed, moving to the bar for his own drink.

"You broke protocol," Leo growled. "We agreed that information would stay in the trash pit we burned it in all those years ago."

Yes, they had. All the paper and electronic recordings of

something the world need never know where the Breeds were concerned. Or they thought the world need never know of it.

"He needs to know." Graeme poured himself a drink, silently grimacing at the delicacy he must use while dealing with Leo.

The Primal would eagerly fight him, pit his strength against the Lions, but both Graeme as well as the Primal were well aware that if it came to such a fight, they would forever be enemies with a man they both held great respect for.

And if they were enemies, there would be no way to protect Katelyn from the creature that would destroy whoever or whatever it took to protect his mate and son.

"He's not your son," Leo pointed out. "When you have your own children, then you may decide what to reveal and what to keep hidden. It's not a decision you may make where my son is concerned."

Except his son was on a collision course with the past, Graeme thought sadly. And that, he couldn't allow Leo to know. The other Breed would kill the innocent to protect the Breeds as a whole, and that he simply couldn't allow.

"Perhaps you're right." He gave the appearance of relenting. "If I crossed the line, my friend, I'll ask your forgiveness."

If he crossed the line . . .

All things were in the wording of it sometimes, he thought.

"What is the girl?" Leo asked then. "She's different. How is she different?"

He turned back to the Leo and gave a weary sigh. "Her mother was a natural analyst, with no opportunity to show her skills to those who could have used her talents." It was close to the truth, he told himself without a drop of guilt.

"Natural human talent, then?" Leo mused, still quite suspicious.

"To the best of my knowledge. If she's anything more than that, my senses haven't detected it, nor have my tests." Once again, close to the truth.

It was all according to when her blood was taken as to whether or not the full scope of her genetics made itself known. Leo didn't need to know that. Not yet, anyway.

"She's Dane's mate," Leo growled then, displeasure whispering through his voice. "I had hoped he'd find a Breed female to mate."

Now, that was interesting that Leo had picked up on that fact so quickly.

Graeme's eyes narrowed on the Lion. "Careful, Leo," he warned him. "Any slight to Katelyn is one to myself as well as my 'other.' It won't be tolerated from you."

Leo stared back at him, that displeasure still apparent. "She's human, and therefore she's weak, easy to target and kill, as we saw today."

"She handled herself well." Graeme shrugged, aware of the game the other Breed was playing: Piss the Bengal off and make him reveal something he wasn't telling. He would have sneered if it wouldn't have given him away.

"So she did, but it doesn't change the fact." Leo nodded, then finished his drink and rose from his chair. "Make certain she's in the medical facility for the second testing phase she's scheduled for, Monday," he demanded. "Elizabeth will test the samples herself on private equipment, just in case."

"Are you going to tell Dane she's his mate?" Graeme asked, wondering how well that would go over as the animal hadn't yet revealed his bond to Dane. "Or ask him why the mating hasn't yet completed when it should have?"

They'd had sex several times, Leo knew. Dane's scent covered her and hers him, but there was no smell of Mating Heat. And if it didn't happen soon, then God help them all.

Leo flashed him a glare. "Why the Mating Heat hasn't begun, I'm not certain. He's a hybrid. It could be something in his genetics. He's not to be told she's his mate until the tests are completed. Push me on that one, Graeme, and we'll have problems. You don't want that."

"It doesn't particularly worry me deep into the night either," Graeme assured him. "I may not be a 'first,' but my 'other' ensures I'm a damned fine match when it comes to a fight, make no mistake there, Leo. And as Dane is yours, so is Katelyn mine. It would do well for you to remember that."

Leo liked to think he was the strongest, that his genetics ensured all Breeds would submit to his will if tested, because so far, none had cared to test him.

"We don't want to be enemies, Graeme," Leo assured him. "Elizabeth would cry and fuss, and that would make me irate. She has a soft spot for you. Don't make me hurt her heart or I'll skin you out and hang your hide on my study wall. She never goes in there."

Graeme was tempted to chuckle at that one. He knew very well that Elizabeth breached Leo's so-called privacy at every given chance.

"Of course, Leo," he drawled. "Ensuring you're not irate is my life's goal."

"Make it your life's goal to keep our secrets secret, then," Leo snapped, as though Graeme's assurance weren't patently false. "And should Dane become nosy, make damned sure he doesn't know exactly what to become nosy about."

As though Dane were some teenager without the will or the intelligence to learn for himself what he wanted to know. Graeme had just made certain he knew what to be nosy about.

But he inclined his head in all apparent agreement and watched as Leo left the suite, closing the door silently behind him.

The Primal let out a low, irritable growl as Graeme finished the drink, then pulled his phone and hit a preprogrammed number.

It was the cloaking tech that worried him more than Dane's or Leo's sensibilities. That was his design, and he was rather possessive. If the Winged Breeds had shared it, well, there would be hell to pay. They may find it hard to regrow those feathers when he finished with them. He'd make certain of it.

But beneath that worry was his grief.

Revealing the truth would only complicate the mating that wasn't. Neither Dane nor Katelyn could force it, but even worse, the vow he made as the "other" all those years ago kept him silent.

The "other" was primal. It was the base essence of who and what he was, and in giving his word while in that form, he'd ensured he could never reveal the secret. All he could do was lead, guide and pray.

# • CHAPTER 14 •

Katelyn awoke Monday morning feeling more herself and her energy renewed. Lying in the bed and watching as dawn made its way on the horizon, she was aware of Dane sleeping behind her, his arm anchoring her to him.

She could feel his heartbeat at her back, the warmth of him enfolding her. She didn't feel the chill that normally filled her, or that sense of feverishness. What she felt was an arousal that was nearly painful, though, she thought in amusement. It had awakened her, like a strident summons, already primed for the man behind her.

And Dane stayed hard, she'd realized. At present, his erection was tucked against her rear, hot and hard, just waiting for her to straddle his thighs and take him inside her. Her need for him had been dulled the day before, the pain and soreness in her body making the thought of sex more problematic than he'd even consider.

Maybe she didn't want to give him a chance to refuse her this morning, she thought with a smile. She could just roll over, take him in her mouth and convince him she was feeling so much better. Well enough to find her pleasure with him and help him find his with her.

She rolled over slowly, her hand moving to his chest, sliding lower, until she slid it down the hard ridge of his cock to the tightening ball sack.

"You're about to get in trouble." The sleepy rasp of his voice brought a smile to her face.

But he rolled to his back, watching her in the dim light as she moved to kneel between his thighs, using both hands to surround the hard flesh and stroke with deliberately slow caresses.

"Keep it up. I won't let you go this time until I fill your mouth with more than just my dick."

His voice was almost a growl. It sent a lash of pleasure striking at her womb and a shiver down her spine as he slid his hand between his thighs and gripped the heavy stalk.

"This what you want, baby?" He gripped her hair with his other hand, pulling her head until it was poised above the throbbing crest.

Her lips parted on a hard breath, her lashes lowering as she deliberately pulled against the hold, looking up at him and running her tongue over her lower lip.

"Are you going to fuck my mouth?" she asked him. "Or just talk about it all morning?"

A chuckle whispered through her senses.

"Oh, Katy, love, I'm going to fuck that sweet mouth until I spill every drop of my cum down your throat." The earthy, erotic threat had her breath catching and her tongue peeking out when he pulled her head to the engorged crest.

She licked over the wide, damp flesh as her fingers wrapped around the width below it. And she moaned at the taste of him. A hint of saffron and wild desert nights.

She loved how big his cock was. How hard and thick it was. As the throbbing head met her lips, she parted them, taking him in her mouth in one slow, heated movement.

Both his hands were in her hair now, clenching, holding her in place. She ached to feel him pumping past her lips, filling her mouth and making her take him. Heat rushed through her body, burned through her womb, wrapped around her clit and built her need for her own orgasm.

The pleasure she found in this, in taking him, hearing his groans, feeling him as he loved what she did to him, was a high she could have never imagined.

She'd never believed she'd have this. It had been her fantasy, her dream for so long, but having him now felt almost unreal. Hard and hot in her mouth, his muscles tightened as she sucked him deeper, licked beneath the crest.

"Fuck, baby." He sounded as entrenched in pleasure as she was. "That's it. Suck me just like that."

She drew him deeper, sucking at his cock with hungry draws of her mouth, her moans desperate and vibrating against his flesh. He kept his hands locked in her hair, restraining her movements, keeping the rhythm where he wanted her. So she teased him with her tongue, flicking beneath it, lashing at the sensitive area. She sucked him slow, worked her mouth on him and fought to break his control.

"Ah God, Katy, when I get my mouth on your pussy, you'll pay for this." He groaned, his hips jerking against her, driving his cock deeper. "I'll make you beg me to let you come."

Yeah, that would take a minute, she thought as she teased, stroked and licked. She flicked over the slit, tasted him and ached for more.

She stroked the hard shaft, sucked him with firm draws of her mouth and moaned as the engorged head came close to her throat.

He tensed beneath her, hips lifting to her sharply, burying him deeper as she tightened her mouth, worked it on the throbbing flesh, sucking as her tongue undulated beneath the engorged head.

She sucked him with all the hunger and need that had tormented her since the night she met him.

"God, Katy, I'm going to come." His voice was deeper, rougher. "I'm going to fill that sweet mouth . . ."

She took him deeper, sucking the flesh with a hunger that made little sense. Because she wanted it. Wanted him filling her mouth.

His hips arched, his hands tightened in her hair, holding her in place, and the hoarse, deepening groans that fell from his lips were her only warning.

She felt the first explosion hit the back of her throat, swallowed and took him deeper each successive one, struggling to take him, to swallow him, until he collapsed beneath her.

He forced her head from the still-hard flesh, where she still tongued the underside, captivated by a tightening, a further hardening just beneath the head that she hadn't known existed.

A second later she found herself on her back, the tank top and panties she wore pulled quickly from her and his head lowered.

There were no preliminaries. He was as hungry as she had been. His tongue swiped through the soft, silken folds, moving up the narrow slit of her pussy. Her taste exploded against his tongue like ambrosia. Like ecstasy itself. And all he could do was crave more.

He pushed his hands beneath her rear, cupped the cheeks of her ass and pulled her to him. He pursed his lips over her clit, kissed it, suckling at it briefly as her hips jerked against his mouth and a desperate wail left her lips.

His tongue flickered back down, licked around the clenching opening to her pussy, teased the opening until her juices spilled to his tongue and nearly sent her careening into release.

Oh God, she needed to come. She was dying; heat was rushing through her system like an inferno, burning her with the building need.

His hands clenched on her ass as he licked lower again, then back to suckle at her hard clit. She was shaking, panting and crying for him as he pressed his tongue against the sensitive bud and moved against it, sending sensation tightening around it as she cried out his name.

He licked her clit, sucked it into his mouth and just when she was certain she would explode, he moved. He licked along the slickened folds, licked over and around the entrance of her vagina, then back to her clit.

Her thighs were shaking with her need for orgasm, her body sheened with perspiration as she heard herself begging. Because it was so good, so hot, and the need was pounding at her senses until she felt was going to go insane from it.

He sucked her clit into his mouth again, his tongue flickering against it, building the torturous pleasure, driving her crazy. She felt her body tightening further, the flames pounding at her, racing over her, and when his lips tightened further, the sucking draws deepening, she exploded.

She felt as though her soul were flying, torn from her body by a pleasure she couldn't have known was coming. Then he pushed her further, higher. His tongue thrust hard inside her, pumping inside her pussy, licking her, a growling moan vibrating against her flesh that had her vagina spasming with the sudden release that tore through it.

She was crying his name, lost in him, dazed from the extremity of the pleasure when he moved between her thighs, draped her legs over his arms and plunged forcefully inside the ever-tightening muscles of her pussy.

She writhed against the bed, held firmly in place, her nails digging into the sheets, back arched as she died a little more. Felt him pumping desperately inside her, his cock shuttling through the ultra-snug tissue, parting it, sending pleasure and pain lashing at her senses until she found herself melting around him, imploding, detonating with a force that threw her back against the bed, and left her struggling just to breathe.

And in a distant part of her mind she realized he was still hard as he slid from her. Ironhard. Not that just-released, has-yet-to-soften hard. But that fully erect, ready-to-fuck hard.

And she knew he'd come. She'd felt it exploding inside her, filling her with his heat.

She watched him from the cover of her lashes as he slipped from the bed and pulled his slacks on, forcing his erection behind the material and zipping them with a grimace before moving to the bathroom.

Seconds later he was back with a damp cloth and towel, and just as he had before, he cleaned the slick excess from between her thighs before drying her with gentle hands.

"It's still early," he told her then. "Go back to sleep. I'll be back in a bit."

He kissed her, a gentle, searing kiss that echoed with lust, before he pulled back, grabbed the rest of his clothing and shoes and left the bedroom.

*Go back to sleep*, he'd said, as though she couldn't be aware that he'd just left her bed, still hard, as though what he'd had with her wasn't enough. Wasn't what he needed.

And Katelyn couldn't do anything but hide her tears and wonder why.

# CHAPTER 15

She now had four bodyguards.

Katelyn stared balefully at the four Bengal Breeds before turning to Graeme.

"I really don't think this is called for," she told him quietly after he introduced them to her. "Four Bengals, Graeme? I know they have more important jobs than following me around."

"Not hardly." His expression was icy as she met him in the restaurant the next morning. "Jonas has had some of his sources in Broken Butte and Window Rock working on the reason for your attack. It would seem you were targeted personally. Word is you've acquired an enemy of late. Someone who's rather irate that you haven't left the area."

She stared at the bodyguards again, Graeme's stone-cold expression, then Dane's savage features. To say he was pissed was an understatement.

She imagined it didn't help matters that he wasn't finding the satisfaction with his lover that he should be. He'd turned to her several times through the night, spending hours touching her, driving her as well as himself crazy with hunger. He was just as hard after ejaculating the second time as he had been the first.

"I have a full day ahead of me, Graeme." She sighed. "I'm due at the house in an hour . . ."

"That has been postponed." It wasn't what Dane said, it was the way he said it. His voice was clipped, the accent clearly present as his jaw tightened over the words.

"Katelyn." Graeme's voice was a bit softer. "You can't possibly move from the security here, my dear. And we can't protect you nearly as well anywhere else."

"The Bureau," Dane spoke up, his expression determined. "I've arranged with Jonas to have an apartment provided for you there. Your assistant is welcome to stay as well."

"No!" She made certain to leave no room for argument but turned back to Graeme instead. She could usually convince him to allow her to have her way.

"Katelyn," Graeme said softly, his green-and-gold eyes shifting as his expression softened with the fondness she knew he felt for her. "I have no sisters. No children. You, Portia, Catherine and Sabra are the same to me as family. Please don't take that risk. For my sake."

She could have refused if he'd demanded or ordered, but he wasn't. She knew how much he cared for them, and the lengths he would go to in keeping them safe. No matter their needs and many of their wants, he had been there for them. And this really wasn't so much to ask.

She breathed out heavily and took the chair Drew had pulled out for her, allowing him to help her slide it closer to the table.

"Very well, Graeme," she acquiesced, though she let it be known she didn't like it. "But I should tell you Portia is starting to go a bit stir-crazy. She was yelling at Rhys this morning and told Drew she was going to skin him and make herself a fur rug. That's a pretty bad sign."

Knowing Rhys, he was driving her crazy, though.

"You know Rhys," Dane commented as he turned his chair to watch her more firmly. "He only gives you peace if he doesn't like you."

She shook her head at that.

"Any idea yet who was behind the attack?" she asked. "Last I heard, mercenaries weren't exactly cheap."

"It's all according to where you hire them," he grunted before looking up as Jonas neared the table.

"We're ready," he told Graeme.

Graeme nodded and glanced at Dane. "Dane knows everything; he can answer your questions." He slid his chair back and nodded to her bodyguards. "Take care of her. I don't think she needs more bruises this trip."

He didn't wait for them to answer but stepped to Jonas with a brief nod toward the door to indicate he was ready.

"Where are they going?" she questioned Dane.

"They received some information on the cloaked craft you saw," he told her. "They're heading to the location hoping to speak to the pilot and find out where he acquired his tech."

"That will be interesting." She restrained her smile. "I guess since the house is off my schedule this morning, I'll assume I can check the construction sites? Or am I under house arrest?"

"I could get so lucky." Dane sighed, his lips quirking as he reached out and tucked a stray ribbon of hair behind her hair. "Damn, you're pretty this morning."

Katelyn felt the flush that worked up her face and was suddenly glad she'd taken more care with her hair and makeup than she usually did. She wore cream-colored slacks and a light cotton blouse with strappy white sandals rather than heels.

Not her usual attire, but she'd wanted to be comfortable while checking on the offices and construction site.

"I should be here when you get back," he continued. "Then I have to leave for Phoenix. There's an event I'm committed to and have to attend while I'm here. Then my schedule should be clear for the next few weeks."

She started to tell him she was heading to Phoenix herself later that evening but, for some reason, held the words back. That and the invitation she was going to make for him to attend with her.

"Kensington's fund-raising party?" she asked, lifting the coffee to her lips and sipping at the hot liquid.

"I'd get out of it if I could," he told her somberly. "But unfortunately, I can't. I should be back by morning, though."

He wasn't going to invite her.

Katelyn kept her expression composed as she nodded at the assurance. "He seems like a good candidate. I like him."

And he was going to win. She'd already told Graeme that Kensington's win would be by quite a few hundred thousand votes. She'd made certain of it.

"He's a Breed proponent; his wife was a good friend of Merinus's before she died of cancer last year. He has several Breeds on his campaign staff as well. They've been quite popular during the time he's spent on the campaign trail," he told her.

And she was quite aware of that but held her knowledge back.

He'd find out once she arrived. She wasn't staying at the hotel and missing that party. She'd put far too much work into ensuring his senatorial success.

She sat and discussed the candidate, his views, his progressive ideas for the state, and through it all she pushed the hurt so deep inside her that she doubted even the Breed bodyguards sensed it.

As she finished her breakfast and another cup of coffee, she glimpsed Portia entering the dining room in front of Rhys and prayed her assistant didn't mention the party to Dane's friend. Not that she'd have any reason to. She was pretty closemouthed even during those times when it wasn't required.

"Time for me to go, love." Dane rose from his chair and leaned down, giving her a lingering kiss before he straightened and headed for the door.

And he still hadn't invited her to that damned party.

"Does he know you're attending the Kensington event?" Drew asked her when Dane and Rhys were well clear of the dining room.

So much for thinking the Breeds had no idea that she wasn't affected by the lack of invitation.

She looked at Portia. "Did you mention it to Rhys?"

"I did not," Portia answered her with a hint of indignation. "I was informed by Mr. Desalvo when I asked if you were going with Mr. Vanderale, that it was something you'd likely not enjoy."

Her receptionist's green eyes were snapping with anger.

"Not a chance I can fit in his world . . . ," she whispered, remembering what he'd told Rhys eight years ago. "I guess nothing's changed."

"Except you," Portia suggested. "You've changed, Katelyn. You don't need his approval to enter his cold little world now, do you? In this instance, you've helped create part of it."

Yes, she had.

But the knowledge that his mind hadn't changed over the years hurt far more than she would allow her friend to know.

"It doesn't matter," she told Portia as though it really didn't. "Get breakfast. It appears our plans for the house have been delayed by the fact that someone wants me dead. We're just checking out the building sites today." She turned to Drew. "Don't take any chances. If you feel the least bit uncomfortable, then we head back here."

He nodded at the order. "Mr. Parker has ordered a heli-jet to be at your disposal rather than a vehicle since you'll be needing it tonight anyway. It's ready whenever you are."

She sighed at the news. Now, wasn't that just wonderful, she thought dismally. Perhaps she was under house arrest anyway. Straight to the sites and straight back via a heli-jet. No more than an hour from the security of the hotel.

At least, until this evening. She was actually surprised Graeme hadn't mentioned the party to Dane.

"Did Katelyn seem upset that you were leaving this evening?" Rhys asked as he and Dane strapped into the Vanderale heli-jet and prepared to head toward Jonas and Graeme's location.

"She didn't." He shook his head, vaguely uncomfortable that she hadn't. "She never cared much for parties when she was younger, though."

"She was never invited to them," Rhys pointed out. "She's attended many of them since joining Tech-Corp."

Dane frowned as he eased the craft from the hotel's landing pad, banked and headed out into the desert.

"Client parties," he murmured. "She didn't mention wanting to attend."

He'd waited for her to say something, dreading it if she had. His time wasn't his own for this particular party. He'd arranged months ago to attend the fund-raising party with Dania Grace, a socialite that he often attended such parties with because it kept other, unattached women from crowding around him. She'd requested he attend the party with her and ensure she had an introduction to the senatorial hopeful. And he'd agreed.

He'd been a fool.

He should have known better. Should have known Graeme would bring Katelyn to Broken Butte at the worst possible time.

"If she sees you with Dania during one of the entertainment reports . . . ," Rhys began.

"She won't," he growled. "Graeme assured me she won't."

"Graeme," Rhys muttered. "I can't believe you're going to trust that shifty-eyed Bengal. He lies for his own amusement."

That was true, but he'd seen his affection for Katelyn, the care he took to ensure she wasn't hurt.

"I don't have a choice, Rhys," he breathed out wearily. "This was arranged months ago. Dania's been a good friend over the years. She's put herself in the line of fire more than once for me when we needed to get into a suspected Council member's party. Canceling at this late date wouldn't be right."

"You could have told Katelyn," Rhys stated, his tone not in the least understanding. "You could have explained."

And if she'd been hurt, if she'd asked him to cancel, he would have. He wouldn't have had a choice. And if he'd seen her eyes fill with hurt, he would have canceled anyway.

"It's better this way," he muttered, wondering who he was trying to convince, himself or his friend? It wasn't working either way.

Dane felt as though he were betraying Katelyn, even though he knew he wasn't. He was keeping a promise, nothing more. The party wasn't a major event this year. A combination fund-raising party and thank-you to donors who had contributed to this point.

The Senate hopeful, Bruin Kensington, had a good chance at winning, Dane admitted. The man had put together a hell of a team. His chief of staff was a Breed, his secretary a Mata Hari who looked like the perfect girl next door, his head of PR was frankly terrifying if one knew her, and between the three of them, the rest of the team worked with well-oiled efficiency.

Now, if he could only manage to get through the party without any problems, then he might have a chance of explaining things to Katy when he returned. He'd swear he'd never do such a thing again, would invite her to the President's Ball, no matter who won, and the party he'd received an invitation to in England with the royal family.

This was going to work out, he told himself.

It had to work out.

But that was what he'd been telling himself each night he made love to her too. The tight, uncomfortable feeling beneath the head of his dick was beginning to piss him off.

He could feel the mating barb pushing to emerge but held back by what, he wasn't certain.

The glands at the side of his tongue weren't swollen or enflamed. There was a vague little itch, but nothing more. But his flesh was sensitive. He'd noticed that morning that shaking hands was damned uncomfortable. Like a thousand little stings under his fingers and palm when he did so. And when he'd shaken the hand of the hotel owner's wife, his skin had actually felt singed.

And each time he'd been forced to shake hands, Graeme's amusement had irritated him further.

The fact that the Bengal knew wasn't lost on Dane. He knew about the party as well. The Primal's gold eyes had flashed in fury when Dane informed him that he wasn't inviting Katy to it. The bastard had actually growled at him.

The smile he'd given Dane just before Katy arrived had been

frankly worrying, though. There had been such a dark warning in it that even Dane's animal instincts had peeked open in wariness.

*Crazy fucking Bengal,* he thought, nearly growling. One of these days, Dane was going to kill him himself.

"I found something on that term you were given," Rhys finally stated in the uncomfortable silence. "But it wasn't just the roughly translated *basilicus humanus rapax hybrida* I found," he stated thoughtfully. "Get this. Two terms, kind of similar, relating to the same group. *Tribus basilicus monstrum.* Three royal monsters. And *tribus insaniae basilicus.* Three insane, or mad, kings. They were supposedly created so differently from normal Breed genetics that they made Graeme look like the friendly neighborhood puppy with a nice pink bow tied around his neck."

He shot Rhys an amazed look. Graeme, neighborhood puppies and pink bows should never, ever be in the same sentence.

"Who's your source?" Dane shook his head at the very thought.

"Well, I haven't figured that one out yet," Rhys answered as he rubbed at the back of his neck and frowned back at Dane. "A contact sent me to a contact, who sent me to a contact." He sighed. "I was directed to the dark web and an encrypted chat. I was asked what terms I was curious about. When I typed in *basilicus humanus rapax hybrida,* they typed back the first alphas, not the first Leo or the first Breed, Dane. In all capitals they typed back, loosely translated, bastardized Latin, the first alphas. Royal genetics, the most powerful predators of the most powerful animals that could be found, with human females whose genetics were altered with yet more genetic material from royal lines. Then they asked if I needed to know more. When I asked if there was more, I got the second term. When I asked about the three mad kings, I was told to find the first feline alpha, Leo Vanderale. Then the chat room disappeared just that fast."

One of the first alphas?

The Leo was the first. Other Breed lines came decades later. At least, records for the additional lines did.

"Leo refuses to discuss the first term. He said sometimes Graeme's musing are just insane ramblings, nothing more," Dane answered as he caught sight of the Bureau's heli-jet not far from a small, ragged canyon cut into the desert floor.

"Where do you want me to go from here, then?" Rhys asked.

As Dane set the heli-jet next to the Bureau's, he watched as Jonas stepped from a shadowed cut in a rising butte opposite the canyon. The Breed didn't appear to be in a pleasant mood.

"Well, let's see if we can't get a little help," Dane stated thoughtfully. "We'll see what Jonas knows. If he knows nothing, it won't take him long to figure it out. He's tenacious like that. And he hates it when he thinks father dearest is hiding information he needs."

And Dane had a feeling time was of the essence, just as he was certain Leo was hiding information they needed. At least, information Dane needed. Why he needed it, he had no idea, but if Graeme was throwing out the bread crumbs, then there was a better-than-average chance it involved Katelyn as well.

# • CHAPTER 16 •

Senatorial candidate Bruin Carver Kensington was considered the underdog when he first came on the scene more than a year ago. A state representative whose wife passed away from cancer just after he announced he was running for Senate, he'd thrown all his passion, grief and energy into what he called "a fight for every Arizonian."

When asked the hard questions, he didn't lie, didn't promise the moon, which he knew he couldn't deliver, even though those running against him did. He didn't slander his opponents, nor did he answer to the ridiculous accusations against him. He simply told the voters how it was. And they had responded.

It was then that, according to him, he'd heard of Katelyn and her ability to put together a team that made winning companies. He wasn't a company, but he wanted a winning team. And he wanted Katelyn to help him create it.

He'd balked over the three Breeds at first. The secretary was a registered Breed, the chief of staff was not, and should that information get out, then she'd know it came from him and he'd lose all Breed support. Period. She'd put her own ass on the line with Jonas to get the man she wanted.

The head of PR was a registered recessed Breed. His genetics were no different from those of anyone who wasn't a Breed. It was his voice, the way he had of speaking, of looking into the camera or at a journalist, that made him a true asset. He was incredible at his job.

Bruin had every chance at winning and the polls were complete in agreement. As Katelyn stepped into the opened doors of the Kensington mansion, she remembered the first time she'd arrived there. Marsha Kensington had passed away months before, but she could still see the effects of it on Bruin's face. He'd loved her. Losing her had nearly broken him. And Katelyn had understood that.

"Katelyn. You were able to come after all." Bruin greeted her as soon as she stepped inside the marble entryway, his handsome face creased in a smile as he held his hands out to her.

At thirty-six, over six feet tall, with thick black hair framing an aristocratically sculpted face and an engaging smile, he drew people to him. A compassionate man, a kind man. She liked that about him.

She let him clasp her hands, barely holding back a grimace of distaste at the feel of his flesh against her. When he kissed her cheek, she almost shuddered in revulsion.

A hell of a response, she thought. It wasn't the first time she'd felt uncomfortable at another's touch, but it was the first time it had been quite so strong.

"You didn't bring a date?" Bruin frowned down at her, his gaze chiding. "What am I going to do about you? You should have a nice man on your arm, a pretty ring on your finger."

She rolled her eyes at the admonishment as she always did.

"My arm and my finger are fine without the two," she assured him with a genuine smile. "I see you have quite a turnout. You should rake in the donations tonight. I've been hearing good things."

"I have a wonderful team," he acknowledged, just as she'd warned him to always say. She did not want Tech-Corp, or her name associated with politics. What she'd done, she'd done because she believed in him, not for business purposes.

"You do indeed," she agreed.

"Come. My lovely sister can do the greetings for a moment. I have some friends I'd like you to meet." He held out his elbow and when she took it, he lowered his head and his voice as he escorted her across the entryway to the elegant steps leading to the ballroom. "On my honor, I haven't mentioned your name, but the fact that we know each other isn't a secret. I have a very good friend who asked to meet you, and I couldn't say no."

Yeah, that happened a lot, she admitted.

"I believe you, Bruin." She tucked her hand in his elbow, thankful the material of his evening jacket separated her hand from his skin.

"And you are looking beautiful tonight," he told her.

✦ ✦ ✦

When Graeme had first made her the offer to work for Tech-Corp, she never wore dresses, didn't know a salad fork from a dessert fork and didn't care to know, any more than she'd known how to wear an evening gown or heels. Now she was dressed in a designer original from an exclusive California designer. The autumn rust color gown was shot with silver and forest green metallic thread. It draped her breasts perfectly while remaining modest, and the fragile straps were barely there and complemented the skin of her shoulders perfectly. The snug bodice ensured there was no danger of the material slipping, and from beneath it, the fall of silk and chiffon to her four-inch silver heels was like a cloud of perfection.

It was one of the most beautiful dresses she owned.

Before she left, Graeme had arrived with jewelry that he swore he wouldn't allow her to leave without wearing. She'd begged him not to make her wear it, but it was so gorgeous.

From her neck to just above her breasts hung a diamond, emerald and golden amber tennis necklace, each stone perfectly matched in size and beauty. At her ears hung matching earrings, beginning with the amber, then the emerald, then a perfectly beautiful diamond dangling from her earlobes. And around her wrist was a bracelet that matched the necklace.

She'd never worn such exquisite jewelry and had to admit, the fear of losing a piece of it had nearly sent her into a panic, until she stared into the mirror.

With her long brown hair piled haphazardly on her head and trailing down past her shoulders, glittering bejeweled pins that matched the colors of the jewelry twinkling in the strands and holding the style where it belonged, her brown eyes and the darker tone of her skin, the entire outfit looked like a dream.

"I can't believe some man hasn't snapped you up yet."

He had, she thought. Unfortunately, she just wasn't the woman he wanted or needed for some reason.

But she'd come a long way in eight years.

She could fit into any walk of life, she knew, from the poorest to the richest, and never know a moment's embarrassment. In the eight years she'd been away from Broken Butte, she'd transformed herself, learned her strengths and weaknesses, and she knew when enough was enough.

If Dane hadn't realized by now that she was the woman he wanted, then he never would. No amount of love or torturing herself was going to change that.

But it hurt. Clear to the very reaches of her soul, she could feel the brutal claws of betrayal digging in deep.

As she and Bruin moved through the throng of guests filling the entry wall and ballroom, they were stopped several times. She knew everyone there, she realized, and they knew who she was. There was no censure, no rejection in any of them. They laughed with her, teased her that she had Bruin next to her rather than some handsome young man, and many asked if she'd received the invitations to their own parties.

It took quite some time to make it to the far side of the ballroom, where Bruin's friend waited. He stood next to the garden doors, drink in hand, talking to another couple as he watched the crowd.

Then he saw her.

Katelyn felt an odd bolt of adrenaline shoot through her system, but she pushed it back ruthlessly. She neither needed it in her head, nor rushing through her body.

"Reign Tallon. Owner, along with his two absent brothers, of Tallon Investments. The lovely Katelyn Chavos," Bruin introduced them.

She'd seen him at the hotel in Broken Butte, she realized. Six-two or -three, with black hair and amber-brown eyes, he wasn't a man one could forget seeing. But there was that something "more" about him as well that she couldn't quite put her finger on.

Closely cropped beard and mustache, his hair growing a little long, the color a rich, raven's wing black. Broad shoulders, trim physique and a hint of power in the body beneath the expensive black tux he wore.

"Ms. Chavos, you're a hard woman to get an introduction to."

Reign smiled with obvious charm as he extended his hand in greeting. "It's a pleasure to meet you."

She accepted the handshake, expecting the same sensations she'd felt when Bruin had touched her. The reaction was milder, not nearly as intense, but still there.

"I'm really not that hard to contact," she demurred, more comfortable in his presence than she should be. "And I've heard some good things about Tallon. It's not often that an investment firm does quite so well with regards to rentals and leases. But you've acquired some excellent properties over the years. I hear you've made a few purchases in avionics and electronics as well?"

"Mostly the software used in them." Reign smiled, tipping his head to the side as he released her hand. "I must say, I'm rather surprised you've heard of us, though. We're very small game in the business and investment world."

"Investment firms are an interest of mine," she informed him as the other couple drifted away. "It's one of the few fields I've not worked in, though I've been approached by several."

Could he be a Breed? she wondered. But that didn't explain that almost déjà vu feeling that swept over her.

"I actually attempted to get a meeting with you last year," he admitted as he slid his hands into the pockets of his slacks and gave her a questioning look from his unusual gaze. "I left several messages with Tech-Corp that went unanswered. My brothers and I flew into Broken Butte a few days ago, hoping to introduce ourselves. But Mr. Parker and Mr. Vanderale have kept you quite busy."

There was a glimmer of knowledge, of compassion, in his amber eyes before he glanced over her shoulder, then back to her. And she read a silent message there. She could turn at her own risk, but what he'd seen concerned him.

Katelyn turned slowly, knowing what she'd see, hating it, preparing herself for it.

Dane stood at the top of the entry, at the top step leading to the ballroom, looking so handsome, so strong, in a black tux, his dark blond hair windblown, his gaze narrowed as it raked over the guests below. And at his side, holding his arm possessively, was the woman he was rumored to have had an affair with the year before.

Dania Grace. Danie to her friends, she always claimed. And she had claimed Katelyn as a friend.

She actually liked the other woman, though she avoided her after she'd heard Danie was possibly sleeping with Dane last year.

The cool blond beauty was the perfect foil for Dane. The daughter of a former American ambassador to England who'd married the daughter of a duke.

The other woman wore a beautiful black gown that whispered over her body from breasts to heels. Diamonds glittered at her neck and wrist, and it was plain to see she had been born into the money that backed her.

She wasn't some poor little waitress who had worked her way up, who had worked for several of the donors present in her position of managerial analyst.

Dania Grace fit perfectly into Dane's life, just as she fit perfectly on his arm. Katelyn bet he hadn't left the other woman's bed unsatisfied, as he had hers.

Katelyn felt sick to her stomach as he smiled down at the other woman, the curve of his lips one of genuine fondness as he led her down the short flight of stairs. Katelyn's throat felt tight, her stomach cramped as she watched them, knowing he'd probably slept with the socialite in the past.

Had he slept with Danie before coming to the party? He would have had time, she acknowledged. He'd left hours before she had; he'd even said he was running late when he stopped by the suite.

So he wouldn't have to fuck her before he left? she wondered.

"Ms. Chavos?" Reign drew her attention back to him, his expression faintly concerned. "Is everything okay?"

She pasted on a fake smile, certain she was dying inside. She was being ripped apart, torn from the inside out.

"There's Dane," Bruin stated, oblivious to her destruction. "And the lovely Ms. Grace. I hear there's going to be an announcement soon between the couple. It's said his father sent for the family heirlooms several days ago . . . Excuse me . . ."

Katelyn fought to breathe.

Her knees felt weak, her body flushed as she fought another surge of adrenaline that would have slipped free.

"Katelyn?" Reign caught her arm, his expression truly concerned as she realized she must have stumbled. Something. "Do you need to walk outside?"

She nodded quickly. "Excuse me."

She brushed past him and stepped past the open door to the garden. She should call Drew, she told herself. Have him find her and get her out of there before Dane caught a glimpse of her.

"Here, you seem chilled." A jacket dropped over her shoulders, the cool material doing nothing to warm her.

"I'm fine." She tried to paste on a reassuring smile as Reign watched her, one hand beneath her elbow, his jacket between her and his flesh. "Please. Go enjoy the party."

"Nonsense," he chided her, his voice curiously gentle. "I was bored to death. I think the world of Bruin, but these parties are as dull as a butter knife. Enjoying the gardens with a pretty girl is much more interesting."

Not with her, it wasn't. She didn't want anyone to see her breaking apart, see the broken, crumbled remains of her pride.

"You're in love with Vanderale," he said softly then. "The man's a fool, my dear."

But was he really? Perhaps he just knew the qualities she lacked in the world he lived within.

She shook her head. "I don't fit into his world." The sound of her own ragged, hoarse voice was a shock. "I knew that, so long ago. I knew that."

"That's rubbish." There was a vein of anger in his tone that she knew should concern her. "The man is so far beneath you as to be laughable."

He sounded far angrier than he should for a stranger, she thought.

Later. She'd worry about it later.

She felt a wave of heat rush over her, felt herself beginning to lose control of the surging energy she knew was going to overtake her. "I need to leave. Please . . ."

"Of course. Do you have your phone?" he asked her. "Call your bodyguard. I'll have him meet you here."

She shook her head. She would not. She would walk out the same way she had walked in, with her head held high. She was not going to slip away from the party as though she had something to be ashamed of. As though she were someone to be ashamed of.

"Katelyn, please allow me to help you?" he asked gently, imperatively, as she turned back to the doors. "If nothing more, allow me to walk you to the doors where your bodyguard can see you."

"I'm fine," she whispered, though she knew she was dying inside.

She shrugged the jacket from her shoulders, aware that he caught it, and reached into her clutch, pushing the small button at the side of her phone for Drew.

She had to get out of there fast.

"I have to go. Now," she whispered, and the doors looked so far away.

"Of course," Reign told her, suddenly gripping her arm and tucking it in his elbow as he began moving. "Let's go, dear. It's not that far. Just ahead. Remember, head held high. That's what you wanted."

Head held high. She wanted that. She could break down when she got to the limo. Or when they reached the heli-jet—it wasn't that far away.

"Tell me your favorite color," he demanded, his voice low as he cut a path through the guests that no one seemed to object to.

"What?" She shook her head at the question.

"Hurry, before those pretty tears fall from your eyes. You'll hate yourself in the morning should that happen," he told her, his voice kind as he led her through the ballroom.

Why in the hell did he care?

"Humor me," he urged her, as though he'd heard the thought.

"My favorite *colors*," she whispered. "Green and gold."

The colors of Dane's eyes.

Her unlucky rescuer cursed, his voice low.

"Mine was always blue," he announced. "A lovely ocean blue. The color of dreams, I always thought."

Katelyn shook her head, her stomach cramping, heat surrounding her now. Her tongue felt swollen and sore while the rest of her body felt feverish, burning with it.

"There's your bodyguard," he told her.

Katelyn looked up, seeing Drew step into the entryway, his eyes narrowed, searching for her. They widened when he saw her, a curse shaping his lips.

"Just the steps now," Reign Tallon announced as he all but carried her up them.

"Katelyn."

She almost stopped at the sound of Dane's voice.

"Katelyn. Wait . . ."

Drew all but dragged her from the businessman's arms as he whipped his jacket around her, revealing the weapon he carried under his arm.

"God, Katelyn, you're burning up," he hissed, rushing her from the mansion into the night air and into the open door of the limo they'd driven in.

"Go!" he snapped at the other bodyguard, and the car shot from the drive, moving fast along the curved drive to the road.

Katelyn laid her head back against the seat, realizing her cheeks were damp with the tears dripping down her face, her breathing rough, gasping.

A wave of pain hit her stomach, more intense than it had been, dragging a cry from her lips as she nearly doubled over.

"Faster," Drew ordered the driver, moving quickly to the seat across from hers and checking her pupils, the pulse at her throat.

She fought to breathe through the pain. That usually worked. Breathe through it, and it would go away. Everything would be okay.

Liquid heat, molten hot seemed to spike straight to her bloodstream, and she cried out at the sensation.

Adrenaline.

She had to push it back. Push it to her brain. Anywhere but her body. There was too much of it. There was no way her body could survive it.

She was only barely aware of the limo jerking to a stop and the lights of the heli-jet glaring amid half a dozen other crafts.

"Come on, Katelyn." Drew was out of the car, staring at her as he extended his hand.

She looked at his hand, then to his face, fighting and losing control of a jagged cry of pain.

"Fuck it," he snarled.

He reached in, pulled her into his arms, ignoring the sudden bowing of her body as every cell she possessed jumped in reaction, screaming in rejection of the touch.

She heard an animal's snarl of fury, and tried to struggle, to escape the pain. But there was no escape. It was everywhere. Inside her, around her, burning through her brain and through her body until she screamed again.

And she screamed his name before she collapsed in Drew's hold, nearly blacking out as another wave of heat tore through her, seared her and burned through her last shred of control.

✦ ✦ ✦

"Katy!" Dane screamed her name as he heard the piercing, agonized cry that echoed around the clearing, watching Drew jump into the heli-jet with her.

The doors closed before he and Rhys could reach her, the craft lifting quickly from the ground as the pilot ignored his attempts to get him to stop. He would have jumped for the landing gear and dragged himself up if Rhys hadn't grabbed his arms, forcing him back.

"Come on, dammit. We have our own, Dane." He ran, half dragging Dane to the sleek black Vanderale heli-jet powering up.

The door was thrown open by the bodyguard Leo had forced him to take and was lifting off before Rhys finished securing the doors.

"Wherever that fucking heli goes, you follow!" Dane yelled as he slid into the copilot's seat and watched the lights racing through the night ahead of them.

"We're only seconds behind them," Burke promised. "Call came in from Jonas. Drew made a call to Graeme that brought out the Primal in the dining room. Goddamn Dane, he went Primal in front of everyone. It was all Cat could do to get him out of there before a dozen other guests saw the Bengal emerge. His roar was heard two floors down when he reached the top floor. Word is he's on the roof, waiting for the heli to land."

Of course the bastard was, Dane thought. He knew something. He knew whatever it was that Dane had scented as he'd nearly caught up with Katelyn. That mix of Katelyn and some unknown scent so powerful, so filled with rage, he'd been shocked.

"I want our Breeds on Graeme's floor," he ordered Rhys. "Call Mother. Get her there, Rhys. Get her there now."

Because something was wrong. Very wrong. And the animal fighting to be free of him, as well as the man, suddenly feared his Katy may not survive it.

# • CHAPTER 17 •

Leo stood at the window of the top-floor apartment he and his mate and two daughters had been given at the Western Bureau of Breed Affairs, his hands shoved into the pockets of his slacks, scowling.

The vague reflection that stared back at him was hard to look at. Most days it was hard to look at. Neither man nor Breed could make the decisions he'd made in his life and still look himself comfortably in the eye.

*Basilicus humanus rapax. Royal human predator.* A rough, loose translation, he admitted. One the scientists had given because they were a mongrel mix of the three.

Those words had been burned into his mind while he was in the labs, before his escape with Elizabeth. He knew what even his human father or his mate didn't. He knew the secrets the scientists had fought to keep even from the Council that funded them.

In those days, the first days of genetic animal-human mutations, the scientists had done many things they shouldn't have. Some of those experiments hadn't even been written down for fear of discovery. What they'd done had been so inhuman, so completely without moral compass or compassion, as to be demonic.

*Basilicus humanus rapax* had been the least of those crimes, he imagined. Royal human predator. Creatures whose animal genetics nearly matched in quantity, their human genetics. Animals, the most fierce of the predators that roamed the Earth, had mutated to the human genetic strand and given birth.

They were, as Dane often muttered, fucking abominations.

They were meant to be abominations.

Abominations who at any time could submit to their genetics and take control of the few thrones left on Earth. They could stand before the people, proclaim themselves kings and fully get away with it.

Even his beloved mate, Elizabeth, was unaware of the true extent of what he was, what their children and grandchildren could be.

Royal human predator.

And he'd escaped, determined in the arrogance of his youth to be free, to love his mate, to have all that humans and animals possessed as their due.

His own Pride. His freedom. Laughter, love, joy.

He would have done the world a greater service had he terminated himself, he'd often thought, in the darkest days, when his mate lay near death from the brutality of those determined to reacquire their creation, or sobbing in rage and pain at yet another miscarriage. There had been far too many of those. Or those dark, desolate days after their sons had died even as Leo and Elizabeth fought to shield them with their own bodies.

They had nearly all died that night.

And now, for whatever reason, that maddened Bengal had given

Dane a piece to a puzzle Leo had prayed would never be re-formed. Then Dane had given it to Jonas.

A clever ploy, Leo admitted. Those with the information knew better than to test his loyalty and his fury by revealing the past to Dane. Jonas was by far another matter.

Leo had always thought Dane was the best of all the genetics he possessed. He'd been raised, loved, faced death more than once, lost friends and lovers and still he knew mercy and compassion. Perhaps that "best" had come from his mother rather than anything Leo had bequeathed him.

Jonas, on the other hand, was everything Leo fought within himself. Coldly logical, without mercy when the need arose, savage when pushed to it. And without fear.

And unlike Dane, he didn't give a flying fuck if the mistakes he revealed Leo had made in his life pissed off or hurt his mother. She hadn't raised him, Leo thought, his grief running deep for that. Jonas hadn't known her mother's love, the lullabies she sang the babies or her tears when he was ill.

He hadn't known a father's guiding hand, or his firm, loving guidance. He hadn't known what it meant to be loved.

He glanced behind him, where his mate, Elizabeth, waited silently, her arms crossed over her breasts as she glared at him.

And she had every right to glare at him.

And behind her stood the son who had inherited the darkest parts of his father, where Dane had inherited the lighter. In more ways than one.

"*Basilicus humanus rapax*. Royal human predator." He sighed. "Is a designation assigned to the first alphas, those Breeds that began the insanity the Council conjured up." He turned back to them. "Royal human predator. They hypothesized that the people of the world were far too attached to their genetic lines, and even more so to their royal lines. The first alphas carried not just the genetics of past kings taken from their descendants, but the actual genetics taken from the bodies they tracked down. In some cases, the quantity of genetic material was high; in some, barely present. But they were able to acquire what they needed."

"Meaning?" Jonas growled, and Leo could feel the apprehension beginning to edge at his son's normally cool demeanor.

"My genetics, if tested deep enough, would give me a throne in two different countries," he answered him. "That's the *basilicus. Humanus,* being humanlike in appearance, coupled with genetics drawn from the descendants of those same kings, to increase the legitimacy of the lineage."

He watched the horror that filled his mate's expression and knew she well understood what the Council had been attempting to do.

"*Rapax,*" he continued. "Predator. They chose the strongest, most fierce of the animal genetics and began mutating, perverting the human genetics, then did the same to the animal with the human genome they'd mutated. They did this to ensure that the resulting fetus wasn't deformed or didn't abort itself. Animal and human characteristics were matched. Strength, cunning and even physical characteristics that would ensure the resulting creature was pleasing to the eye were mutated with an exacting hand." He sneered.

Jonas watched him with cool detachment. "Not surprising." He finally shrugged. "We knew they used genetic material from long-dead royalty. Del-Rey Delgado, the Coyote Coy, is a prime example."

Leo shook his head. "There's a difference, Jonas," he snarled. "Delgado has the normal ratio of human-animal genetics. Like five percent animal to ninety-five percent human, and the ratio of genetic material from long-dead leaders to the genetic strand present in the sperm and ova being mutated was only three percent. In the Breeds that came after the first alphas, scientists targeted specific genetic strands for strength, fighting ability, physical appeal or charisma. They mutated the genetics to fit the idea of the Breed for a specific role. The first alphas, though, matched all criteria with a near-fifty-fifty percent of each species. Where the human genome was weaker, it was mutated with the stronger Breed genetics. Where it was already strong, it was made stronger. Charisma was strengthened, plus physical appeal, strength, fighting ability, intelligence, ability to make rapid strategic decisions." He allowed that force to expand within him. "The ability to lead and command." He growled in Jonas's face with a sudden release of all the power he knew he held at his command.

His son jumped back, eyes widening, the claws that had begun emerging retracting, the silver storm brewing in his eyes abating for a second.

Elizabeth cried out, jumping in front of her son as though to defend him before Jonas pushed her back and watched his father warily.

"They put all of that into one Breed. That is what I am," he yelled back at his son. "One of the first alphas. Not the first, Jonas. I was but one of those creations engineered to take over this fucking world and give it to those who paid for our creation."

Disgust welled in him as it always had. The knowledge that he was designed. Engineered. That he was to exert the brutal strength he possessed against those so much weaker than himself.

As quickly as he'd thrown that power at Jonas, he pulled it back, forcing the surge of the instinctive animal back to his brain, where it powered an intelligence few could grasp.

The Breeds were just learning what a Primal Breed was, but to learn what an alpha Primal was, was another thing entirely. And each of the firsts were natural alpha Primals.

Jonas stared at him now, silent, absorbing what he was learning.

"Hybrids." Jonas pushed his fingers through his hair with a shake of his head. "What was the resulting effect of the hybrids?"

"Dane is the only hybrid born. With you and Callan and the other Breeds created from the sperm and ova taken from me and your mother, the DNA was mutated to hold more human than animal genetics. Dane holds his power more naturally and hides much more than even I can sense," Leo answered him. "But he's unaware of what he possesses or of the creature that inhabits his body. So far, he merely draws from the strength he inherited. When that happens, it's like adrenaline suddenly pumps into the body with a punch of force that can become addicting. Channel it to the brain, and the mental and intellectual awareness are increased exponentially. And that's where it's naturally supposed to rest. Dane came by the ability to do that as a toddler with amazing control." Perhaps too well, Leo reflected.

"And those first alphas?" Jonas asked, and Leo swore he could see that boy's mind working at an incredible rate, just as Dane's so often did. "How many were there?"

He breathed out heavily at the question, the past rising in front of him filled with the blood as well as the brotherhood.

"Seventeen." He ignored Jonas's and Elizabeth's shock. "I have a brother, full brother, born as a fraternal twin, but he could pass as identical. Bengal, Siberian Tiger, Northern Rocky Mountain Wolf, Alaskan Tundra Wolf, Plains Coyote, North American Cougar. Each a twin set. Each still living as of our meeting last year."

"That's only fourteen," Jonas informed him.

"Yes, it is." He looked down at Katelyn's tests once again and knew the son he so loved may soon hate him.

"What of the other three, Leo?" he demanded.

Yes, what of them?

"Then there were three," he said softly. "The greatest of us. The strongest. The most powerful. And our commanders. *Tribus insaniae basilicus.* The three mad kings." He looked up then, and silently admitted to the trepidation filling him. "They were away on a mission, unable to return and stop us when we began our escapes. They were the greatest of us all, because they were all of us," he told them. "DNA of the greatest of royal blood, and DNA of seven of the greatest predators all living within the bodies of three men. They were all of us, and they were mad. Monsters walking in human skin." He looked at the tests again, then looked back to his wife. "And Dane's mate is the child of one of them. She's the child of a monster. And she'll draw them out from wherever they've hidden for over a century. When she does, they could destroy the Breeds. And they'll enjoy it."

As he finished, his phone rang. Glancing at the caller ID, he connected the call quickly and brought it to his ear. He listened, eyes widening, aware that Jonas could hear the same thing he did.

Dane was on his way, following Katelyn, who had collapsed at a party and was rushed away by her bodyguards. Dane was certain he scented Genetic Flaming, and he needed his mother, Leo and every Breed that followed the Vanderales on Graeme's floor at the hotel.

In the background, Leo heard a roar that sent ice racing through his veins. That wasn't a Breed's roar. It was a Primal's.

As he spoke, Jonas's phone as well as Elizabeth's rang.

"We're on our way, Rhys," he promised. "Tell Dane we'll be there."

"I need my bag," Elizabeth barked at Jonas. "Have my equipment loaded in another heli and flown out behind us."

"Bring her here," Jonas snapped. "It would be easier."

Elizabeth shook her head. "She'll be lucky if she makes it to the hotel. If she does, I can stabilize her until you get there. Hopefully." She threw Leo a hard, furious look. "You and I will deal with your secrets later, mate. For now, you will support our son, and by God, you will do so with all honesty should he ask it. Are we clear?"

He stared back at her curiously.

"Are we clear, Leo?" she yelled back at him, baring her teeth like a Breed.

"Yes, mate," he promised her. "We're clear. With all honesty."

It wasn't like he had a choice now.

He stared at the tests again and shook his head before following her, collecting her medical bag from Jonas, then rushing to the heli-jet parked on the landing pad on the roof.

They would all be far better off if the girl died. All but Dane. And because of Dane, Leo would do all he could to protect her. Which was the reason he'd sent out the emergency code the day before to the other thirteen first alphas who had escaped with him. And the reason why three dozen Congo Breeds would be converging on the hotel within an hour.

For his son and the woman he feared would die in Dane's arms.

# ✦ CHAPTER 18 ✦

Graeme paced the hotel rooftop marked with two separate landing pads for the heli-jets often landing there. He paced and he stomped, snapped and snarled.

The "other," as he called the Primal, was fully awake now and merged with him. And the Primal, just as Graeme, was filled with grief and rage for what he knew was coming.

How did one take the life of a child they loved? he asked himself with overwhelming grief. Even to save her from an agony the likes of which even Breeds had never known.

God, how he had fought this day arriving. For eight years he'd used every ounce of knowledge he had or could steal from others to find a way to halt the horror he knew she was going to suffer.

It was that beast that had known what the twenty-one-year-old child was when he first met her. He'd known, known the dangers she could face, and couldn't countenance such a gentle, fragile soul being alone and defenseless when her genetics awoke and ripped her apart from the inside out.

The Primal had actually wept tears, taking it as his duty to end her life when it began, before she entered that place where the agony was even more inhumane than a vivisection.

He and the Primal had sworn they would be there for her, ensure no others harmed her and that when she took her final breath, she would take it knowing she was loved. Even if it was by a maddened Bengal Breed who would shed his tears for her.

God help him. He didn't want to do this. He didn't want to see the fear and the pain in her eyes and know that he had been unable to save her. That he'd finally figured out what it would take and had been unable to give her that gift.

He had figured it out too late.

He had tried. God above knew he had tried. He had been so certain nothing could save her, only to learn that she might have a chance. When he'd matched the hormonal elements of her and Dane's samples, Mating Heat had sprung to brilliant life. Then he'd added that to the madness of her genetics after adding just her latent mating hormone.

At first, it had been just incremental changes. But as Graeme had added the combined mating hormone in progressive doses, the added animal hormones had faded away and only the feline had remained.

Dane could have stopped this. He could have accepted his mate and allowed her to live long before she'd known the first measure of pain from it.

But seeing her mate with another woman on his arm, knowing she hadn't claimed his heart and his heat, had been too much for the contradictory genetics just waiting to destroy her. For the mate who wanted nothing more than to be accepted by the man she'd given her heart to so long ago.

It had happened far too soon. She would have had another year, perhaps more, to ensure the Mating Heat and have what she needed to survive.

If she hadn't seen her mate with another . . .

If her mate had just given her the mating hormone that somehow he had managed to hold back.

His head tipped back and the beast roared in agony, the Bengal's screams echoing across the desert as he fought to let it out, to expend some of the rage building inside him and tearing at his chest.

He hadn't lied to her. His love for her was as deep as a father's for a child. It had been the Primal who had forced his return to that restaurant all those years ago. The Primal who had begun caring for the saddened young woman first. Graeme hadn't had a chance at guarding his heart against her.

He cursed Leo Vanderale and the vow the other Breed had demanded from his "other," years before he'd known Katelyn existed. His sanity had visited for just a short time, during a time that Graeme found Leo, searching for something, anything, to help ease the madness inside him. And he'd learned Leo's secrets, and the secrets of the mad kings. Secrets Leo had demanded the "other" make a vow to never reveal.

Because of that vow, this sweet child would die.

He would never be the same after losing her, he thought painfully, wiping at the tears the Primal shed. Each day he would miss her laugh, her smile. He would miss the world as he knew it, with her in it.

As he stood there attempting to get a handle on the emotions ripping him apart, he felt his Cat step onto the landing pad and turned to her. His mate. The most precious of creatures to him. Surviving this would be impossible without her.

"I don't have the answer," he whispered brokenly as he wrapped his arms around her and held on to her, both as the Breed as well as the "other." "I can't find it, Cat. I can't find what saves her. Only he could have saved her. And he wouldn't. He wouldn't allow it . . ."

Dane would die.

Graeme knew that in his soul, and he was fairly certain by the time Katelyn passed, Leo would know it as well, but he doubted that young man would do more than await the killing blow.

Dane Vanderale saw himself as a hero.

A hero willing to sacrifice a life with his mate to save the Breed world.

Katelyn had needed a villain.

For only the villain would sacrifice the world to save his mate.

Or his child.

"I can't save her, Cat," he whispered again. "I can only end the pain before it becomes too great. And I fear I can't even do that."

"I know." She leaned back, touched his cheek as the tears whispered down it. "You love her. Which was far more than anyone else was willing to do. You love her, Graeme. And she'll carry that with her . . ."

He pulled back, clawed hands wiping at his face at the sound of the heli-jets in the distance.

*Of course the bastard followed her*, he thought with a snarl, seeing the second craft following. Dane had caused this. His having another on his arm had forced Katy's Breed instincts to fully emerge, which had forced her genetics to fully flame into life.

He should have had time. There should have been more time. If only Dane hadn't betrayed that sweet child's heart.

As the heli-jet landed, he rushed for it. He was there when Drew threw open the door, only to catch Katelyn's delicate body as she threw herself from the opening.

He clasped her to him, holding her to his chest as she fought to run from the pain, to escape the intensity of it. Her whisky eyes were more golden than brown, her face paper white, terrified and confused.

"Dane. Dane please . . . ," she sobbed, incoherent now, lost in that world where nothing was sane, nothing was right. A world where only pain exists.

There was no blacking out from it. There was no escape; the animal-infused adrenal hormone assured that.

He was only distantly aware of the sight of the tears on Drew's haggard face. That Breed had been forced to hold her down, to restrain her as she fought him, mindless grief tearing at her soul as her awakening genetics tore at her body.

And she cried for the bastard who refused her as Graeme rushed into the entrance to the hotel and jumped the flight of stairs to the top level, where his suite was located.

A Breed waited with the door open, and Graeme rushed through it, running along the corridor, aware of the Breeds lining the walls and not really giving a fuck.

The Leo's insurance that his perfidious son lived once Katelyn took her last breath, he thought, turning into the suite that had been set up in the eventuality that it would be needed.

Graeme believed in backup plans, but he'd honestly believed this one would not be needed.

She screamed Dane's name again, begging, pleading with him to make the pain stop. And Graeme wept. As he secured the restraints about her body that would keep her from throwing herself from the small bed to the floor, he wept with her, sobs tearing at his chest as he touched her cheek, silently saying goodbye.

A feline snarl curved her lips, and a second later a wolf's cry escaped her throat. Her fingers formed claws, though her nails had no actual claws to use.

"Drew. Keep Portia from here," he ordered, his own voice ragged as he scented the other woman attempting to get to the suite. "Tell those Lion Breeds restraining her I'll skin them myself for touching her," he roared.

Drew rushed from the doorway to get to her, and Graeme couldn't stop another sob from shattering his chest as Cat rushed into the room with him. "Leo and Elizabeth are here. As are Elyiana Morrey, Nikki Armani, Delgado's specialist Katya Sobolova and Amburg."

He nodded. He'd called them in that evening when the Primal's senses warned him this would come soon. He wouldn't have long. If he was to save her from the worse of the nightmare coming, he would have to take her life soon. The others were here to record the need for it, not because they could aid in her survival.

He looked around at the equipment he'd brought in, the store of all possible combinations of concoctions he'd created over the years. Nothing he'd matched her blood and hormones with worked after he'd added the madness overtaking her. Nothing but the addition of the latent hormone he'd swabbed from beneath Dane's tongue just days ago.

She screamed for Dane again as the scientists rushed in and stopped in shock while Leo and Elizabeth pushed past them. In the hallway, he could hear Dane, his roar vicious, filled with a rage that was terrifying to hear and echoing in the hallway as he approached.

Graeme lifted his head and stared back at Leo, tears still falling to his cheeks. "I kept my word," the Primal spat at him in soul-hating fury. "I told none of your secrets. Now she pays the price . . ."

Would Dane have released his animal to mark his mate if he had known?

The Primal had made the vow to never tell those secrets, before it had ever known what it was to love a child. The Primal's vow couldn't be broken. Only Graeme's. And for that, he would hate this man forever.

Leo shook his head, watching as her head tipped back, a howl then a strangled feline scream tearing from her as horror filled his expression.

She screamed out for Dane again, begging him to ease her pain. Her voice broke, so ragged that even hardened Breed scientists looked on helplessly.

"Genetic Flaming," Elyiana suddenly snapped, glaring at Graeme. "There's a therapy for this."

The Primal laughed in savage mockery. The "other" was fully present now, weeping along with Graeme and demanding Leo's blood.

"Should you tell her, or do you release me from my vow?" the "other" demanded.

Grief and sorrow twisted Leo's expression, and he gave a short nod. "You're released from your vow," he whispered.

"*Progidium tribus insaniae basilicus,*" it growled in a torn, enraged voice, staring at Leo. "Child of the three kings. Is there still a therapy?"

She paled as he glanced at her, her lips parting with such fear he almost found it amusing.

She had heard of them. Of all of them there, he figured she would be the one who had heard the tales of the three mad kings. And he had been right.

In that moment Dane burst into the room, his fingers clawed, his gaze demonic. His face looked nearly transformed to that of the lion. Flatter nose and cheekbones, amber eyes obliterating even the whites.

He appeared broader, a bit taller, savage and primitive in his rage as he easily threw off the Breeds who tried to hold him back. To protect him from the sight of his mate.

The Primal he had become was exceptional. Powerful. Such an amazing specimen of animal and human combined by an inhuman rage.

What a shame. There weren't enough Primals as it was, and this one would die.

The creature paused in shock; those eerie amber eyes locked on its mate.

"Dane . . . !" Katelyn arched till he thought her bones would snap, her eyes opened wide, burning blue now with shards of gold as she fought the restraints.

Her screams grew more ragged, more desperate. Blood now stained the entrance to her nostrils, while a bloodred tear spilled from her eye.

"Katy." The creature's voice was jagged, a monster's rasp, as he rushed to her, his arms surrounding her slight body, jerking, writhing in agony.

She fought the restraints, her body bowed and she sobbed. Sobbed for a man unwilling to love her enough to give her his heat in time. And now it was far too late.

"Her organs are being ripped apart," he stated with an icy lack of mercy as Dane tried to hold her, his accusing glare turning to Graeme. "Bones are attempting to harden, adrenal hormonal fluids are pushing inside muscles unable to take the force . . ."

"Make it stop," Dane demanded, and the commanding resonance in his voice was deep, strong. "Make this stop, Graeme."

Rage was burning in the eerie green of his eyes, the mix of gold and emerald, which had overtaken the whites and burned with his fury.

"I can't . . . ," the Primal snarled in agony and spilled his tears once again. "There's nothing I can do but ensure she doesn't experience the worst of this horror. That she be relieved of this agony before her organs begin ripping in half . . ."

Elizabeth cried out in denial even as she attempted to read the various reports and results of the tests Graeme had done over the years.

Leo let loose an alpha Primal snarl that still did not match the sheer power of his son's.

*Fucker.* It was too late for anger.

"Fix this . . ." The demand in Dane's roar was a horrible thing to see, and even harder to deny.

It was possible, Graeme thought in some surprise, this Primal had the power to even overthrow his father.

Not the mad kings, but a first alpha possibly.

How surprising.

◆ ◆ ◆

Dane held Katelyn to him, feeling, sensing the heat burning in her body, the agony radiating through her mind. He had never, in all his years, seen such pain. Felt such pain.

This was his mate. His mate.

His to protect.

"Dane . . . !" She screamed out again, but her voice was too weak, too ragged to give it much force. It was all the more destructive for its weakened state.

She arched, her body bowing. Feline snarls, canine growls. It made no sense.

"Breed," Graeme's Primal said across from him. "One of many. A child of the three mad kings." He was released from his vow. But it was of little comfort. "They carried the genetics of all of us. Her body, her senses, even her very cells cannot decide which Breed she is or should be. So they're all fighting to emerge."

He stared at Graeme in shock. How could it be possible?

His gaze went back to his Katy, a sob breaking in his chest as his senses were lashed with the mating hormone that had begun spilling to his mouth as the primal creature threw itself past his control.

He could feel her, sense her and the horrifying pain wracking her body. Never had he sensed such agony. Like a thousand daggers digging at her insides, lava hot, flames pouring inside her, vicious claws ripping at her mind.

She couldn't endure it. God, how had she endured it this long?

He was going to lose her. He could feel it. No body, Breed or human, could survive this. None should have to endure it.

"It's some kind of Genetic Flaming," he heard one of the scientists say behind him.

*Little fucker could have saved her. All he had to do was mate her . . . She dies because of him . . .*, the Primal raged, but the words weren't spoken aloud, he knew.

*Would telling him have changed anything?* his father's uncertainty whispered behind him.

"I love you, Dane . . . ," she cried out, a bloodred tear drifting from the corner of her eye. "Always . . . love you . . ."

The words spilled from his mate's lips, part animal in sound as she thrashed in his arms.

He could feel her reaching out to him, letting him feel everything she felt for him. So much love and acceptance. Such a sense of personal unworthiness, of an inability to give him what he needed . . .

"No," he whispered. "No, Katy . . ." Because she had known he hadn't found that final release with her, that he'd held back the mating, unable to loosen the reins he had on the creature inside himself. Or his fear of what it could mean to her safety.

"Dane, we can't allow her to continue like this," the Primal Breed snarled across from him. "Her agony is worse than any vivisecton a Breed has ever known. Say your goodbye to her, then step aside. I'll do what no mate should have to . . ."

Because he loved her as he would his own child. He'd take her last breath, mourn her, then send her mate to join her.

Dane knew the Bengal's thoughts, his intent. He'd only allowed her to suffer as she had because he knew Dane would not accept her death otherwise. And Breed Law would have convicted him without the proper acknowledgment that he'd committed the act out of mercy.

The Bengal would use those lethal claws, stain them with the blood of Dane's mate and take her from him forever . . .

The roar that left Dane's throat wasn't one he had control over. It tore through his head, echoed around him. His heart was breaking in ways he'd never imagined one heart could break. His soul was fracturing, and he knew, no matter Graeme's actions, he would never survive Katy's death. The sound was filled with agony. Filled with loss and impending doom. Whatever happened to the woman, the Primal would quickly follow, even if it meant taking his claws to his own throat.

Every Breed who heard that sound, heard that knowledge.

Behind him, his mother sobbed his name as the Leo fought to hold her to him as his own grief threatened to escape.

"Too late for Mating Heat . . . ," the Primal Bengal warned even as Dane felt the mating hormone growing ever stronger, coating his tongue, refusing to be swallowed. "It's just too late . . . Please, Dane. Give her your goodbye and stand aside . . ."

So he could take her life.

So he could still the pain, and the beat of her heart forever.

"Katy. Baby, please . . . ," Dane whispered with jagged despair, lowering his lips to hers, feeling the heat blazing through her body, destroying her. "Please, Katy. Don't leave me. Please don't leave me."

Tears. He watched as several fell to her cheek.

His tears.

"Please, Katy . . . ," he whispered.

His mouth was so filled with the mating hormone that had spilled from beneath his tongue during the flight from Phoenix that his mouth felt numb. It burned, a blaze of heat like the hottest chili peppers he'd ever eaten.

He had believed the chilis were her taste, a part of her alone. But he tasted it in the mating hormone, the spiciness, the reminder that she was a part of him.

And she had never known the taste of it. Never known the honey-and-spice scent of their mating, or the way it filled the senses.

He could feel her slipping away from him, feel the horrible flames burning her alive, the genetics causing her organs to begin to collapse. Graeme was right: He couldn't allow her to suffer that. Couldn't let his mate die within a nightmare of inhuman agony. And he cried for both of them. Unashamedly. His tears fell to her face, to his lips.

His lips covered hers, his tongue spreading the hormone across her lips, feeling it gather faster, swelling the glands beneath his tongue and spilling to her mouth.

His Katy.

Oh God, how could he have let this happen?

He'd known when she was twenty-one. An instinct he had never been able to explain demanded he kiss her each time he saw her. But he hadn't tasted the hormone. Or he hadn't *allowed* himself to taste it.

The Primal slashed at his mind, his chest, the rage pouring through him increased until he felt he was dying with her. There, in that room, his mate strapped down to keep from harming herself, Breeds surrounding him to see his shame and his loss. He, one of the most powerful among them, had destroyed his mate.

He wouldn't leave her. He'd hold her there, their lips touching, his tongue stroking hers, wondering how their combined mating would have tasted. How their lives could have been so much different.

Because he had loved.

He had loved. He had mated. And he'd refused to acknowledge it because of the risk to the Breeds and his fears for their freedoms.

He had let his little mate burn . . .

God help him, he should have let the world burn instead . . .

# CHAPTER 19

The Primal Bengal was preparing himself, pushing aside grief, loss, hatred. Everything but the love he had for the precious child who had stolen his heart.

His claws curled, his fingers extended.

He would take them both with the same blow. Dane's Primal stared back at him, his demand pouring from him, a scream of rage every Breed in that hotel would feel. Know. He would die with his mate, and that was his choice to make.

"Dane, no . . . ," Leo whispered brokenly behind him, feeling his son's determination to pass from the world at the same time his mate did. "Please, God . . ."

And Elizabeth. Leo was forced to hold her to his chest as she fought, grief filling her, her pain that her son would leave along with his mate, one only a mother could know.

She cursed Leo. She begged Dane. And still, the Primal her son had become only stared back at Graeme, and the message was clear. If he still lived when his Katy's last breath was taken, if his blood wasn't spilling along with hers, then Graeme would die.

And he just may be strong enough to accomplish that, Graeme thought.

To take her from this world was to show her the greatest love, the gentlest mercies. His hand lifted as the Primal mate held his lips to hers, the scent of his mating hormone strong, the most powerful the Primal Bengal had ever scented. So much strength feeding to his mate, the genetics, more lion than human infusing her, spilling to her mouth, taken to her stomach to make its way to her blood . . .

As Dane gave a latent, vicious growl, Graeme swore he could scent those Lion Primal hormones, stronger by the second as they began to hit her bloodstream, to overtake the adrenal hormone spreading such chaos through her body . . .

Graeme's head jerked up as his claws neared the Primal's throat and the vein that throbbed fast and strong beneath the tough hide; even the Primal paused, that once-unknown sense of hope exploding in their senses at the knowledge of this unknown variable.

Until tonight, Graeme, not his "other," had never sensed the Primal lurking inside Dane.

Dane had shown no tendency toward natural Primal elements, that meant the Primal had emerged to save his mate. Just as Graeme's had. Such emergence always occurred because only the Primal could save the mate the Breed had claimed. Only the strongest Breeds, those with the most powerful elements infusing their genetics, could make that transition.

He stared at the hybrid Primal Lion in amazement. He hadn't sensed this in the Vanderale son, and perhaps he should have at least expected it. Jonas, the Breed created from the Leo's seed and his mate's ova, was Primal. But he'd sensed it in Jonas for years. He was a natural Primal, the strength of the animal in him searching for an outlet, so to speak.

Dane had never shown the slightest inclination of it.

The Vanderale playboy and Breed activist? He played a convincing game of the spoiled heir who had no true intention of taking over his father's business, nor of having inherited the power the first alpha Leo came by so naturally.

And Dane's Primal was surprisingly powerful. Exceptionally so.

So powerful that as a Lion Primal, his mere presence commanded attention. The Breeds standing around him would lay down their lives for him now, with no more than a thought from this creature.

No, perhaps he was natural, Graeme reassessed. He just hadn't felt the need to emerge until now.

And he had emerged with such a strength and raw primitive power that Graeme found himself astounded. Second by second, the raw primal scent of the mating hormone grew. Increased. And by the second, Katelyn was taking more of it into her bloodstream as the animal fought to survive for the mate, whose cries echoed in her head with such desperation.

As Dane's Primal gently took his mate's lips, tears wet his cheeks and a tender purr vibrated from his chest. Only mates purred, and they only purred for their mates and children. The sound was beautiful to hear, as Graeme could attest each time his mate purred for him.

And with that kiss, tongue to tongue, the mating hormone spilling from the swollen glands, the power in it only growing in strength as it met the hormone her glands spilled as well, Katelyn stopped fighting.

Within mere minutes, she began to still and ceased the bucking and attempts to scream.

And that was where the change was so damned incredible.

Graeme could smell the mating hormone. Not the mating scent produced from it, but the hormone itself. Chilis and honey, a hint of saffron and that intriguing mix of the desert that surrounded Broken Butte.

His gaze went to Leo as the alpha Primal held his mate to him, the sounds of her weeping, her pleas and curses receding in the distance as Leo concentrated every sense he had on his son and the woman Dane was now marking with such strength. Power poured from the Leo, wrapped around his son as he sought to understand what was going on as well.

But his gaze met Graeme's and Graeme could feel his amazement, feel the hope beginning to build in the father, that the son just may be stronger, more instinctive and determined than the genetics flooding his mate's body.

Graeme's head turned with a jerk, his gaze spearing to Elizabeth as her mate held her in his embrace and she cried for the son she feared she'd lose when his mate was taken away.

"Elizabeth," he hissed. "Stop your crying. Now."

Leo growled a warning at him, but she stilled, fighting the agonized sobs as the others in the room turned their gazes on him.

"Swabs," he demanded, knowing they needed to understand, to figure out how this worked. If the kings had known how to save their children, then he had no doubt they would have come to him already. "Several. Quickly."

As he spoke, Jonas entered the room along with Dane's other brother, Pride leader of the Feline Breeds, Callan Lyons.

Jonas was in Primal form, Callan had yet to pull his Primal forth. It was closer, though, the raw threat of the death of his brother's mate, reaching into the primitive heart of the Breed and drawing it forward.

They were there for their brother. Callan had flown in the moment he'd learned Dane may need him, and as he watched, confusion filled his expression.

They all watched Graeme now, though mostly in suspicion.

Elizabeth rushed to gather the sterilized swabs as the other experts in the field of Breed physiology and medical care moved to pull together syringes and swabs for perspiration and began prepping Graeme's equipment to begin testing.

"Graeme?" Leo watched him with a glimmer of hope as well in his golden gaze.

"Don't you smell it?" Graeme hissed, his mind beginning to run possibilities and outcomes and all the myriad tests needed. "Can you scent the mating hormone, Leo? That is not the scent of Mating Heat, wasted upon a dying mate. That is the mating hormone itself."

Leo's eyes widened as he stepped closer, then moved back at once as the scent filled his senses.

"Dane. You must listen to me." Primal to Primal, Graeme's "other" spoke to the creature Dane possessed. And that creature believed he was giving his mate that goodbye kiss that there was no coming back from. "Can you sense the change, Dane? Do you feel her?"

His head lifted marginally, his nostrils flaring, the gold brightening in the green depths of his eyes as his gaze lifted slowly to Graeme.

"Feel her," Graeme urged him. "She's easing. Her breathing is freer. Do you feel it?"

Dane looked down at his mate once more, touching the side of her face with the back of a clawed finger, and Graeme could feel him reaching out to her with all his Primal, Lion Breed senses.

"Mate." The sound was broken, the animal rising inside him so primitive, so primal, his voice was even more animal than Graeme's Primal.

"Dane, we need blood, swabs." He extended the swabs to the

Primal, knowing it would never countenance another male touching Katelyn just yet. "Your mother can help if you need." He nodded to Elizabeth.

Dane's head lifted.

"Mother." The Primal's voice, so hoarse and filled with power, it could become the stuff of nightmares. "The swabs first. Quickly."

Because that scent of renewed pain was returning.

Katelyn moaned, and Dane jerked the swabs from Graeme's hand and quickly swabbed Katelyn's tongue. Beneath it, across the sensitive taste buds. The second he used against her cheeks, the roof of her mouth, before taking the second set from his mother and quickly swabbing his own.

His lips were on Katelyn's again as he extended the cotton-tipped instruments outward, his entire focus on Katelyn, on forcing more of the hormone into her.

"Take it, Katy," he snarled against her lips a second later. "You will take it. Draw it from my tongue, mate. Now."

His lips slanted over hers, his tongue pressing between them and Graeme watched as her cheeks finally moved, just a bit. Weak, nearly lost to the effects of the brutal Genetic Flaming. But she was doing as her mate demanded. Drawing on his tongue, suckling the hormone from the swollen glands beneath it.

The scent of it thickened, cloying now with a heavy infusion of pure animal genetics.

The other scientists worked to test the monitors and prepare IVs. But when Elizabeth moved to draw her blood, Katelyn jerked against her touch, a fragile cry drawing a warning growl from Dane as he bent over her.

"Dane, please . . . ," Elizabeth sobbed. "Please let us help . . ."

There was no mercy in the creature. It had no father, possessed no mother or siblings. It belonged to its mate alone. And in the Primal's world, nothing but nothing touched his mate and caused her pain.

"Wait," Graeme warned the mother when she would have protested.

He fought to connect with the Primal through his own as he had when it had first gathered its mate in his arms. But it resisted, refusing to allow force, to hold his mate down as she was given yet more pain.

"Dane, we need that blood," he growled, focusing on the Lion Primal.

But Dane only extended his own arm.

Once several syringes were collected, Graeme was on the verge of cursing, because each time Katelyn seemed settled and they attempted to draw her blood, another of those pitifully weak cries would part her lips, and Dane's Primal would snarl in vicious warning.

"We need that blood," he snarled again, even his own Primal reacting in frustration.

He stood holding the syringe, staring at Katelyn's arm, willing to risk death if he thought he'd be successful, but Dane never took those eerie eyes off Graeme as he continued to force the hormone to his mate's system.

Then the Lion Primal lifted his gaze, looking beyond Graeme's shoulder to the entrance into the room.

His head lifted from the kiss.

Leo emitted a sound, half growl, half snarl, and filled with a threat of violence as Graeme glimpsed the tall, raggedly dressed man who entered the room.

He wore jeans that were snagged and ripped in places, had a beard that was several days old. Thick dark brown hair was pulled back and tied in a ponytail at the nape of his neck. A well-worn black T-shirt with a popular motorcycle emblem, heavy boots and a leather jacket.

He was clean, but Graeme decided that was the best that could be said about him. Behind him, the second, nearly identical in looks, but his clothes were newer. Rather than boots, he wore fringed leather moccasins, jeans and a T-shirt with the name of a heavy metal rock band from the past splashed across it. Behind him, the third was dressed in a black tux, his hands shoved in his slacks pockets, his expression weary and saddened.

Three men, three nearly identical faces, and yet so much seemed to set them apart.

Strange, he thought, because his Primal "other" hadn't sensed an unknown threat, Breed or human, anywhere close. Not human, he finally realized. There was little human to these three, but what they were he hadn't yet decided.

"Not here," the Leo suddenly snapped. "This is no place for your vendetta. You don't know . . ."

"That she's my daughter?" The unkempt Breed stepped forward, his lips quirking somberly, sadly, as he watched Katelyn and Dane.

His head tipped to the side, his eerie brown gaze assessing as he watched Dane for long moments before turning his gaze to Leo once again.

"Interesting, my friend," he said softly. "A strong, fine son you have. Clearly a mate worthy of her."

He slipped his leather jacket off and handed it to one of the two Breeds standing behind him. His whisky brown eyes sparked with reddened depths as his strong, savagely hewn expression softened and he stared down at Katelyn.

"The syringe, Primal. She'll allow my touch." The demand in his voice wasn't impossible to ignore, Graeme's Primal calculated, but it wasn't required either. And the sheer strength, the aura of pure power the Breed gave off, was one to be cautious of.

Graeme extended the syringes. "Three . . ."

"Full." The mad king nodded. "I remember the protocol."

He took the needle and approached Katelyn, reaching out slowly to steady her arm.

He stroked his palm down it first, a barely heard croon leaving his lips as he seemed to be easing her, an assurance, the Primal sensed, his animal to hers, that there would be no pain. To still.

"We are of the same blood," he whispered, his fingers gently gripping her wrist, massaging the flesh over the vein that beat there. "You are flesh of my flesh. Blood of my blood. And you are, daughter, dearly beloved."

The croon sounded again, and Graeme realized it wasn't just coming from the father but from the uncles as well.

"Just a slight pinch, baby girl," he whispered, placing the needle at her arm. "But Papa's here to make it all better, just as your mate will ease your pain and lead you back to life."

The blood was drawn quickly, and as each vial filled, it was handed to Graeme.

When that last vial was handed over, the father placed his thumb over the small entry point rather than taking the bandage Graeme extended to him.

"I can sense her," her father whispered as he frowned. "Such fear . . ." Anger sparked in his reddened gaze once again. "Leo, take your mate and leave this room," the king demanded, never taking his gaze from Katelyn. "Your suspicion and hatred for us are bleeding from you, and it's upsetting her. She senses it and suspects she's the reason for it. That you do not find her worthy. It's weakening her. Her entire focus must be on allowing Dane's heat to fill her. And to heal her."

"You're not in Primal form," Leo growled. "You can't possibly know that."

"I am always Primal," the father whispered then. The king turned to Graeme and arched a black brow in query. "I'm Basil, by the way. This lovely child's father." He stroked his hand along her arm again. "I can sense her fondness for you, and yours for her. As her mate is occupied, will you tell this stubborn Leo what you sense as the Bengal Primal?"

As gentle as the voice sounded, as nonthreatening as he forced it for Katelyn's sake, Graeme could feel it touching his Primal's instincts and the demand in it, the pure force, had Graeme shaking his head.

"You had only to ask," he grumbled in irritation before giving his head another shake and staring across the bed Katelyn lay in, to Leo. "He's not here to war, Leo. And he's right. Katelyn senses your aggression and believes it's toward her. You're frightening her."

Dane stilled, breathed in deeply, then lifted his head and turned to his father.

He didn't say a word and Graeme couldn't see the look he gave the Leo. But the father gave a sharp nod of his shaggy head, and within the next heartbeat the tension and aggression Graeme had felt in the room began to dissipate as Leo settled himself, forcing his emotions to calm.

Katelyn eased a bit more as Dane rested his head against hers, staring down at her with such regret and guilt it was heartbreaking to see.

"She marked me that night after I hurt her heart so deeply," he said softly. "Her tear against my hand. That tiny reddened mark I've carried for so long. And I her, when I tasted her tears and my tongue touched her cheek." He brushed his cheek against her, that tiny mark a bit redder than it had been days ago, Graeme noticed. "And still, I walked away. Enraged. Furious that there was no heat, that I couldn't take her with me." His eyes closed as her breathing seemed to ease a bit more. "For so long I feared finding my mate. Vanderales must never be revealed as what they are." And that was no more than the truth. "I would have walked away from her, denied myself what is mine by nature, to save you all." He lifted his head, his clawed fingers touching his mate's lips before he ran the backs of them across her cheek. "But I'm no hero after all. If my mate ceases to exist, then so will I. I cannot allow her to cease. To burn away in my arms. I won't."

Basil continued to whisper whatever sound it was he sent to his daughter as the backs of his fingers caressed down her arm again.

"She's strong," Basil whispered, his whisky-colored gaze meeting Dane's as Graeme sensed the pride he found in Katelyn. "Her love for you is strong. Enduring." He smiled sadly. "Vastly forgiving."

She was his daughter. She carried his royal blood, his unmatched genetics, and she'd inherited his strength. There was no one on this earth as worthy as she . . .

And she would sense it as well, Graeme thought. She knew they were there. Every word being said, every emotion or impression she could pull in, she focused on. Anything but the pain.

She was still in pain, the genetic-infused adrenaline continuing to pour into her system. The genetics of seven powerful predators still attempting to control the body they inhabited all at once.

The Genetic Flaming wouldn't stop until every strand of her Breed genetics became active. And she would be strong. Her mate was spilling his lion Primal genetics through the mating hormone, ensuring that her lion genetics reigned supreme. Her father was a mad king, the youngest born, Graeme was guessing. He breathed them in, allowed his lips to part, his tongue to taste what his nostrils pulled to him.

"Stop attempting to dissect my genetics, Bengal," Basil ordered him, his voice whisper soft, without a single ill emotion or intent. But what Graeme sensed in that order had him grunting in irritation.

"How long have you known about her?" Graeme asked him then, knowing if he disappeared, Katelyn would want to know.

"Only this past week," he admitted, regret touching his expression but not his emotions.

There was nothing for Katelyn to sense but his acceptance, his joy in having found her. Every emotion the emerging Breed she was becoming sensed from this parent was only the best of what a parent should feel.

"My brother didn't lie to her at the party," he stated. "We've wanted to meet her for a while now. Her work in managerial analysis is outstanding. We wanted to discuss the possibility of working with our main office, creating a team that can manage without us for long periods. When we arrived in Broken Butte, I took one look at her, and I knew." The gentleness of his expression, the way he stroked her arm, stood by her side protectively, spoke volumes. "She's as beautiful as her mother. She looks just as my Amora did when I met her. She's as kind and as caring. Perhaps when she awakens and she's feeling better, we can discuss the untruths so many told her about the woman who gave her life."

As Dane watched the king carefully, he lifted Katelyn's hand, laid a gentle kiss within her palm and folded her fingers around it.

"The next few days will be difficult," he told Dane, keeping his voice soft, nothing for Katelyn to worry about. The world around her was marshmallows and puppies and not to be feared. "You must stay at her side as the Primal because the strength in that mating hormone is her only chance at survival. She can't travel until she's healed completely unless you want her to know more pain."

Still, Dane only watched him.

"Will you tell her I will find her again soon? Once she's healed and able to deal with the truth of who I am without dealing with her body attempting to change at the same time."

"Not my place," Dane growled. "If she remembers and asks, I'll tell her what I know. If she doesn't, then you can deal with her when she meets you again."

The king chuckled at the obvious threat.

Basil turned to Leo then as the elder Vanderale watched him suspiciously, obviously holding little trust for the Breed he'd once fought beside.

"We'll talk soon, Leo. Never fear." He gave Leo a vaguely mocking grin. "And we've always known where each of you are, even in our maddened states. Perhaps you should contact your brother, allow him to come out of the shadows a bit. He has a mate awaiting him."

Leo frowned back at him.

"No, the other firsts haven't mated." Basil sighed. "It's a shame really." He glanced at Dane. "You've done well with your mate."

"And you?" Graeme asked, when Leo wouldn't. "Have you?"

"Sadly, no," Basil said softly, regretfully. "It's not often that the madness retreats long enough. A few years at most." He looked back at his still silent brothers. "We're called the mad kings for a reason, Bengal." He looked back at his daughter. "Hopefully, she and I can talk before that madness occurs again."

He turned back to the Breeds awaiting him and nodded as they watched silently.

"Take care of my daughter, Lion," he told Dane as he left the room. "For all your sakes."

The Lion Primal watched as the three Breeds left, their very presence pulling at the Breeds they passed, as though they should follow them, protect them. Each Breed knew the animals hiding in the appearance of a human body.

What they recognized as well was the very bearing, the air of regal presence and power.

Those creatures could destroy the world, Dane thought, or they could help remake it. If only they could stay sane long enough.

He definitely had questions he needed answered by his father. There was so much Leo had hidden from him, information he needed, answers that awaited, that could possibly aid the Breeds. Aid his mate.

All that would have to wait, though.

For now, he could feel the hormonal adrenaline punching into her system again, threatening to undo everything his mating hormone was attempting to repair within her fragile body.

The presence of the genetics of the seven powerful species pouring into her was too much for her body to contain. For each species there were adjustments to make to the body, the organs, all differing, all fighting for supremacy. It was literally ripping her apart from the inside out until the primal mating hormone hit her system, the lion coding working to erase all but the lion genetics as the adrenaline hit her system.

Taking her lips again, he gave her what she needed, purring in approval as she fought for the strength to draw it from the glands beneath his tongue.

He could hear her whispering in his heart, feel her tears and her lack of confidence in her worthiness to be his mate. She wasn't the one that lacked worthiness, he assured her. It was he who wasn't worthy, who had no right to demand this from her, but he was the one nature had given her.

And was that a spark of amusement he felt in the bleak darkness of her pain? Of course it was. She was strong, determined. She wouldn't leave this world without a fight. And he was going to make damned sure she didn't leave it without him.

# CHAPTER 20

A week later, Dane realized that Katelyn was slowly edging back to awareness. She wasn't awake, but she was aware, drifting in that shadow place where the pain was just a nuisance and she didn't have to force herself into nothingness to escape it.

The primal hormone he had been feeding into her system through each kiss had worked to stabilize her body before it began overriding the alternating and often opposing DNA strands that tried to come alive within her. Healing her became a secondary task for the hormone. As long as her internal organs remained functioning, then the hormone concentrated itself where it was most needed.

They'd been able to move her via heli-jet from the hotel to the Bureau of Breed Affairs twenty-four hours after the primal hormone had first hit her system. There, his mother, Elizabeth, along with the other specialists, was able to analyze the changes in her DNA structure as well as the damage to her internal organs.

The healing was going much slower once she was stabilized and the primal hormone began working at the genetic level to subvert all but the Lion Breed hormone in her DNA. The rest was still there, a part of her, though no longer strong enough to become active.

She was healing. Her internal organs had at first shown massive damage, with some tears in her brain matter as well.

The tears were completely absent now, thankfully. And the other damage, though serious, was slowly showing improvement.

She was still in some pain, but it was manageable. The fact that she still had a ways to go wasn't in doubt, but neither was the knowledge that it wouldn't be long before she was on her feet once again.

In that time, Dane had learned more than he'd wanted to know about his father and Graeme's only other experience with one of the daughters of the so-called kings, as both Leo and Graeme revealed the secrets they'd kept.

The first was a young woman Katy's age who Graeme had found in France and brought to Africa, curious about the anomalies he'd sensed in her. By the time they'd arrived at the safe house Leo had directed Graeme to, the young woman, Millicent, the Bengal called her, had begun slipping into Royal Genetic Flaming.

Leo hadn't seen it before, but he'd seen the results of it one other time, decades before, and he'd known the girl couldn't survive what was happening to her. In an act of mercy, Leo had assumed his Primal form and taken the girl's life.

Graeme had demanded answers, but in giving them, Leo had forced his "other" to vow that he'd never reveal what he heard, nor would he ever bring another such child to Leo. It was his responsibility to do what needed to be done.

Once the Bengal Primal had given its vow, Leo had taken him to the compound deep in the Congo, and there, Graeme had learned far more than he'd wanted to.

Then Leo had burned all proof of the three kings and the fourteen first alphas. Seven different Breed species, twins, who the kings had forced to separate by another such Primal vow because they would have been strong as a group, and the kings, in their madness, feared the others would rise against them.

They were allowed to gather, once a year, for forty-eight hours, no more, and were barred from conspiring against the kings at any time.

Once a vow is given while in Primal form, it can't be broken. No amount of torture, even risk to his mate, could force that vow free. A Primal existed for his mate alone, but even for his mate, that vow couldn't be broken. It could only be released by the one the vow was given to. A release Leo had been given no choice but to extend after the kings made their appearance.

Now, sitting next to his mate's bed, he picked up her hand, felt the warmth of it and brought it to his cheek.

"Hey, beautiful," he spoke softly, holding her hand to his lips. "I'm here, baby." Blinking back the moisture in his eyes, he pressed a kiss to her palm. "Someone stopped by to see you. He's rather insistent."

Dane could feel the powerful creature at his back, and it was highly uncomfortable.

"Katelyn Regina. Awaken."

The fucking power in that voice had his teeth clenching.

"I said you could see her, not force her to wake up." Dane could feel the Primal power gather in his gut, pushing forward.

Katelyn's lashes drifted open, settling first on Dane, her gaze drowsy, but her eyes . . . deep, dark pools of whisky brown. They weren't Primal eyes, but they glowed just the same.

Then her gaze lifted to the one behind her, a frown settling on her brow.

"Give me just a moment, Dane." Basil made it sound like a request. Likely for Katelyn's sake.

Thankfully for all of them, Dane imagined, he'd anticipated the other Breed wanting to be closer to her.

He rose from where he sat in the chair next to her, moving behind it instead as Basil took his seat and Katelyn's hand.

Silence filled the room but for the faint hiss and beeps of the monitors connected to her fragile body.

Basil pressed her hand between each of his, and Dane could feel awareness surging toward her, surrounding her, covering her.

A faint croon came from the other Breed's lips, not quite a lullaby and not quite a purr, but the sound of it brought a faint curve to Katelyn's lips. She was soothed by it; that was all that mattered.

"We have much to talk about when you're able." The soft cadence of his voice was gentle, filled with love and regret. "But we can't talk if you don't heal. Stop fighting it." The demand was given in a harder tone, but still one filled with love. "If I have to return, I will force the acceptance, do you hear me? That would be unpleasant for both of us."

Dane tensed, his gaze going to Katelyn and catching the little pout that formed at her lips.

*What the hell?*

"Should I tell your mate what you're doing?" he asked her. "I believe I will. Perhaps he can make you see reason before I do."

She swallowed, her expression becoming distressed.

"Scared . . . ," she whispered, moisture beginning to sheen her eyes. "Hurts . . ."

"Yes, it did hurt," he crooned. "But that pain is gone now, and it will never return. What's left is your fault. Your mate's kiss can't heal you if you continue to fight it. Before it can heal the internal wounds, you must first accept the Breed emerging inside you. And you are the reason that hasn't happened."

Dane stared down at his mate, understanding now the strange disquiet he felt whenever he discussed Katelyn's test results with her medical team. This was why.

Her gaze tried to break from her father's, but Dane could literally feel the Breed enforcing it.

"You are the daughter of a king." The arrogance in that statement was bone-deep. "You are the daughter of Amora, the wife I loved. I will not allow this disrespect. You will not deny that part of yourself, when your mother so loved both of us. She didn't deny me, and neither will you."

Katelyn blinked slowly. "Wife?"

"My wife," he said again. "When you're strong, healthy and healed, then I'll return. I have pictures to show you, and I will tell you everything you want to know about your mother. But only after you've healed."

He held her gaze for long seconds, then rose and bent and kissed her cheek gently.

"You are loved, little princess. By many. Now heal for us. Especially for your mate," he whispered, though the demand in his voice was clear.

Straightening, he turned to Dane. "She's stubborn. So was her mother. Sometimes, she'll need to be gently reminded that she's important. For some reason, no one but that crazy Bengal bothers to convince her."

It was a reminder, Dane knew, that he'd walked away from her. It wasn't one he needed, but he accepted it all the same.

"You're powerful, Dane. Likely far stronger than your father once you begin honing your strengths," Basil told him, and it sounded like a warning. "Your father was one of our best strategists, but he was never working alone where the good of the Breeds and their survival was concerned. The others were doing their part as well. Stop struggling against that power, and learn from it. Allow those who came before you to guide you, stand at your side and teach you what they know. Only then will that incredible strength and knowledge you'll one day possess be of any good to you, to your mate and to those who follow you."

A conclusion Dane had already come to.

Basil's lips quirked in a grin. "Leo and the other first alphas are busy attempting to figure out how to defend themselves against myself, and my brothers, Magnus and Reign." He chuckled. "We've had decades to kill them if that was what we wanted. We just made certain they stayed in fighting shape. Didn't want them getting lazy, now, did we?"

Dane had already heard of the many skirmishes the Leo had fought against one or more of the brothers. They hadn't sounded friendly.

"Look at it this way: My brothers and I basically had fourteen youths who had yet to control their impulses or their tempers in battle." Then grief crossed his face. "If only one of us had been sane during the years your parents lost their babes." He shook his head wearily, resigned at the past, perhaps. "Breeds believe if they don't mate, they'll continue aging, but they do not. Nor are they finished developing physically as well as instinctively. With the vast range of genetics they possess, that will take a while."

"And how long does this age delay last?" Dane asked.

To which Basil shrugged. "I haven't a clue, my young Breed. But neither myself nor my brothers have mated, and we still haven't aged. So when you learn that answer, perhaps you'll let us know. Or perhaps Graeme shall. That Bengal's genetics are not far from mine and my brothers'. The one who envisioned him and created his basic genetics was either dangerously lucky, determined or just that intuitive. Or, I fear, all the above."

A surprising piece of information, Dane thought. And he wasn't quite certain what to do with it.

"Perhaps you'll find it within you, as well as your brothers, to give us what knowledge you do have," Dane suggested.

Basil's lips quirked in amusement. "Perhaps." He nodded. "Until then I'll give you this. The ones who attempted to have Katelyn killed will bother her no more. The mercenaries who were hired were contracted by a small group of businessmen interested in delaying or hopefully destroying her project in Broken Butte. The problem has been taken care of."

The primal instincts that raged inside Dane demanded more than being "taken care of." "Are they dead?"

"We have need of them if Leo makes the announcement I believe he's going to make," Basil stated with no apology or further explanation. "For now. They will live. I will deal with them when the time comes. She's my daughter, and I'll take this responsibility."

"If I learn who they are, Basil, they'll die," Dane warned the king, not really caring what the other Breed wanted. "And that's a promise."

The Breed merely nodded, but Dane had a feeling he and his brothers had made certain their small group of businessmen were well hidden. At least until Basil decided when it was time to kill them.

"I'll leave now." He glanced back at Katelyn, his expression softening as he gazed at her sleeping countenance. "She'll be up and moving soon. And no doubt driving you crazy once again. Give her some babies. She longs for them as only one could who was created to be a mother. And they'll keep her busy."

With that, he strolled from the room, shrugging his leather jacket back on and slipping silently from the suite. Within seconds, Dane realized he could no longer sense the Breed in any way, not by scent or presence. And if he tried, Dane knew he could detect the placement of every human and Breed currently within the walls of the Bureau, and for a short distance outside it.

To completely hide himself as well as his scent so effectively should have been impossible. But the Leo had warned him that they were able to do so. To sense them took not just alpha Prime senses but training. And he wondered if Leo was aware that Basil had managed to slip past him.

◆ ◆ ◆

Dane watched hours later as Graeme stepped into the bedroom in Primal form. The Bengal, when in his "other" form, as he was prone to call it, could be an intimidating sight. He'd never intimidated Dane, but they'd known each other for quite a while, and Dane had liked to think he knew the Bengal's limits.

It was only now he realized how very wrong he was. With his own primal senses unleashed, he drew in information as he'd never imagined he would.

Slouched back in the chair on the opposite side of Katy's bed from the door, one foot propped on the edge of her mattress, he watched the Breed step to the other chair and sit down silently.

One large hand touched hers, the elongated claws razor-sharp and deadly. As they brushed across the back of her hand, though, they didn't so much as leave a scratch.

Dane now knew why Graeme was so wont to touch with the tips

of his claws. Sensory information came in differently there, more defined, more focused than it did in other ways.

Heavy brows arched over the Bengal's gaze as he glanced at Dane.

"She's doing much better," he all but whispered. "The genetic conversion is nearly completed. I had guessed earlier that it would take much longer."

Dane gave his sleeping mate a rueful look before moving his gaze back to Graeme. "She was fighting it. Fearing the pain would return. She had only to be convinced otherwise."

Amusement gleamed in the golden eyes of the Primal as he shook his head at the information. "A stubborn one is our Katelyn. How did you figure out what she was doing?"

"You didn't know?" Dane asked, curious that Graeme seemed unaware of it.

"If I had known, Dane, I would have told you," he answered querulously. "Her health is rather important to me. I wouldn't have held that information back."

Perhaps there were some things Graeme didn't know after all.

"Basil Tallon slipped into the suite earlier. One minute I was alone and enjoying a drink and a bout of self-loathing, and the next, the door opened and in he walked. He was rather put out I was allowing her to delay her recuperation, as he put it."

Graeme frowned, the stripes crossing his face and extending past his shirt seeming to darken. "I didn't sense that he was here. Cat and I were just down the hall with your parents. None of us sensed him."

"Don't ask me how he did it." Dane snorted. "Even I didn't know he was approaching the suite until he walked in."

"The three brothers are extremely powerful." Graeme sighed. "It's hard to push back against them and deny an order they're intent on.

No wonder the first alphas are so wary of them. Though I fear if the kings wanted them dead, then dead they be."

"Right!" Dane agreed with a short exclamation. "Basil admitted as much."

Graeme turned back to Katy, his gaze, his expression softening. "It will be hard to watch her grow to love him. I've been the one she's looked to for such support these eight years."

Dane shook his head. "She loves you. I don't think anyone will replace you in her heart. But she has a great capacity for love and an ability to give everyone their due."

"She's an angel," Graeme whispered, the rough, preternatural voice almost reverent as the creature he was stared down at Katy with pure confusion. "When my 'other' first sensed her, we wept, certain there would be no way to save her. It was one of the periods of sanity that I was granted before mating Cat. The 'other' would have to retreat to step into the diner, to be absolutely certain of what it sensed." Regret twisted his features. "Leo and I had seen the horror of another daughter one of the kings had sired, as the Flaming hit her. Once Leo realized what was happening to her, he was forced to take her life. The pain was inhuman, Dane. Far worse than what you witnessed with Katelyn when you burst into that room."

His father had told him about the girl. Graeme had found her in France during one of his sane episodes, as he called them. He'd sensed something odd, "wrong" about her, Leo had told him. Graeme had rushed her to Africa and arranged to meet with Leo in a safe house there. By the time they arrived, the Flaming had already begun.

"I would have taken her life before she left Broken Butte," the "other" spoke in a demon's rasp. "But she had known only sadness and no sense of worth her entire life. And she was far worthier than any who she had touched with her kindness, only to feel nothing but brutal rejection." Rage flickered in the Bengal's deadly gaze. "Even from her mate. She deserved to know something more. So I arranged to keep her with me, to allow her to grow that exceptional mind of hers, and feared each instance that I sensed the Flaming. I taught her to channel the adrenal hormone, to push it to her brain rather than allowing it to hit her organs, where it would amplify and begin the genetic awakening. And I connived, plotted and planned the best way to force your instincts to relent and mate her when you saw her again."

Dane merely stared back at him, resting his cheek on his upraised fist, drawing in the information Graeme unintentionally allowed free as the last of his grief and rage expended themselves.

The "other" had been helpless against the pure gentleness it sensed within Katy, and Graeme hadn't had a chance once the insanity released him and the "other" retreated. She had already been accepted by the Primal as part of his heart; Graeme could do nothing less.

"I returned for her several days later," Dane revealed. "I told myself I was going to make certain she was offered a better job, that she would move into a safe house I owned in Broken Butte. I made a very detailed plan for her, and not once did it include mating her." His lips kicked up in a resigned grin. "But I would have mated her, Graeme." He stared back at the Breed forcefully. "She nearly died because you jumped the gun and took her from me. She would never have had to know such agony as what she experienced."

"Is that what you're telling yourself?" The mockery in the Breed's tone was infuriating. "No, Dane, you were so intent on saving the Breed race from itself that you would never have given in to it. Say what you will, convince yourself of what you must, but I know that, to the depth of my quite ragged heart. She would have come into the Flaming, and Leo would have known what it was. He would have been forced to take her life before you ever allowed the creature you harbor free. Until you watched her life bleed from her body. And wouldn't it have been too late then?"

"You're wrong," he snarled back.

The very idea of such a scenario was instantly rejected by Dane, but he could feel a prick of suspicion. Could Graeme be right? God help him, surely, he wouldn't have allowed such a thing to happen.

"You're a good man, Dane." Graeme sighed then. "Intuitive, strong. Determined. Honorable. The best of everything a Breed should be in many ways. But holding back your strength and primal awareness to ensure no one suspected Vanderales were Breeds was your steel core. Protecting your family at all costs. Even to the point of walking away from a mate should you ever find her. Who could have guessed such consequences existed?" Graeme stared sadly at Katy. "Or the untold agony she would have faced if she had faced the flaming alone. Even in your primal form, you couldn't have known. Any more than I could have known with Millicent."

The unthinkable had nearly happened, though.

"What of the other girls?" Dane questioned what he was already sensing. "Portia and the other two?"

He was quite curious at the response Graeme would give him.

"They're not daughters of the kings," Graeme revealed. "I'm certain Portia is Leo's niece. So certain, I did all I could to keep her from Leo. Sabra, I suspect, is the daughter of one of the first Bengals. Catherine, I believe, is the daughter of a Tundra Wolf. They're all recessed at present. They'll go into Genetic Flaming soon, though, if they don't find their mates. Thankfully, the therapies Morrey and the others have created will aid them through it. It's only daughters of the mad kings who face such horror. I pray there are no others."

Portia was indeed Leo's niece, and Leo was well aware of it. Dane had ensured it.

"Get them here in the next twelve hours," Dane told him, straightening in his chair as he sensed Katy moving closer to consciousness. "They need to be protected when Leo makes his announcement."

He still wasn't certain about the wisdom behind the decision that had been made.

"They'll be here in the next few hours, actually," Graeme told him, his claws brushing against the back of Katy's hand once again. "Portia ensured that when she heard Katelyn's screams and was unable to get to her, she called the other two, who dropped their current projects and are now on their way. The four girls are incredibly close. They look to Katelyn often."

Of course they did, Dane thought. She was their alpha. Even with all their genetics recessed, they'd still respond to that. Their Breed senses were sleeping, not dead. And Katy was incredibly strong and protective. Just as any true alpha was.

"Is she primal?" Graeme asked Dane then. "I know she's strong. Incredibly so. But just as with you, I can't sense one inside her."

Dane merely shrugged. "If the creature is there, it will show itself in due time. In her time. For now, the mating hormone is doing its job and ensuring other strands of DNA are inactive while building her lion base. She's still about forty-eight hours from being healed, perhaps a week before regaining full strength. As soon as she can travel, we'll make the journey to Leo's estate. The announcement will go out then, revealing Mating Heat, the aging delay and the Vanderales as Breeds. We can only pray we all survive it."

Dane and Katy would take his sisters with them and keep them safe until Leo and Elizabeth could return for them. If they could return to them.

Dane wasn't so certain survival would be possible. At one time, he'd believed such an announcement was the best course for the

Breeds, but omitting his family's status. And Leo had been violently opposed to admitting to any of it.

With Dane's mating, they had few choices, though, and his parents were united in their refusal to allow Dane to fake his and his mate's deaths and retreat to the compound in the Congo for however long they lived.

"About that." Graeme sat forward then. "I believe I may have an alternate answer to that. One that doesn't require much travel at all, and complete safety. Not just for you and your mate, but your sisters, your parents and my girls as well, along with several hundred other Breeds."

"Caves," Katy mumbled then.

Dane looked from Katy to Graeme.

"She's quite intelligent, just as I told you," Graeme murmured. "Would you like to hear my plan . . . ?"

# • CHAPTER 21 •

THREE DAYS LATER

Dane watched as his father breathed out heavily, then picked up the mobile device lying in front of him. There was a single number programmed to send out an alert to every Breed and human he'd targeted over the decades.

The ground had already been laid with those humans the first alphas held incriminating information on. They were aware of what was held, and they knew the role they must play to ensure that information remained hidden.

Mates and children had already been sent to secure, fortified locations in the event every projection that had been run in that room proved to be completely erroneous.

Leo sent the notice. **Four hours.** The next went to news services around the world to be prepared for a special announcement that would be broadcast from the Western Division of the Bureau of Breed Affairs by the Federal director, Jonas Wyatt and the Vanderale family.

The final preparations wouldn't take long. They showered and dressed in fresh clothing, made their way to the makeup technicians and, within four hours, reporters who had arrived at the Bureau were shown into the journalists' area and Jonas, Leo and Dane stepped behind the security partition as two dozen reporters stood expectantly from their seats.

Stepping to the wooden podium in front of the Bureau of Breed Affairs background, Jonas stared back at the journalists. Imposing, commanding, he was a force to be reckoned with, and he made no apologies for that.

"There will be two announcements made," Jonas informed them. "I'll make the first; it will take approximately fifteen minutes. Once I finish, Leo Vanderale will make his announcement, which will take approximately another fifteen minutes. You'll hold your questions and be shown to a conference room where you'll have the time you need to compose your questions before being shown back to your seats. You can contact your news desks or other reporters while there, but when you're called back, your time will be up." When he finished, a dozen Breed enforcers stepped in, creating a loose ring around the reporters. "When the time for your questions comes, they'll be taken one at a time, beginning at the front row and going around. This will be a calm, organized briefing, ladies and gentlemen."

There was no "or else."

And he began.

Around the world the news was watched in silent shock, amazement, by some in fear, terror, others in curiosity and anticipation.

Mating Heat was real. The mating mark existed, and those who were mated experienced an age delay that, to date, had been counted to one hundred and forty eight to perhaps one hundred and fifty years. Hybrid children had a natural age delay, which began around twenty-five in females, thirty in males, the oldest hybrid having reached seventy years of age with the body of a thirty-year-old. If a person has no wish to be mated by a Breed should nature decide they were mates, then they should make certain not to become intimate with one. It was that simple.

Why did they wait so long to bring that information to the public? Their scientists, doctors and geneticists needed time to understand the phenomenon, how it worked and if it was possible to reverse. They knew now, after two decades of research, that it couldn't be reversed or engineered to use for any sort of medical advancements. It worked between mates, period.

In the twenty years they'd fought to understand it, that was the extent of it.

"I'll step aside now and allow Mr. Vanderale to make his own statement. Then we'll bring the foremost experts on the phenomenon out. Human and Breed scientists, geneticists and immunologists as well as some titles even I have trouble pronouncing." He turned to Leo. "Mr. Vanderale."

Leo stepped to the podium and before he spoke, slowly he began to peel away the facial prosthetics he used whenever he wasn't in a completely secure setting.

Reporters' eyes widened as the man, believed to be nearing seventy, stood tall, regal and in his prime within minutes.

"Allow me to introduce myself," he said, his voice resonating with strength, power and command. "I am the Breed known as the first Leo." His twin stepped through the door leading to the podium and stood with him. "Or should I say, one of the first alphas. There were fourteen of us. To my knowledge, we are the only survivors. We escaped in our thirtieth year, and the hell we knew before escape was just the beginning . . ."

The world listened.

They saw his tears when Leo spoke of the babes his mate lost when a Council soldier's bullet tore through her abdomen. The decade it took for her to heal, then the twins born a decade later. Twin sons who'd died as he and his mate tried to shield their bodies during a midnight attack.

The babes had died. He and Elizabeth had nearly died.

Their son, Dane's birth, his age and the birth of their twin daughters.

His statement was nearly thirty-two minutes, but no one objected.

When he finished, he stepped back and looked to his left as the door to the back room opened and scientists and specialists stepped forward. The first, his Elizabeth. When she stopped next to him, she stared into the cameras and, as Leo had done, slowly removed sagging skin and fine lines. The gray had already been washed from her hair, and when she finished, the beautiful, fresh-faced twenty-eight-year-old she had been when Leo first mated her emerged.

There were twenty Breed scientists, fifteen human surgeons and specialists who had worked with the Council and/or with the Breeds exclusively. Several of which were believed dead.

"You'll be shown in to the connecting conference room." Jonas stepped forward and extended his hand to the doors Breed enforcers were opening. "Prepare your questions carefully, concisely. You'll be called back in, in approximately an hour. A list of the specialists you'll be introduced to will be provided for you as well as their credentials and their history within Breed research and physical care. Till then."

Jonas nodded to the reporters as they stood silently, their expressions amazed, some shocked, as they were escorted to the conference room.

A room the three mad kings watched and listened to intently. They smirked as several reporters ran electronic detectors programmed to detect the sensitive and highly mobile listening devices known as nano-nits around the room, and checked the devices Breeds provided to create a completely spy-proof room. All that worked, they believed, were their mobile devices to contact their offices or other news services.

When it was over, the Breeds had been in front of the cameras more than ten hours. Within the first hour, senators began arriving for the question session. Within three hours, government leaders and ambassadors to other countries arrived as well for the live interview, their questions hastily prepared.

Around the world, Breeds were in hiding or making their way secretly from the countries that continued to try to imprison or impose restrictions on them. Government labs emptied out, soldiers standing aside as Breeds under testing were rushed from confinement to waiting vans, heli-jets and planes.

As the world was held in thrall, they made their escape from the restrictive countries in an exodus so coordinated, smooth and without violence that later, it would be called completely remarkable.

The Breeds had fought to honor humanity's demands for nearly twenty years while living in fear of their secrets being exposed and destroying all living Breeds. Those in confinement had stayed to preserve the lives of those who were free. Many had died in their efforts, and those instances were documented and ready to be released.

Across the world, small towns, major cities and political hubs, a century of planning, of markers taken, information gathered and held for when it was needed were paid out. Political leaders, major CEOs, presidents and even a king or two, assured the world they weren't in the least worried about this new development. They'd been aware of the rumors and even some cases, the proof of both the Mating Heat as well as the age delay, and had trusted the Breeds to learn all they could about it.

When it was over, Breeds everywhere would know that the first Leo had ensured Callan's success when he stepped forward. And now they were praying he'd ensured the success of this, their greatest weakness, their greatest strength, revealed as well.

When the questions were answered, then doctors and scientists were escorted out first and slipped seamlessly through hidden tunnels and escape routes built into the building rather than the suites it was known to hold. As reporters and political and government officials were escorted out, the entrance doors were closed, and as they watched, metal barriers rose from the cement foundation along doors and windows on the first two floors. Balcony doors and upper windows were similarly secured by reinforced steel that slid silently, protectively in place. Just as the DC-based Bureau had done as well.

It was assumed the upper hierarchy and their mates were protected behind those barriers. And they were wrong.

Breed Leaders had been working in synchronicity for two decades to ensure if this day came, they would have a chance at survival. That mates and children were protected to the best of their ability.

Once safely in secure locations, they had no choice but to sit back and to wait. Safety wouldn't be an overnight assurance, and it wouldn't come without its dangers. But for now, all they could do was wait for an indication of the public's reaction.

And they could pray, the mad kings reminded them, pray hard.

# • CHAPTER 22 •

Dane came awake between one breath and the inhalation of another, aware that something had changed in the hours that he'd slept next to his mate.

When he'd come to bed the night before, she'd already been asleep. Exhaustion had forced her to make her way to the bed as she and Graeme had been going over possibilities as information kept pouring into the underground communication center Graeme had created in the desert.

The caves were separated from those that ran under the Reever estate, where he kept a small working lab. Over the past year he'd been slowly converting a completely lone set of caverns he'd found even deeper unground just in case the day came of a possible Breed war with a world that had suddenly turned on them.

That hadn't happened yet, but they still weren't certain that it wouldn't.

Dane had seen Katelyn to their bed, tucked her in and, as the Primal surged forward, extracted another of those kisses that made him insane with the need to have her, slow and deep, the taste of the mating hormone infusing both their senses and giving him a glimpse of the pleasure that could be found with her.

Fuck, it was all he could do to pull away from her and force himself to return to the huge cavern converted to a conference-slash-communications room.

Dozens of televised feeds played out on the monitors hanging along the walls, or placed on long worktables. Every news station in the world played within that room, Dane swore.

Files littered the tables, arranged in one long line on another wall. Reports, dossiers and projections were stacked, fanned, arranged in what appeared to be a haphazard mess but Dane knew was anything but.

When he'd made it to bed himself and curled around Katy, his head was still spinning with all the information and discussions still being carried out.

The three mad kings were indeed mad.

They hadn't slept the entire time they'd been there. The firsts were nearly as bad, though he'd caught several of them napping.

As he slid from sleep to awareness, though, reports and the projections were the last things on his mind. The only thing he could think about or consider was the feel of Katy's lips along his chest, her inquisitive tongue taking long, slow licks of his flesh.

The room was still dark as his eyes opened and the unique Breed sight shifted, allowing him to see her as she rose over him, straddling his abdomen as his cock rose, thick and hard, demanding attention.

She wasn't in heat, he knew. The scent of Mating Heat, nor his mating hormone was infusing the arousal filling his senses, but fuck if he cared. When her lips came to his, he didn't give a damn.

He'd worry about that later.

He gripped her hair with the fingers of one hand, holding her to him as he felt the humid, wet heat of her pussy kiss the highly sensitive head of his cock. Her juices were thick, heated, her arousal creating a lush, slick invitation to ecstasy.

"I was dreaming of you," she whispered against his lips as she rubbed against him, her moisture spilling to his flesh, tempting him to throw her to her back and take her like the animal he could become with her.

"Shall I ask what you were dreaming?" he groaned.

She shook her head slowly, her hips shifting until the snug, heated entrance to her inner flesh pressed against the swollen crest of his cock in a move that had his entire body tightening.

"Not yet," she whispered, her voice low, resonating with need. "Later. You should ask me . . . Oh God. Dane. You're so thick. So hard . . ."

Her cry tore a groan from his chest as he jerked beneath her, exerting every shred of control he had to allow her whatever she wanted. However she wanted. She deserved to tease, or to play, or to take her pleasure however she chose. He wouldn't protest. He'd give her whatever she asked.

With her head thrown back, her breasts swollen and tipped with hard, pretty pink nipples, she looked like a goddess. Her hair fell down her back in tempting waves and perspiration sheened her feminine curves.

He forced himself to stay still, in such pleasure it was nearing agony as she worked the bloated, engorged head inside the tight entrance of her body, her moans echoing around him like the most erotic music.

"You're like iron," she panted before a little mewl of rising pleasure left her throat. "I never know if it hurts, or just . . ." A short little cry left her lips again. "Or just so good it hurts."

It was slow, erotic torture.

Dane's hands fell to her thighs, and he forced back the demanding growl that wanted to vibrate in his throat. A vocal command to take him, to let him hear her cries as she peaked on that pleasure/pain he could sense pouring from her.

He could feel her pleasure as he felt his own. The ultra-snug entrance flexing around the head of his cock, as the flared crest parted her flesh, forcing its way inside her as she moved, shifted, working herself on it.

She was taking him with the same greedy lack of speed that he'd kissed her with for the past two weeks. Slow, deriving the fullest extent of the pleasure that could be drawn from the experience.

"Dane . . ." She whispered his name, a little whimpering sound that had his abs tightening, his muscles growing taut as he forced himself to hold back for her.

"What, baby?" he growled, on fire for her, burning from his balls to his very soul as she took him with exquisitely slow shifts of her hips.

"I can't . . ." She shook her head, moving more firmly on him, taking him by the barest increment as a low sob fell from her lips. "I can't think . . ."

"Don't think," he groaned.

God, that was the last thing she needed to do.

She growled then, her nails curling against his chest, where they rested, her eyes flashing with golden fire as he stared up at her.

She shifted, rising then lowering, taking more of him as another of those ecstatic little cries passed her lips.

"I need . . . ," she cried out. "Oh God, I need . . ."

Gripping her hair, he forced her head down, her lips to his, and snarled against them. "Take what you want, mate," he demanded, then forced his tongue past her lips, curling it around hers as he felt his primal instincts suddenly flare awake.

The glands beneath her tongue were swollen and heavy. He could sense the mating hormone building there, but it had yet to spill to her mouth, to his kiss.

Her pussy was weeping on his dick, her moisture coating it though she'd barely managed to take half the flared crest inside her.

Another sharp little feline growl sounded in her throat as his tongue stroked over hers, under it, uncertain of her need, but knowing neither of them could hold out long.

The Primal was awake inside him now, and he wanted to shake his head, force him back as he felt his cock growing stiffer, thickening as she shuddered in his hold.

He tried to force the creature back to his subconscious, force it to retreat, but the sensuality that flooded his senses wasn't going to be denied.

Katy took his kiss, her tongue licking against his, crying out as he drew it into his mouth and suckled it, trying to ease the hormone from the glands. He'd never heard of them only filling but never releasing.

His hands gripped her hips now, his own lifting to her, working his cock against the ultra-slick opening, taking her by increments as her muscles locked around his flesh.

Tender feminine tissue rippled over the head of his cock, caressing it, sucking at it.

She cried out again and he nipped at her tongue, desperate to taste the mating hormone as it spilled free and mixed with his own to create the Mating Heat.

He wanted that mating. God help him, he ached for it. And his own "other" was demanding it, rising inside him and threatening to overtake him as Dane held her to him, working his flesh inside her, groaning at the sheer bliss as her muscles fisted around him.

Feline Breed males possessed a mating barb that emerged, locking the males inside their females at ejaculation and spilling a hormone that aided conception and eased the more painful aspects of a female mate's heat.

The female mate possessed something even more destructive, though. The hormone secreted through their feminine moisture tightened their vaginal muscles around the erection pushing inside her, sending little rippling waves through them that gripped and sucked the male's cock inside.

It was pure fucking ecstasy.

"Give it to me," he growled against her lips, catching her tongue again, desperate for the taste of her, for the mark her kiss would make on him.

She shook in his arms, all that sizzling energy that was so much a part of her pouring inside her now. But it wasn't painful. And it was destroying her control as well as his own.

When she jerked back from his kiss with a little feline snarl of impatience and challenge, he froze. Tensed.

*No!*

He fought to hold the Primal instincts back, to cage them inside him. But she was daring him. That sound was like a red flag to every particle of the animal inside him.

Before he knew his intent he moved. Gripping her waist, he had her off him and on her knees as he came behind her, one hand pushing her shoulders down and holding them to the bed as he wrapped his arm around her hips and came over her.

The head of his cock pushed inside her, giving her the full, engorged width of it as his teeth locked in the flesh of her shoulder.

She screamed. But it wasn't pain he felt pouring from her. It was a hunger, a need that had no name, no description. All it had was the pure desperation building inside her.

The incisors locked at her shoulder were longer, piercing her flesh just enough to spill his hormone directly into her system as he began thrusting inside her.

With each impalement he went deeper, stretching flesh that had known only the barest male possession. Those men had no hope of comparing to the one that held her heart. The one invading her flesh, her senses, as he was now.

Her fingers formed claws and dug into the mattress beneath her as she bucked into each thrust, as desperate for more of him as he was to give himself to her.

Each thrust was hard, calculated for the maximum sensation and penetration. And with each thrust he felt more of her senses opening to him, pulling him inside her as the beast raging inside him did the same with her.

By the time he pushed his full length inside her, he could feel the mating barb close to the surface, just beneath the head of his cock, hardening, trying to push free.

And that last thread of control snapped.

Katelyn arched, her back bowing as blinding sensation erupted through her body. Once Dane managed to push his full length inside her, it was as though both of them lost themselves.

She tried to scream, to beg, to plead with him . . . but he knew. He knew what she needed, and he gave it to her.

Deep, hard, his cock pounding inside her and forcing her inner muscles to take him, to accept everything he had to give as her moisture grew more heated, slicker.

She could taste him: chili peppers and honey and a hint of saffron and with it, an added taste. As her tongue ached, the little swollen glands beneath it began spilling a taste that made no sense. It was almost honeysuckle.

As it began to fill her mouth, Dane's hand tightened in her hair, and as he fucked her with hard, deep lunges, he pulled her head back to catch her kiss, and that taste.

He caught her tongue with his lips, drew on that taste in a kiss so sensual, wild and deep, that nothing else mattered. Because it increased the pleasure, the sensations. Pleasure so sharp and intense it mixed with pain. The more he drew from her, and she drew from him, the hotter the room seemed to get, and the more intense the sensations became.

Each impalement, each stroke of pure sensation burying inside her muscle sent flash points of electric sensation to sizzle over her body, wrap around her clit, pierce her womb. It pushed her higher with each thrust, until she reached a pinnacle where she simply flew.

The explosion tore through her, and in the next breath Dane buried deep one last time, tore his lips from hers and bit into her shoulder again as she found his arm, biting him in turn.

She was shaking, bucking against him as she felt some added pressure against the tight walls of her pussy, a rippling, hard caress, then a further stretching, and the liquid hot jets of his release.

She couldn't survive it. She knew she couldn't.

She swore her spirit lifted from her body, twisted with his, and she lost herself. Each hard convulsion of sensation that shook her tore a cry from her, burned her, remade her then pulled her back to earth with slow, rocking waves of so much sensation that she wondered if that was what it was like to die.

✦ ✦ ✦

Dane felt the barb lock inside Katy and heard the primal snarl that left his lips as his mate's kiss infused his system, mixed with it and assured the creature instincts acknowledged the mating.

She belonged to him.

She had always belonged to him.

The woman lying exhausted beneath him, her pussy still locked around his pulsing flesh, would never know the touch of another man's lust, never allow it to infuse her scent. She was his . . .

He let her collapse beneath him, his soul suddenly so filled with her that he knew he could never survive without her.

He sensed her, not in pictures or thought, but in an essence so elemental it made no sense. Not just his mate, not just his woman. He felt the life she longed to hold, and knew it was a part of him as well. He felt her need to hold their child even as he felt his release spilling to her womb and the life awaiting there, laid in place by the Breed hormones that had changed her, shaped her, created her.

Before a new day finished, his Katy would hold sweet, precious life inside her body.

Their child.

He didn't try to stop the tears that dampened his cheeks. Didn't even attempt to hold them back. He'd waited over seventy years for this woman, for a dream he'd never believed he could have. And no matter what the next day brought, he swore to that new life, he'd protect it, and his mate, with his last breath.

Just as Leo had protected Elizabeth.

Just as he had tried to protect his own children.

And he could only pray, with everything inside him, that the decisions they'd made would secure the Breeds' future. Because only by securing the lives of the Breeds as a whole could he ever secure his own child's.

◆ ◆ ◆

Basil Tallon lifted his head from the files he was concentrating on, closed his eyes and allowed the knowledge to pour inside him.

It was something none but perhaps his brothers could sense.

And Leo.

He opened them again, staring at the Apex First Leo, seeing the tension in the Leo's shoulders, the way his head lifted and he seemed to gather the knowledge around him.

Yes, this Leo knew as well.

Basil hadn't sensed the mating, hadn't scented or heard the sounds of it that he knew would have been filled with desperation. No, he'd felt it. That odd "something."

He'd felt the conception.

He'd felt his daughter's child come into being.

Basil's heart seemed to expand, and the love he felt for the daughter he'd never known, hadn't realized until mere weeks ago existed, deepened to the depths of his soul.

He'd so loved her mother, and he realized he'd known the moment Amora's body had taken his seed and allowed it to find a home inside her womb. He'd known that second of his child's conception as well.

Basil felt his brothers move behind him, each gripping his shoulder, acknowledging only through touch what they sensed.

"I'll be damned," Graeme whispered from the table across from him, no more than a breath of sound, and an acknowledgment, as Leo made his way to them.

The others had left the room hours before; only the five of them—himself, Leo, Graeme, Reign and Magnus—had remained behind.

He and his brothers had drained their well of tears decades ago, but it seemed Graeme and Leo still were able to spill that emotion from their soul.

"Poor kid." Graeme cleared his throat after a moment. "An insane grandfather, another who's far too arrogant for words, two uncles no more sane than their brother. Damned good thing I have a bit of sanity left. She'll need me."

They stared back at him, and Basil realized he felt some outrage. Something else he hadn't believed he had left inside him.

"Bengal, you define madness even more than the mad kings," he growled.

To which Graeme only inclined his head in agreement before meeting Basil's gaze and saying, "You can be Paw Paw. I get to be Yo-Yeaux."

# EPILOGUE

The cave system Graeme had found on the Navajo Nation's lands was extensive and deep. There were clear pools of fresh water several levels below the earth, veins of gold and gems that had never been touched. There were even several intact dinosaur skeletons still lodged in the walls of the roughly hewn "halls" that were cut into the dense stone connecting the caves.

Graeme had spent years, he confided in her, running pipes, electricity, and lights, but he admitted the vast cave system and its connecting walkways had already been there, just waiting for him to make use of them.

As she walked, she fought to make sense of all the changes that had happened so fast. There was so much that she had never been prepared for, never imagined could happen. She'd always known that the problems she had with the rush of adrenaline weren't normal. It was too debilitating. Too extreme. And she'd always feared it would become worse.

But she'd never imagined what it actually was.

Katelyn had just returned from a walk within the upper walkway, aware that someone was waiting for her. As she stepped into the living area of the two connecting caves Graeme had given them for their stay, she wasn't surprised by the Breed standing in the middle of the surprisingly comfortable area.

She'd known he was there. She could feel his presence before she even neared the room.

Stepping inside, she faced him. This man that shared her blood, who had loved her mother. The father she'd always wondered about, ached to know.

"You've been avoiding me," he stated, sliding his hands into the front pockets of his loose jeans as he faced her.

The action might have denoted discomfort in other men, but not in this one. His shoulders were straight, his gaze direct. His expression as arrogant, perhaps even more so, than Dane's.

"It wasn't avoidance," she admitted, facing him and allowing her gaze to take in the incredibly powerful figure in front of her. "I need time to think, to come to terms with your existence, I guess. I had always assumed you had died as well. After all, why else hadn't you come looking for me after my mother's death. You would have known she was pregnant."

He'd said he'd only known of her in that week before the Genetic Flaming had nearly killed her. But he'd married her mother, she'd heard him tell Dane as she lay drifting between consciousness and that dark, sheltered place where pain didn't exist. He'd known her mother was pregnant when he'd left to help one of his brothers. Why hadn't he found her?

He gave a slow nod.

"I was told you had died as well." Grief flashed in his gaze. "The woman she shared her apartment with was quite certain of that, but admittedly, I had already begun slipping into madness at the time. I didn't ask questions. I left before I could kill her on the spot." He gestured to the easy chair beside him. "I brought pictures for you. Pictures of your mother and myself. Our wedding . . ."

He didn't show discomfort or any sense of uncertainty, but she swore she could feel a hint of it.

She glanced away for a moment, fighting her tears.

"I loved your mother, Katelyn," he said then, his voice rougher than before. "No mating could have made me love her more. Her death was an act of senseless violence. A man high on drugs determined to rob the store she worked at. You slept in the back room, barely a month old from what I've recently learned. No one who knew your mother was aware that you hadn't died as well. She didn't have many friends, though. Only two who I was aware of. But I know she loved you the moment she knew she carried you inside her. And I loved you as well. And I grieved for you. Just as I grieved for your mother."

She could hear the emotion in his voice. She could feel it slipping from him, filling the room and wrapping around her.

And in it was his love for her. That emotion tugged at her, urged her to him, and soothed the anger and feeling of desertion she'd been dealing with. He was a Breed unlike all others with the exception of his two brothers. A man plagued by periods of madness so extreme that he locked himself away when he felt it beginning to fill his mind.

Graeme, Dane and Leo had given her quite a bit of information over the past days. They'd answered her questions as fully as they could, never once urging her to talk to her father, but never advising her against it either.

This was her choice, Dane had told her. A choice only she could make.

"I needed you." The tears broke free, despite her attempts to hold them back. "I was so different no one wanted to love me. No one cared until Graeme . . ."

"No, child, the Santiagos loved you." He stepped to her, lifted her chin and stared down at her, his expression filled with pain. "They longed to care for you as a daughter, but by then, you were too wary. Their sons longed to be your brothers, and often carried bruises from the fights they entered over slights to you. Your foster father, John Moran, loved you enough to leave you the house and business he owned, but his cousin cheated you out of it. You were loved, but you knew, deep inside that you were more than any of them could imagine. So you held back. The animals that filled you, fought within you, you leashed them, until the good and sweet nature that was so much a part of you, could survive. And that nature held you back."

His hand lifted, his fingertips brushing her cheek and the tears that dampened her cheek.

"You are so strong," he whispered. "The best of your mother, my Amora. Your love and gentleness for those around you is like a beacon of warmth. But you're also determined, resilient, and fully capable of facing any enemy. You've proven this in the job you sought. You have protected your friends, guided them, enabled them to face a life they never believed they could have, even as you faced it yourself." A weary smile crossed his lips then. "You needed your father because he was your father. You never needed him to survive. Even had Graeme not arrived, you would have found your way to a place where others saw you, respected you. There is no doubt of that."

And he was certain of that.

She could feel that certainty, feel his belief in it, his doubtless belief in her.

"No Breed, whether recessed, unknowing or fully aware of what they are, can have a life without hardship, pain, loss." He brushed her hair back, his expression gentling, softening until she could see the man her mother must have fallen in love with. A man who knew love, knew tenderness. "No child of a mad king can even be assured of life period. But you, Katelyn." His smile was filled with pride. "Look at who you are. Look at the life you created for yourself. The Breed that couldn't forget you, no matter the distance between you. The maddened creature who gives his loyalty to none but his mate. And one of four young women he names as his daughters. But above them all, Katelyn, that insane Bengal loves only his mate more than you. And yet, you cannot see how very unique you are to all of us."

But she could feel it. Like a wave of warmth surrounding her, joining the warmth that filled her from her mating with Dane, the knowledge that she was loved, accepted. A father's love wrapped around her as well, his pride in her, his joy. His sorrow that he hadn't known, hadn't protected her.

"Come, let me tell you of your mother." He took her hand and drew her to the couch, picking up the box of pictures and placing it on the coffee table in front of them. "The camera loved her. Almost as much as I . . ."

And that was where Dane found them hours later. Their heads together as Basil spoke softly, telling her of the woman who loved him, who loved her child. Somehow, he'd managed to find a friend of

Amora's who had pictures of Katelyn with her mother. Not a lot, but enough to show how very proud the mother was of the daughter.

Father and daughter had both shed tears for the wife, the mother lost to them.

Dane slipped from the room and gave them the time they needed to form the beginnings of the bond that both of them needed.

His news could wait. They had time. Hope. Love.

And that was all that mattered.

## ✦ BREED GLOSSARY ✦

**Genetics Council:** The secretive organization that funds, collects donations from like-minded humans of excessive financial abilities and applies those funds to the creation, training for war, and/or experimentation of genetically altered humans whose DNA now contains vast qualities of animal DNA.

**Breed:** A human whose conception occurred using genetically modified sperm and/or ova, modified with animal genetics.

**Primal Breed:** The strongest, most savage and primitive of the Breeds. The Primal can be drawn from any personality type but, once awakened, will ensure the Breed is the ultimate alpha. It's the most primitive of the Breeds, drawn free from the innermost core of the animal genetics. The Primal is the strongest, the fastest and most savage parts of the Breed.

**hybrid Breed:** Any child born of a Breed and human is classified as a hybrid of both.

**hybrid Primal:** A Primal who arises in a hybrid Breed. All the qualities of the Primal Breed but integrated so deeply, so interwoven with the

Breed that its civilized savagery is dangerous to whoever is pitting itself against the Primal. The voice draws whoever's listening, its paranormal power over the human senses is natural and convincing as none other is. The hybrid's awareness within the Breed shows in the brilliant color of its eyes, its voice; its ability to instantly recognize a problem and calculate the best response makes it incredibly dangerous. Reasoning capability is off the charts, as is intelligence and its ability to succeed in any situation. It can hide in plain sight within the Breed, and only Breed senses can accurately detect it. Humans have no defense against it and only the rare few can detect it.

**Apex Primal:** The natural metamorphosis of an Apex Breed or First Alpha to the primal animal intelligence and strength of the combined genetics. The top of the Primal hierarchy.

**Breed mates:** Any Breed or human tied to the other through the mating hormone that activates in the glands beneath the Breed's tongue. There is only one mate, and if he/she is lost, it's unknown if the Breed can or will mate another.

**recessed Breed:** Showing no Breed genetics through regular blood screenings and having no Breed senses. Can only be detected through a genetic screening at the deepest level.

**hybrid recessed Breed:** Born with no apparent Breed genetics. Evidence of Breed mutation can be found only on the deepest level genetic screening.

**hybrid anomaly:** Shows no Breed genetics even at the deepest testing level. These genetics only become known if Genetic Flaming occurs.

***Basilicus humanus rapax*:** Very loosely and roughly translated to royal human predator, which the scientists used to define the First Alphas. Proper Latin translation was not used because the Breeds it defined were considered an abomination even by the Genetics Council.

**Apex Breeds:** Also used to define the first alphas.

**First Alphas:** The first of each genetic species created using nearly fifty percent human to fifty percent animal genetics. The strongest and most powerful of each genetic species of Breeds.

***Basilicus humanus rapax hybrida*:** A child of the Apex Breeds or First Alphas.

***Tribus insaniae basilicus*:** (very loosely translated bastardized Latin) The three mad kings. Three Breeds created using the genetics of royalty as well as seven different species of predators. They experience long periods of madness and try to confine themselves when it happens.

***Progidium tribus insaniae basilicus*:** (very loosely translated bastardized Latin) Child of the Three Mad Kings. A hybrid recessed child of one of the Three Mad Kings.

**Mating Heat:** Chemical, biological and pheromonal reaction between a Breed and his or her mate. This causes extreme arousal, the inability to allow another's touch, other than the mate's during the first, extreme period of the heat.

**mating hormone:** The hormone that collects in the glands beneath a Breed's tongue and sometimes along the invisible hairs of their bodies that creates a bonding reaction in the mate.

Effects: Extreme arousal, painful sensation when touched by another, aphrodisiac properties, the inability for mates to refuse the touch of their mate. An almost addictive need for the taste of the hormone that comes with a Breed's kiss.

**hormonal glands:** Located beneath a Breed's tongue. Once the Breed's animal senses and/or recognizes his/her mate, these glands fill and spill a hormone that transfers to the mate in a kiss or bite. The taste of this hormone is individual to the Breed and its strength varies.

**hormonal therapy:** Created by Breed scientists and geneticists to aid in the control of the hormonal effects and help prevent conception. It varies in the ability to diffuse the arousal but it's never one hundred percent effective.

**Genetic Flaming:** Sudden flaming or awakening of once recessed Breed genetics. Usually occurs between age twenty and twenty-three.

Effects: Body temperature over 107 degrees, convulsions, hallucinations, enraged growls or snarls, attempts to bite or scratch, extreme pain, chills, sensory overload, et cetera.

**royal Genetic Flaming:** Sudden Flaming or awakening of genetics with the offspring of a mad king.

Effects: Inhuman pain. All seven species of genetics fight for supremacy within the body, causing organs to become irreparably damaged. Death has been the only known end of this Flaming.

Suspected Therapy for royal Genetic Flaming: Once it occurs, only the primal strength of a hybrid born from one of the first Leos has been known to cause recovery. The mating hormone produced by such a strong Primal forces only the genetics that match the Primal's to take precedence within the body. As in Katelyn and Dane's mating, Katelyn became a Lion Breed.

**nano-nit:** Tiny electronic bug that records video and/or audio. Attaches to an electrical source such as a lamp. Voice activated. Records until the internal hard drive is full, then will move along an electric current to a device capable of transmitting out or accessing internet, where it then uploads its information to a predetermined location. Almost impossible to detect or to catch once it activates without high-level advanced signal detectors or transmitting dampeners. Most interference devices are highly irritating to Breed senses.

**Breed Laws:** Laws that govern Breed societies, which are autonomous from the rule of national or state governments. When any crimes are committed against, or by, Breeds, then the Breed society has the option of trying them within the Breed society, under Breed law.

**Federal Bureau of Breed Affairs:** Oversees the Breed communities, protests or actions against Breeds and all government payments to the Breeds as a whole.

**director of the Federal Bureau of Breed Affairs:** Oversees all departments within the Bureau and chairs any committee created or assigned to oversee any part of the Breed communities. Present Federal director is Jonas Wyatt and the assistant Federal director, Rhyzan Brannigan.

**Western Bureau of Breed Affairs:** The offices located in Window Rock, Arizona, and under the guidance of the Federal Bureau of Breed Affairs. Current director is Rule Breaker, with the assistant director, Lawe Justice.

**Sanctuary:** The first protected Breed community created. Located in Buffalo Gap, Virginia. Under the leadership of the Pride leader, Callan

Lyons, the recognized head of the entire Breed race in the United States and his Prima, Merinus Lyons.

**Haven:** The protected Wolf Breed community in Advert, Colorado. Under the leadership of Lupus Wolf Gunner and his Lupa, Hope Gunner.

**Citadel:** The protected Coyote Base in Advert, Colorado. Sits overlooking Haven. Under the leadership of Coy Del-Rey Delgado and his Coya, Anya Delgado.